THE
CHOICE
I MADE

BOOKS BY CYNTHIA ELLINGSEN

The Choice I Made

Marriage Matters
The Whole Package

THE STARLIGHT COVE SERIES
A Bittersweet Surprise
The Lighthouse Keeper
The Winemaker's Secret

THE
CHOICE
I MADE

CYNTHIA ELLINGSEN

bookouture

Published by Bookouture in 2021

An imprint of Storyfire Ltd.
Carmelite House
50 Victoria Embankment
London EC4Y 0DZ

www.bookouture.com

ISBN: 978-1-80019-234-8
eBook ISBN: 978-1-80019-233-1

To Butch and Kathy Ellingsen,
for the precious memories at Sela Woods

PROLOGUE

My darling child, one day you will understand that the heart is only as fragile as the choices we make. I tell you this now—we will make surprising decisions for love. Ones that can tear our heart out and leave us begging for answers. The most painful choice I've ever made, my dearest, was to say goodbye to you.

CHAPTER ONE

Tristan stood for a moment in the doorway. Then he chuckled. "I have to hand it to your family. Talk about a sales job."

"What do you mean?" I asked, setting my purse on the kitchen counter.

The counter's wood grain was as rustic as our small cabin. My grandfather had handcrafted each detail of the place nearly fifty years ago and I had craved its serenity for ages. I could hardly believe we were finally going to spend a few days here.

Clearly, my husband didn't feel the same. He'd made passive-aggressive remarks starting the moment we left Chicago and increasing in irritation the closer we got to Wisconsin. It was hot, I was tired, and as my mother liked to say, I'd had it.

"What do you mean by a sales job?" I demanded.

Tristan opened and closed cabinet doors, looking for a glass. The man drank water constantly, because he'd committed to consuming a gallon of it a day for his latest health plan. He eyed the tap water with suspicion before downing it, then gestured at the living area with the empty glass.

"This place. People pay thousands of dollars a week to rent a shack with a good view. It's impressive."

The 'good view' was a picture window that overlooked Lake Florentine, a freshwater lake surrounded by fir trees. It meant mist with morning coffee, the glint of sunshine on the water during an afternoon book, and a deep sense of peace with every blue heron that skimmed the surface. People were more than willing to pay for that, but of course Tristan had to question it, since he was mad about leaving his cultivated world of structure and steel behind.

"It's hardly a shack," I said. "It's six hundred square feet."

My dad had assigned us one of the couple's cabins, complete with a separate bedroom and master bath. The queen bed was cozy as a cocoon and the bathroom had a deep soaking tub that overlooked the lake. There were carefully selected personal amenities like organic soaps from the high-end local soap company, a game closet in the living room, and a curated bookshelf.

The cabin was adorable and I was baffled that Tristan refused to see that, especially since Wood Violet Resort had been in demand longer than he had been alive. My grandparents had bent over backwards to build a legacy and my parents had followed in their footsteps. Countless celebrities and CEOs had stayed here, and they had never uttered a word of complaint. In fact, they came back for more.

I looked at my husband, not sure what to say. He was leaning against the kitchen counter, his arms crossed. It was his successful adviser pose, the one he used to impress upon new clients that he was strong, confident, and up to the challenge of managing their money.

"It's not a shack," I repeated.

"Does it have a television?"

"You know it doesn't."

He grinned. "Then it's a shack."

"Tristan, people love this way of life. They need it to recharge and rejuvenate. To get back to nature."

"They couldn't just go camping?" he asked.

Irritated, I looked down at my watch. My father had wanted to talk to me before I went to see my mother, but I still hadn't heard from him. Check-in day was always slammed and he would be putting out one fire after another, but he'd insisted on meeting up before I went to find her. That had me worried, because it was possible the situation with my mother was worse than what he'd told me on the phone.

My parents were famous for keeping me and my sister in the dark about major issues, especially me, since I was the youngest. It didn't matter that I was in my early thirties and trusted to legally represent some of the largest insurance companies in the country. I kept telling them they did not need to protect me, but they refused to listen or, maybe, to believe it.

I walked over to the large welcome basket on the table to unpack it, trying not to slap the items onto the counter. Organic raspberries, roasted almonds, dark chocolate with sea salt... My parents worked hard each season selecting the perfect treats. Was Tristan going to make fun of that, too?

I dabbed my shirt against my face. The cabins did not have air conditioning, as the windows were designed to allow a cross-breeze from the lake. I opened them and breathed in the outdoors. Pine, moss, and something darker, like the decay beneath a fallen log.

I turned to face him. "You don't have to be here, you know."

"Hey, don't say that." Tristan joined me at the window. He smelled too clean, like sporty cologne and laundry detergent. I moved back to the welcome basket.

"Let's not start our trip like this." Tristan followed me to the table and brushed a strand of hair out of my eyes. "Your hair looks pretty."

"My hair?" My hand fluttered up to touch the wispy strands.

The honey highlights had been done two weeks ago, along with a new cut that fell just above my shoulders. It hardly mattered at this point. My hair was the last thing on my mind.

He rested his lips on my head, then sighed. "Look, I'm just a poor boy from the country." He pulled back to look at me, his dark eyes sincere. "I get it that rich folk like to shell out to pretend to be normal, but they could go to the spa or one of the million other places around here. It's impressive that your parents can still bring in a solid clientele based on the old-fashioned camp model. I really am impressed, Julie."

"Thank you." It was almost embarrassing how much it meant to me to hear him say that, but I'd wanted to share this with him for so long.

Wood Violet was a part of my soul. Tristan and I had been married for three years now, and had never made it here together. Our work schedules didn't match up and in the rare moments they did, he wanted to go somewhere big like Greece or the Cayman Islands. The fact that we had four days here together was magic to me and it scared me to think he might not feel the same.

"I'm glad you like it," I said. "I was worried you were mad to be here at all."

"Of course not." Tristan pushed up the sleeves of his white T-shirt, revealing strong forearms. He'd made his country boy remark: there were moments when it was easy to imagine him on the farm, cutting hay or roping cattle. "I'm ready for the great outdoors."

I'd probably taken his mood the wrong way. My temper was short because I had wanted to come immediately after my mother had a stroke, but I had to finish a case at work, which set me back ten days. That, coupled with the constant crush of the city, had put me on edge. I probably needed to cut him some slack.

My watch buzzed.

The Hut in ten minutes?

"Dad texted." I was halfway out the door when I realized Tristan wasn't behind me. "Come on. He won't have a lot of time."

"You two should be alone. I'll get unpacked and go for a run." He grinned. "It's not like I can watch TV."

Maybe it was for the best, since they'd have to play catch-up. This way, we could just get down to business. My dad had made it sound like everything here at the resort was still under control in spite of my mother falling ill, but I wanted to make sure. The past few years had been complicated enough for the hospitality industry. It would be an uphill battle for my father to make this summer a success without my mother by his side.

I followed the woodchip path through the fir trees to the lake. The smell of the water became stronger and I paused before stepping out of the forest. Taking a deep breath, I ran my fingers over the dainty pine needles of the nearest tree. Then, I straightened my shoulders and headed down to the dock to hear the truth.

The Hut, as my family called it, was one of the only places at the resort where privacy was possible. During the busy season, my parents had worked eighteen-hour days and if we were near the guests, we were expected to shake hands or make small talk. The Hut was born to give us a few precious moments as a family to sit and be together.

The cozy wooden shanty was open air, and located at the end of a dock that once anchored fishing boats. My grandfather had built a small wooden gate at the entrance and attached a sign that read 'Closed to Guests'. Sure, anyone could step over it but no one did, so it felt safe, private, and away from it all.

I found my father on the wooden bench, a sweating cup of iced tea by his side. He must have heard the echo of my footsteps against the wooden planks of the dock but he didn't stand until I stepped around the corner.

His tanned face split into a smile. "Look who rolled in from the big city."

"Dad." It made my heart happy to see him.

His salt and pepper hair was short, neatly smoothed back from his forehead, and he'd always had a slight five o'clock shadow. He looked as fresh and sporty as ever, dressed in his Wood Violet Resort branded white golf shirt, a pair of navy shorts, and Italian loafers. There were heavy bags under his eyes, but those had always been there, and the deep laugh lines right next to them made up for it.

My father looked like a man who'd just heard a good joke or was just about to tell one. I hugged him as tight as I could.

"Chicago's got some of the best restaurants in the world." His voice was gruff. "Why are you so skinny?"

"It's been busy." Images of missed lunches, hurried dinners spent reviewing paperwork, and a consistent diet of soy nuts and smoothies from the shop below my office flashed through my head. "How are you?"

"Staying up late, counting beans and berries." My father settled back on the bench. "You know, I cried like a baby two hours ago, thinking about you being here."

The words made me get a lump in my throat but he'd already moved on, regaling me with stories about the neighboring resorts, their scandals and updates, and the new pastry chef they'd hired to take over for my mother. I knew he was working up to the situation and finally, he glanced at his watch.

"I've gotten thirty text messages in the last ten minutes," he said. "But we need to discuss your mother."

Ducks traveled across the water. The mama duck led the row, proud as could be. "How is she?"

"I didn't want to tell you over the phone." He took a long drink of iced tea. "Your mother isn't mobile."

The smooth surface of the lake nearly tunneled out of my vision. "What?" I whispered.

My mother had always been like a bumblebee, buzzing around, trying to make life sweet for everyone. If she wasn't busy with guests, managing the garden, or cooking pastries, she was dancing with my father or having a heart-to-heart with me and my sister. I'd assumed the stroke had caused some facial paralysis and maybe exhaustion, but not this.

"Why didn't you tell me?" I demanded. "I would have come right away."

"I didn't want you to rush away from your life."

The look I gave him was nothing short of outraged. "That's not your call."

I had stayed in Chicago because I had switched firms eight months ago and my new boss, the partner I worked for, insisted I stay to finish my current case. I'd fought against a settlement with a man who had sued two other companies in the past two years. The lawsuit had settled anyway. If my dad had told me it was more than "a minor setback," I would have left immediately. Really, it's what I should have done in the first place. There had been too many times in the past few years where I'd been too busy to return my mother's call or even answer a text. It chilled me to think she had to have a stroke to get me to look up from my desk.

"How is this supposed to make her feel?" I demanded. "That I'm just now showing up?"

He shrugged. "It's what she wanted. She's embarrassed, she's scared, and she hoped things would go back to normal."

I squeezed my hands tight. "Does Kate know?"

My sister lived across the country in Portland, was six months pregnant, and had two-year-old twins.

"Your mother didn't want to worry her."

Kate was going to hit the roof. The first few days following the stroke, she'd talked to my father at least ten times. He'd convinced her that everything was fine.

"What do you mean by 'not mobile'?" I asked.

"Her left side is paralyzed. The doctors think she can recover movement, learn to use her body and walk again, but she has to put in the work. She's depressed, in a way I've never seen."

It was hard to picture, since my mother had always been the most optimistic person on the planet.

My father stared out at the water. "It will be good for her to see you. She seemed a little off before all this happened but wouldn't talk to me about it."

"How?" I pressed.

"The week before the stroke, I found her by the edge of the lake, burning a stack of papers. She was crying."

"What was in the papers?"

He hesitated. "I don't know. We've been cleaning out the records closet, transferring old paper records to digital. I'd moved the shredder in there but the closet gets so hot. Your mother decided to burn some of the papers at one of the bonfire rings instead of shredding them, claiming that the heat from the flames cooled her down compared to the heat of the closet. I should have known something was wrong then."

"It's not your fault," I told him.

The limit to our power to stop bad things from happening was a constant conversation in my line of work. The risk management teams that handled a large grocery store chain, for example, had a responsibility to protect their customers. Things happened, though. Same with life. My father couldn't have prevented this, and I didn't want him to blame himself.

"When can I see her?" I asked, taking his hand.

"Whenever, now that you know the whole story." He looked at his watch. "She's been sleeping a lot, so don't be surprised if she's napping when you get there. Just wait it out."

"How are you going to manage the resort?" I asked. "Without her?"

Before, I'd assumed my mother would help out behind the scenes but now it seemed that the success of the resort rested solely on my father's shoulders. He couldn't handle it alone.

"I've hired an operations manager," he said. "He's slated to arrive tomorrow. Our marketing director plans to take on a stronger role, as will several of our employees."

The breeze blew, stirring up the mossy scent of the Hut.

"Can Grandpa help?" I suggested.

My grandfather had handed the ownership of the resort to my father nearly a decade ago, when my grandmother died. He didn't want to run it without her so instead, he opted to travel the world. He was in his early seventies, in good health, and plenty of time had passed. It was possible he'd help out.

"He's in Ireland right now, on one of those bus tours." My father took a sip of iced tea. "That's more his speed at the moment."

"The resort is a lot, though, and you still have to take care of Mom..."

"There's a nurse that comes in twice a day, and someone from Physical Therapy."

I wished I could stay and help out, but there simply wasn't time. A new case would be waiting for me the moment I got back.

"You have your own life," my father said, as if reading my mind. "We're fine, Julie."

The guilt that squeezed my heart was intense. Not to mention the idea that my family had gotten older, that my home had changed, and I was not ready to accept that.

Out in the center of the lake, a fish jumped, the drops of water from its back sparkling in the sun. It landed, ripples spreading out around it. My father and I sat together until the surface smoothed, then he got to his feet.

"Try to enjoy your time here," he said. "It's a far cry from city life but I hope it will do."

The crush of the concrete and the pressure to work harder pulsed in my mind. That feeling seemed so far from here; from the sweet scent of firewood burning somewhere on the beach, laughter in the distance, and the lazy hum of summer.

"Yeah." I fought against the catch in my throat. "I think it will do just fine."

CHAPTER TWO

The path that led to my parents' house crossed through the main area of the resort. It would be bustling with guests from the check-in area, the dining hall, and the water shuttle that transported guests to the golf course across the lake. I was guaranteed to bump into people I knew, either recurring guests or our staff, and I needed a couple of minutes to process all of this privately.

Oh, who am I kidding? I need time to burst into tears.

The thought made my eyes smart and with a clipped pace, I took a path that led deep into the trails of the forest. I didn't want to cry in front of my mother. It would upset her and, worse, she would offer me support, which was not at all how this should be.

The air became cooler as the canopy of trees thickened above me. Smells changed. Fresh water gave way to the scent of pine and fungi, and even the salt of my skin. The closer I felt to tears, the faster I walked, determined to keep it together until the coast was clear.

Five minutes passed, then ten. Finally, I was so deep into the forest that it was silent, save for the call of an occasional bird, the buzz of the insects, and the sound of my breath. Spotting an old tree that had fallen off to the side of the path, I sank onto its rough trunk and waited to cry but the tears wouldn't come. The pain remained stuck in my throat and refused to let go.

The gnarled branches above scratched against one another, shifting shadows around me. The back of my neck prickled. I sat as still as possible and listened.

In the city, I was always on high alert but I'd let down my guard, despite having grown up knowing the dangers of the woods. Wood Violet was one hundred and forty acres, and my family had left a large portion of it untouched. Wildlife had the freedom to roam and something as small as a lynx could still be dangerous.

Twigs snapped behind me and I grabbed for a large stick, scattering leaves and dirt. I pivoted to see a brown rabbit race from the underbrush, chased by another. They were playing, probably mother and child. Clearly, the city had set my blood pressure much too high.

Or maybe not.

There was a rustle off to my left, and a thin figure in a dark shirt slipped behind a pine tree. My adrenaline kicked into overdrive.

"Hey," I shouted, fumbling for my phone. "I'm calling security. They'll be here in two minutes."

Not entirely true. The resort's security terrain vehicles could zip through the trails, but it would take longer than two minutes, assuming I could get reception out here at all.

"Wait!" A teenaged girl rushed out from behind the pine tree. She was thin with dark hair pulled up in a tight ponytail, and she carried a small backpack. "Please don't call security."

I lowered my stick, heart still pounding. "Sorry, you startled me. I didn't expect anyone to be back here."

It did worry me to think she was in the forest alone. She'd probably dodged family togetherness to drink or smoke, but my mind had clicked over to the liability. If she got attacked by an animal or tripped and broke her leg or encountered an ill-intentioned stranger, the resort would most likely be held responsible for the outcome. Guests had always been welcome to roam free but based on some of the lawsuits I'd seen, it might be time for my parents to issue a warning about walking in the woods alone.

"You shouldn't be out here by yourself," I told her. "It's always a good practice to use the buddy system in the woods."

"The buddy system?" she repeated.

Dropping the stick, I walked towards her, surprised at the hint of mockery in her tone. As I got closer, I realized the girl smelled like she hadn't showered in a few days. My sister had gone through that phase as a teenager, too, and dirty-hair smell was a sense memory I could live without.

"Do you know how to get back?" I asked.

The girl tossed her hair. "Follow the path. It doesn't really require GPS."

"Good point." I smiled. "Well, I hope you have a nice walk."

"It will get better when I'm actually walking."

"Then I'll leave you to it." Turning, I took the trails back towards the main area, irritated at her attitude.

I doubted she would have talked to me like that if her parents were present. Well, maybe she would. Wood Violet guests were usually nice but also very privileged. They wanted to do what they wanted when they wanted, and even though I felt she shouldn't be out here alone, it wouldn't be a good look if this girl complained that I'd ruined her good time.

It was so funny to slip back into that mindset. I'd grown up worried that I would do or say something to disappoint one of our guests. It helped now, I guess, when it came to dealing with some of our more demanding legal clients.

Tightness filled my chest at the thought of my job. The move to my new firm had been a big step up in terms of money and prestige but it was grueling. The moment my next case started, there wouldn't be a second to spare. I was hardly unique, most people worked just as hard, but I wished I enjoyed it more.

The sun was bright when I made it out of the forest and onto the main lawn. It was twelve thirty, the time most people were in the dining hall for lunch, so it wasn't that busy, and I was less likely to bump into a familiar face.

I had just cut across the main area past the fountain when a deep voice called me. "Julie!"

The anonymity had lasted all of ten seconds.

The attractive man waving at me seemed familiar, but I couldn't quite place him. He was tall, with broad shoulders and curly, golden hair. His eyes were bright blue and when he smiled, I knew him in an instant.

"Chase Gibbs," I said, even though he couldn't hear me.

The Gibbs family had stayed at the resort every summer for nearly a decade. My sister and I had always liked Chase and his older brother, Garrett, but the summer I turned twelve, Chase and I became something more. He gave me my first kiss and many more to follow, and I was heartbroken when the season ended.

That fall, we'd exchanged a flurry of postcards and earnest letters, and he'd sent me a heart-shaped necklace for Christmas. Yet when the following summer approached, Chase sent news that his parents planned to cruise the Orient rather than visit the resort. They signed him and his brother up for sailing camp, and I hadn't seen him since.

"Chase!" I headed towards him. We came to a stop on the path and smiled at each other. "I can't believe it's really you."

The last time we were together, he was fumbling with the snaps on my bra. It probably wouldn't be appropriate to open with that memory.

"It's great to see you," I said. "What are you doing here?"

It was so strange to see the grown-up version of him, since the younger version had taken up so much real estate in my heart. I'd forgotten how his eyes had a subtle downturn that made him look melancholy until he smiled.

"I'm writing a data storage book." The lake was radiant against the green of the manicured lawn and, gesturing out at it, he grinned. "However, I'm starting to suspect I might be taking a vacation."

"Writing about data storage doesn't sound like much of a vacation."

"You must not read much for pleasure."

His delivery was so dry that I laughed out loud, something I hadn't done enough lately.

"So, you went into tech." I looked up at him, shielding my eyes against the sun. "I would have thought ice-cream would be more your thing."

His parents had started a hugely popular organic ice-cream company in northern Wisconsin. It was distributed nationally, stocked in high-end shops throughout the Midwest. I'd seen it in Chicago several times over the years and had thought of him.

"Yeah, I'm a part of the company. Just taking a break to work on some passion projects. Because nothing says passion like—"

"Data storage," we both sang, and laughed.

"It's good to be back," he said. "I've bumped into so many people from our old crew here."

"Who have you seen?" I asked.

Back when we were younger, there had been a whole group of kids that came here each summer. We'd spent hours together playing in the lake, doing raft floats, challenging each other on the ropes course... it was great to think that some of them had returned.

"I've bumped into Saxon, Leo, and Tilly. Tilly has a whole bunch of kids. Four, I think, but there could easily be fifty based on the noise."

The names of our old friends were as familiar to me as my own.

"I hope I'll get to see them. Is your family here?"

"I'm not married." He looked down at his feet. "That sort of... fell apart."

"No, I meant your parents and your brother."

I didn't want him to think I was prying in his personal life.

"My parents aren't here." He hesitated. "My brother died. I guess you hadn't heard."

"What?" I said. "No."

I could see Garrett perfectly in my mind. Tow-headed, laughing, and pulling a bluegill out of the lake. He had always been so full of mischief, so full of life.

"When did he die?" I asked.

"Last fall. Heart attack. It was unexpected."

I hadn't seen either of them in twenty years, but the news made me sad. The idea of losing my sister... I couldn't imagine.

"Chase, I'm so sorry."

I almost hugged him but didn't. My parents had always made it clear that we were to be professional with the guests at all times, and not to assume a level of intimacy. Chase and his family had meant a lot to me in the past, but that was a long time ago. Now that I was older, I recognized the imbalance of power, but back when we were kids, none of us had noticed.

"Will you be here for a while?" I asked.

"The whole summer."

"That's amazing." Spending a few months here sounded like a dream. "I'm only visiting for a couple of days. My mother —"

He glanced at his watch. "Sorry. I have to take this call."

"Of course," I said quickly. "It was great to see you."

He gave me a half-wave and stepped away. It felt wrong somehow, considering he and I didn't have cell phones back when I knew him. But time marched on, and so did people.

I was glad I hadn't embarrassed myself by giving him a hug.

The bees buzzed around the flower beds at my parents' house. My stomach dropped to see that my father had installed a ramp for a wheelchair on their front porch. I ran up it but then stood on the porch for a moment, unable to go in.

Walking into my parents' perfectly ordered house, with the fresh bouquet of lilacs that sat on the mantel in the entryway, had always been a heartwarming experience. The current reality would be different. My father had warned me that he hadn't had the time to keep up with the house, and that it wasn't the way I was used to seeing it.

That warning did little to prepare me for the chaos that met me inside the front door. There was a stack of mail that stood about five inches on the entryway table, unpacked delivery boxes, and several pairs of my father's shoes. Moving into the living room, I stared at a mess of clutter. Water glasses lounged next to the chair where my father often worked, along with food wrappers, and worst of all, a folding table set up with more medicine than I would find at a pharmacy.

The house smelled musty and almost sour, a far cry from the fresh, sunshine scent it typically had. I would have to clean it from top to bottom while I was here. Maybe I could ask a member of our staff to continue to step in every few days for extra pay once I was gone.

It had to be upsetting to my mother to live like this. She'd always taken so much pride in her home, her appearance, and all the little details that made life beautiful. Heart pounding, I headed back to the bedroom to find her.

The whole house looked like the entryway. It proved how overwhelmed my father must be, because in any other situation, he would have picked up after himself. In my parents' room, the curtains were drawn against the sun, the air conditioning whirred, and my mother was asleep, covered by a heavy quilt.

I perched on the rickety wooden chair next to her bed, watching her take in the shallow breaths that lifted her thin ribcage up and down. My mother had always been so pretty and put-together, with a smile that didn't know a stranger. Now, her blonde hair had grayed at the roots, she didn't wear any make-up, and she'd lost so much weight in such a short period of time that her skin looked sharp and drawn. The sour smell that had permeated the house was stronger in the bedroom, and I wondered how often she'd been bathed.

The same chaos from the rest of the house was evident here, as well, with dirty tissues that rested next to a used cup of water, and a vague feel of dust clouding everything. It made me angry that my mother's room hadn't been made a priority, so I rolled up my sleeves and got to work, quietly cleaning it from top to bottom. The flower garden in the front of the house provided me with a cheerful vase of daisies that I set by the bedside table, along with lilacs that I placed in the front hall.

I settled into the chair next to the bed and stared at my mother, trying to imagine what she'd gone through in the past few days. Her life had changed in an instant. She'd been so independent, such a warm spirit to everyone who crossed her path. It didn't seem right that someone so kind had to go through something like this.

Her eyes fluttered open. "Julie." The word was garbled as she struggled to speak it and tried to smile.

My father had told me what to expect but I wasn't prepared for how it would make me feel. Her left eye was dipped at the corner, her mouth shaped in a crescent, and her cheek seemed lax. I took her hands. They were warm and smooth in mine, but I could barely feel the pressure of her left one. It took me a moment to understand why, as if my brain refused to accept the fact that so much had changed.

"Mom," I whispered, climbing into bed and pulling her into a tight hug. Frail as a baby bird, her heart beat wildly against mine. "I'm so glad to see you."

"Julie, you have work." Her words were halted, but I could understand them.

"I should have come sooner." I propped her against a backrest pillow. "How are you?"

"Frustrated." My mother looked around as if she needed something. She nodded as I handed her a glass of water with a straw.

The world felt upside down as I watched my mother take cautious sips, struggling to keep the water in her mouth. It ran down her chin, and quickly I went for a towel. The embarrassment in her eyes made me look away.

I reached for the book on the bedside table. "Would you like me to read this to you?"

She leaned back against the pillow. "Talk about you."

I told her about my job and Tristan, making it a point to emphasize how hard I'd been working so she would understand why it had been so hard to catch up with me.

"I'm so happy to be here," I said. "Dad's been doing a great job handling everything."

"He needs good health." My mother looked exhausted as she struggled to form the right words. "To dance, to love."

"Dad needs you." My voice was firm. "He always will."

Her shoulders slumped, as if too tired to continue the topic.

"Do you want to lie back down?" I asked.

When she nodded, it was a challenge to not show my surprise. Pulling the quilt up to her chin, I tucked her in. "Get some sleep."

I shut the lights off but left the door open. In the hallway, I leaned against a wall decorated with family photos and closed my eyes, fighting back a sense of despair.

My mother and I had only been together for fifteen or twenty minutes but in that short period of time, it was easy to see how upset she was by the stroke. The idea that she was suffering not just physically but also emotionally broke my heart. I wanted to be there for her, to comfort her, and it hurt to think just how little time I had here to do that.

CHAPTER THREE

My sister was sitting out on the back deck of her massive home in Portland when I video-called. Her two-year-old twins were busy playing in a sprinkler, and she turned the phone so I could see their chubby bodies splashing in the water. I felt that familiar sense of failure that Tristan and I were no closer to having children than the day we got married.

"They're adorable." I pulled the throw pillow on the couch close to my stomach. Tristan had left a note that he'd gone for a hike, and the cabin felt empty without him.

My sister's face was as full as the moon, and flushed with the heat of summer. We were both blonde, but her thick curls had darkened to a deep honey tone with this pregnancy. It had been a year since I'd last seen her, and it was my turn to make the trip.

"How is Mom?" Kate asked. "Dad says everything's under control, but what do you think?"

Her face became stormy as I gave her the update. She sat in silence, and I couldn't tell if she was blinking because the sun was in her eyes or because she was about to cry.

"I can't believe this," she finally said. "I've talked to him like, fifty times. He convinced me everything was *fine*."

"I think he wanted to believe it was."

"Which is ridiculous." Kate took an angry drink of sparkling water. "He should be by her side, not dealing with Wood Violet. How are they supposed to handle running that place, especially with this happening? It's too much, and you can't be bothered to help, so what are they supposed to do?"

I winced. "Kate, it's not that I'm not willing…"

"So, you'll stay?" she demanded.

"For a few days." Kate tossed up her hands, and I said, "I have to get back! I have a job."

"Take some leave. You still have freedom, the kind that won't be there when you have kids."

So many of my friends in Chicago had the same mindset. Like I had absolutely nothing to do because I didn't have children. They didn't have the slightest idea how hard I worked, how little free time I had, or the fact that it wasn't my choice that I didn't have a family.

Kate set the phone on the patio table. The way she'd balanced it gave me a bigger picture of her, and I saw that her body had grown fuller than the last time we'd spoken. She fanned herself with a paper plate as we glared at each other.

"I'd be on a plane in a heartbeat if I could," she told me.

No doubt. Kate was the type of person who had birthdays and anniversaries programmed into her phone, a florist on speed-dial, and a batch of homemade chicken soup in the freezer at all times. The fact that she couldn't help was probably as hard for her to deal with as finding out the truth about how incapacitated our mother really was.

One of the twins called for her. "I have to go." Kate got to her feet. "Let me know what you decide."

"There's nothing to decide," I told her, but she'd already hung up.

The phone call put me in a bad mood. The fact that Tristan still wasn't back at the cabin at six forty-five, when I'd made it perfectly clear that dinner started at seven o'clock, frustrated me even more. I had already showered, put on make-up, and slipped into a yellow silk dress that fluttered as I paced across our small living room, debating whether or not to head to the main lodge without him.

I couldn't do that, though. It would start an unnecessary fight and we'd had too many of those lately. Picking up the phone, I called him and it rang right outside the window.

"Thank goodness," I said, rushing for the door.

Tristan walked in with his hair wet and his body covered in sweat. "You look nice." He immediately went for some water, and leaned against the counter as if settling in for a long chat. "That was fun. I went over to the obstacle course, the one with the tires and ropes? It's a good workout. Took a dip in the lake afterwards."

"Can't wait to hear all about it. We have to go, though. Dinner's at seven."

He raised an eyebrow. "What's the rush? I still need to hear about your mom."

"It's a formal dinner." I slid on my flats. "Let's go or we'll miss it."

"The food won't walk away. We'll get there." Tristan found the bag of almonds from the welcome basket, crunched on a handful, then gulped another glass of water before heading back to shower.

I leaned against the front door, fighting back a wave of annoyance. We'd rushed to dinner with his clients countless times. It was always so important then. Somehow, he made me feel like the idea of a nice dinner at the resort was vaguely foolish.

There was no time to address that, though, because it would lead to a fight, and we'd be later than we already were. At this point, I just wanted to get there.

He came out of the room at seven, looking handsome in a pair of navy slacks and a perfectly fitted blue button-up shirt. Taking my hand, he said, "Let's go."

*

The lodge looked lovely, as always. It had been built out of enormous oak trees and the logs made up the interior walls. The ceilings were fifteen feet high, which gave the space an open, airy feel, no matter how many guests were seated at the round tables that filled the room. It was also one of the only buildings at the resort with air conditioning, so it was comfortable. Wooden candelabras hung overhead, the electric candles as cozy as starlight.

Since we were late, the appetizers had already been served. A cheerful buzz of conversation encompassed each table as the string quartet played classical music in the background.

Tristan tensed next to me, probably as he realized that I wasn't making it up; we really were late. There were several recognizable faces in the room, like the pitcher of a pro-ball team and the president of a Chicago beer distributorship. It was the perfect place to network, and Tristan seemed frustrated when we were seated at a table of older couples, well past the age of moving their money to someone new.

An ornate serving of tuna tartare sat waiting for us in front of our place cards.

"How long has that been sitting there?" Tristan asked, folding his napkin into his lap.

"Since seven o'clock," I said pointedly, and picked up my fork.

I'd only had time to take two bites before it was whisked away and replaced with a summer salad with mixed berries and goat cheese. The tuna was great, as was the salad. I was pleased to see that the quality of the food was still strong, in spite of what had happened behind the scenes.

Scanning the room, I spotted my old friend Leo sitting with his wife and two young kids. They looked exactly like him, with their freckled faces and shocks of red hair. Seeing his kids made me think of what my sister had said this afternoon about me not having a family.

Most of the time, I put the thought out of my mind, but when faced with friends my age so far along in the process of raising kids, it made me feel like a failure. It didn't help that Tristan and I were completely incapable of communicating about it. The issue had become a hard seed of bitterness between us and, so far, we hadn't gotten past it.

During the main course we made small talk with the couples at our table, but now, as the waiters bustled away the plates that had held grilled scallops on garlic risotto, we finally had a moment to talk to each other.

"How's your mother?" Tristan asked.

"It was hard to see her," I admitted.

Once I'd told him about the visit, he asked a thousand questions I couldn't answer about the general plan for her recovery.

"There has to be something concrete in place." He wiped his mouth with the corner of his napkin. "There needs to be some markers, some set goals."

"We didn't get that far." I sipped at my drink, a brandy old-fashioned. It was something I only drank at Wood Violet, because it reminded me of my grandmother. "For now, my mother's just trying to accept it."

"Do I get to see her?" Tristan asked.

"Why wouldn't you?" I asked.

"It might make her uncomfortable," he said. "If she's embarrassed, she might only want to see you and your dad. You should ask her."

There was a tap on my shoulder and I turned to see Chase. He was sunburnt but well-dressed in a lightweight navy suit, a pair of tortoiseshell glasses, and a white shirt with the top button undone. The rebellious button reminded me of the bow ties his parents made him wear to dinner, typically in bright colors patterned with sea animals.

"No bow tie?" I asked.

He looked confused, then laughed. "Thanks for bringing up my worst nightmare. Listen, I'm sorry to interrupt but I wanted to apologize for taking that call today. It was a scheduled board meeting but I'm sure it seemed rude."

"You don't have to apologize," I said, embarrassed. "You'll actually get me in serious trouble with my parents for saying that. You're our guest, not the other way around."

"Either way, I wanted to let you know." He glanced at Tristan. "Hi, I'm Chase Gibbs."

"Tristan Scott." He looped his arm around my shoulders. "What brought you to Wood Violet, Chase?"

"Nostalgia. It's been years since I'd been here, but it's still a part of who I am." He looked at me. "I'm sure you feel the same."

"Completely," I said.

I'd tried to explain the nostalgic appeal of Wood Violet to Tristan a hundred times but it was impossible to share with someone who hadn't been there. Chase had heard the loons call across the lake, smelled the muck where the frogs hung out, and tasted my mother's homemade sorbet. He had experienced the moments that were forever imprinted on my DNA.

"So, what do you do, Chase?" Tristan asked, moving the conversation to equal ground.

"Oh, this and that." He shoved his hands into his pockets. "I own a mom-and-pop ice-cream company. Before that, I spent a few years in computers."

"You took over the company?" I said, surprised.

"Yeah." Chase adjusted his glasses, looking vaguely embarrassed. "My parents wanted to move on. I closed the deal by offering them a lifetime supply of sugar." The string quartet had been replaced by a jazz band, who started to warm up on the stage at the front of the room. "Speaking of which, you two enjoy your dessert. Tristan, it was nice meeting you."

Tristan waited until he'd walked away and then said, "Who was that again?"

"Chase Gibbs. He was my first kiss. Isn't that funny?"

Tristan laughed. "Well, we all have to start somewhere."

"Tristan," I said, irritated.

I'd meant it was funny as in strange, that life had come a full circle, and my first love was now meeting the man that I'd married.

"I'm kidding," Tristan said. "He seems like a solid guy. Man, though. Those tech guys get a little money then they think people want to hear what they have to say."

I cringed, hoping no one had overheard.

Money had never been a problem for Chase. In fact, if I told Tristan the name of the 'mom-and-pop' ice-cream business he owned, Tristan would probably seek him out later and try to sell him on his finance firm.

There was a resounding crash as the jazz band started to play and the lights went up on the stage. The couples that had come to the resort for years applauded and got to their feet, moving to the dance floor. The bright flash of sequins and fluttering silk floated across the floor, like an instant reenactment of *Dancing with the Stars*.

Tristan looked baffled. "What just happened?"

I smiled. "Dancing." Suddenly, I spotted another good friend from my childhood on the dance floor. "There's Tilly!"

Back when we were kids, she'd been that sun-kissed girl with a pop-up collar that all the boys were in love with. I used to think she was the coolest thing in the world. She was still sun-kissed, with dimpled cheeks and a quick smile, but now tall and willowy. Her husband seemed to be counting the steps and she beamed up at him.

The adoration on her face touched my heart. It was the same with so many of the other couples. My father liked to joke that Wood Violet had saved a thousand marriages. It brought people back together to a simpler place, and allowed them the time to reconnect.

The older lady to my left touched my arm. She had an elegant posture, and a sheer, navy scarf draped dramatically across her shoulders.

"This key lime pie is divine." She dipped her fork in, then waved it at me. "Your mother has outdone herself. I don't know how she always makes such a perfect crust."

I tried a bite. It was good, the perfect combination of tart and sweet, topped with fluffy whipped cream.

"I'm so glad you like it," I said. "Our new pastry chef must have used her recipe. My mother is actually taking a step back this year."

The lady nodded. "Health reasons?"

"Yes. We're hoping she'll be up and about in no time."

The rumors had to be circulating amongst the regulars. My father had not kept the stroke a secret, but he was not broadcasting it, either.

The woman patted my hand. "Well, please tell Mac and Lilian that the DuMae family is hoping for her swift recovery."

"Thank you," I told her. "That will mean a lot to my parents."

"Shall we?" Her husband set down his napkin. Mrs. DuMae rested her bejeweled hand in his and they headed out to the dance floor.

Tristan watched with interest. "Does this happen here every night?"

"Wednesday and Saturday." I thanked the waiter as he refilled my coffee.

"Your father's out there. He's good."

My father led a woman across the floor, spinning her and making her laugh. He'd always danced with the older women while my mother handled dessert but at the end of the night, my parents had been known to dance together once everything was closed down, along to music from a portable radio. My sister and I had loved spying on them through the window but we always ran away if it looked like they were about to kiss.

"My dad is a good dancer. My grandparents were electric, though. Showstoppers. They used to perform this one number to kick things off and then everyone would join in."

Tristan grinned, and got to his feet. "Let's do it."

My shoulders tensed. "Tristan. You know I don't dance."

Somehow, I had managed to avoid dancing for most of my adult life. Dancing embarrassed me. I had no rhythm and, no matter how hard I tried, I didn't like it. Tristan knew that all too well, because I'd even refused to do a couple's dance at our wedding.

"Come on." His dark eyes were playful. "No one will pay attention. I'll lead."

I took a bite of pie. "There are tons of people that would love to dance." Discreetly, I pointed out an older lady at the next table over. She sat alone, tapping her fingers to the music. "It would make her day if you asked her. It would make her year."

"I want to dance with my wife." Tristan's tone became irritated. "Look, you wanted me to have the Wood Violet experience. This is part of it. Let's go."

I could see his point. It was just frustrating that this was the part of the Wood Violet he wanted to embrace. There were so many other options, like a walk in the woods or a late-night dip in the lake, but it had to be this.

"Fine." Cheeks flaming, I got to my feet. "I'll try."

The second before we were about to step onto the floor, my father waltzed over with a television actress who starred in a well-publicized sitcom. She was my age, stunning, and instantly made me feel short.

"Tristan, would you do the honors?" he asked.

Tristan seemed more than happy to accept, and my father walked me back to my table. "So, I have news. The operations manager I hired is no longer coming. He had a family emergency."

My stomach dropped. "You're kidding."

I'd asked my father to text me his résumé. It was impressive. He'd worked with several high-end hotels and had spent a year managing private villas in Lake Tahoe, which meant he had the experience to jump right in.

My father wiped his sweating face on a handkerchief. "The emergency popped up when he failed to negotiate more money."

"Dad," I said, in disbelief. My father loved negotiating but now was not the time. "You don't need a bargain, you need help. It will cost more to deal with the stress."

"Nope." He gave a firm shake of his head, after smiling at a couple headed to the dance floor. "It's a character issue. He knew our situation, waited for the final hour, and planned to call the shots. That's unacceptable."

My father would not have a good opinion of some of the insurance companies I had been defending. I took a drink of water, trying to cool off the sick feeling in my stomach that showed up every time I thought about work.

"So, what's the back-up plan?" I asked.

My father paused. "Our marketing director wants a bigger role." He rested his hand against the back of a chair. "It didn't seem like the best fit, initially. She won't need much training, though, so it should work."

His wording concerned me. "What do you mean, not the best fit?"

"Well, we needed that extra body," he said. "One to focus on operations, and the other, marketing. Putting it all on one person is not ideal but it will work out." Linking my arm in his, he said,

"Come greet people with me. I want to show them that I've got the best daughter in the world."

We had just started talking to a family from New York when a member of security texted. My father excused us from the conversation and led me outside. The sudden silence of the outdoors was a sharp contrast to the lively gathering inside.

"What is it?" I asked.

My father flagged down Matt, the security guy who had texted him. Matt was about my age and also worked on the police force. By the set of his jaw, he was not happy that any type of disruption had happened on his watch.

"What happened?" my father asked, climbing into the cart.

"It's the main office, sir." Matt took the cart out of park. "Someone broke in."

CHAPTER FOUR

My father jumped into the second row of the cart, indicating that I should, too. I hesitated, since I didn't have my phone.

"You coming or not?" my father asked.

Tristan was most likely still on the dance floor. With any luck, I'd be back before he missed me. Just in case, I borrowed my father's phone to text him as the golf cart bumped over the path, my father firing questions at Matt.

"It's a broken window," Matt said. "That's the extent of it, and it doesn't appear anything was taken. However, someone started to look through the records closet. Something must have spooked them, because it looks like they left pretty quickly."

"Did they trip the alarm?" I asked.

"The alarm?" Matt's voice was dry. "That's a good one."

"Dad." I couldn't believe what I was hearing. "You don't have an alarm system?"

"We haven't needed an alarm."

"You're a business," I said. "Of course you need an alarm."

The fact that my parents did not have a security system was a surprise. Yes, they had a team of security but that was a completely different story. Maybe I thought that way because I lived in the city instead of out in the woods, but it felt like common sense.

"There's nothing of value in there," my father said. "Except…"

"What?" I asked, when he hesitated.

"Information. People's data. Years of it. That's why we're transferring our files to an online platform, so that we can make it secure."

Yes, there were people and places that would be interested our guest records, but I couldn't imagine someone would break into our offices for that information. The records closet had files that dated back to the seventies. It would be impossible to waltz in and collect any specific piece of data.

"That seems like a lot of work," I said. "If you're a criminal, why steal paper documents when it's probably so much easier to steal information from other places online?"

The building was lit up as we approached. The golf cart stopped and my father jumped out. It chilled me to think someone had been in there that shouldn't have.

"Were you the one who turned on the lights?" my father asked Matt.

"Yes." He nodded. "I also swept the entire place and searched the perimeter."

Pointing the bright beam of his flashlight at a window low to the ground, he said, "This is the point of entry." The glass was mostly gone, like someone had thrown a rock and then torn away the sharp edges before climbing in. "Point of exit was the main door. It was left unlocked."

The main door had one of those locks that could only be turned from the inside, or with a key. My father examined the window, then Matt led us to the door that led into the building. I hesitated, but since the two were already walking through, it seemed safer to follow than to stand outside, in the event that the person who broke in was still lurking.

The main office building had always felt cozy to me as a child and I tried to focus on that, instead of my nerves. The office had a thick, navy blue carpet, and there had always been a full jar of candy that sat at the main desk, filled with cinnamon discs, butterscotch and Hershey's Kisses. My mother had slipped me one every time I came to the office for a visit.

Now, the big jar was nearly empty but I snagged a Hershey's Kiss before following my father and Matt to the records closet. The room was cramped and hot, especially with the three of us in it. Several boxes from the early 2000s had been taken down, rifled through, and left with their lids off.

"Can you tell if anything has been taken?" Matt asked.

My father sifted through some folders. "No. There's no telling if something's missing if you don't know it was there in the first place." He stood up. "Should I file a report?"

Matt shrugged. "Up to you. I think it would be beneficial, in case there's a further problem. This could have been practice, to see whether or not you had security and if the other buildings are as simple to get into. My primary concern is…"

"The cabins." My father nodded. "The guests."

The lack of crime made Wood Violet feel like a place that was perfectly safe to roam but maybe it wasn't. My friend Tilly jumped to mind, since she was here with four children. Why would she pay a fortune to stay here if there was any chance it would put her family at risk?

"Dad, has this happened before?" I asked.

"This is the first time."

"Then we have to do something so that it doesn't happen again," I said. "I can't even imagine the response if word got out about this."

"I agree," he said. "People won't stay here if they don't feel safe, but it would be nearly impossible to break into the cabins. The windows don't open."

It was a good point. The windows only opened six inches, unless the latch was disengaged for an emergency. The distance allowed guests to keep their windows open at night. It would be impossible to access the latch from the outside, even if the screen was cut.

My father rubbed his hand against his cheek. "Let's report it but keep it quiet. I'll double the security staff and we'll keep a close eye on things."

"You need to have a security system installed in the main buildings," I insisted. "Tomorrow or Monday, latest."

My father shook his head. "It's not how we do things here."

Matt shined his flashlight towards the broken glass that littered the floor. It sparkled like the surface of the lake in the sun. Shutting off his flashlight, he turned to my father.

"With all due respect, sir, I don't think you have a choice."

Matt drove me back to the lodge while my father met with the police. As we pulled up, I could see the guests dancing, the colorful dresses muted in the fogged picture window. The scene was so festive compared to the image of that broken glass.

Inside, the lodge smelled like after-dinner drinks and expensive perfume. Tristan sat at a table on his phone. Spotting me, he got to his feet and indicated the door. "Sorry," I said, kissing his cheek. "Did you get my text?"

"Yes, I did." I could tell by the way he held his shoulders that he was irritated at being left alone for so long.

"I'm really sorry," I said, once we were outside. "It was a mess."

Keeping my voice low as we walked back into the woods, I updated him on the break-in. He whistled.

"That's bad timing," he said. "Your parents don't need that right now."

"I know," I said. "The thing that was the most frustrating was that they don't have security. They have security teams, but no cameras."

We made it to our cabin and stood out front, in the moonlight.

"Well, here's the good news," Tristan said. "Your father has handled this place for years. He's not going to let anything happen to it."

I wasn't sold. My father was so busy keeping an eye on everything that something was bound to slip through the cracks.

"What's the bad news?" I asked.

"That you're going to worry about it no matter what I say."

I rested my head against Tristan's chest, letting the steady beat of his heart soothe me. The stress of it all was exhausting, and I appreciated the chance to feel safe in his arms. Moments like these made wonder whether our fights had any true weight, since he knew me better than anyone else in the world.

"What do you say we go inside?" he murmured.

I nodded, knowing full well I'd be fast asleep by the time my head hit the pillow.

Less than an hour later, I was awake again. The dark silhouette of the trees leaned into each other outside the window and I pulled my pillow close. Tristan lay next to me, snoring, with big plans to run three miles at sunrise. There was no way I'd have it in me to join him, since my mind would run a marathon all night.

For some reason, I was struggling with guilt, like I was the one responsible for the trouble that had hit my family. Two months ago, I'd defended a chain grocery store against an older woman who slipped on a broken juice bottle and hurt her back. The settlement barely covered the cost of her medical bills.

The woman was on a fixed income and had no living relatives. The store was negligent, but my client knew she had no idea how much was due to her in compensation. The fact that I had helped them to pay her as little as possible had made it hard to sleep for weeks.

Now, I wondered if the things my parents were going through was my punishment. I knew that the answer was no, but that didn't make it any easier to accept the fact that my mother was suffering and she didn't deserve it. No one did, but in situations that involved health, accidents, or a broken heart, life called the shots. We didn't have the luxury to choose our preferred outcome.

Chase Gibbs jumped to mind. He had to be struggling with the same issues, while trying to accept his brother's death. My mother hadn't died, and I would be forever grateful for that. Still, it was upsetting to see her have no choice but to let go of her life as she knew it. I wished I had the time to stay here and help her through it.

That's why I had gotten so mad at my sister for asking me to stay. I wanted to, more than anything. But what could I do, quit my job?

I knew what Tristan would say to that. He'd tell me that my parents were adults and could handle the situation on their own. That there was no reason to ruin everything I'd worked so hard to achieve. I was now at one of the most elite firms in the city and it made no sense to throw that away when my mother had my father to help her through this.

The old-fashioned clock by the bed read three a.m. I stared up at the ceiling, listening as the forest settled into the night. The creak of the trees in the breeze, the rustle of the insects against the screens, and the slow silence as nature came to life. The absence of sound also caught my attention—there were no cars honking, or elevated trains rumbling past, or groups of people rushing to get somewhere.

Rolling over, I closed my eyes, squeezing them tightly against the moonlight.

The hardest part is making the decision to do the right thing.

Not true. The hardest part was being able to recognize what the right thing really was.

CHAPTER FIVE

The next two days, I spent the majority of my time with my mother but met up with Tristan to hike, swim, and kayak in the moments she needed to rest. Monday night, there was a campfire and sing-along down by the lake. Tristan went to bed early because he wanted to wake with the sun for a jog but I decided to follow the smell of roasted hot dogs down to the water. There, at least fifteen small fires stretched out along the shore.

Children chased each other through the sand with the wooden sticks meant for roasting marshmallows. The orange glow of the flames reflected in the faces of our guests, while the old and young sat on the logs and chairs set out for the evening. The guitarist strummed softly by the water and when the time was right, he would play sing-along favorites until late.

I'd only gotten a quarter of the way down the beach when a voice called, "Julie Lenox! Get over here."

It had been years since anyone had called me by my maiden name. Turning, I saw a bundle of blonde hair rushing towards me. Tilly swept me up in a hug sweet with campfire smoke and expensive perfume.

"It is so good to see you." She flashed the pert smile I hadn't thought of in years but remembered in an instant. "I have been counting the seconds. Get over here, sit down, and I will personally toast you a marshmallow."

The heat of the fire warmed my cheeks as I walked up to a group around the fire that included Chase, Saxon, Leo, his wife, and Tilly's husband. Saxon made me look twice. He'd always been this skinny, quiet kid but he'd transformed into an incredibly attractive, rugged mountain-man.

"Julie Lenox." He kissed my hand, his gaze lingering on mine. "Do you know how many love poems I wrote for you?"

Tilly swatted him away. "Back off, she's married."

Saxon winked. "The good ones always are."

I actually blushed, probably because it had been ages since anyone had bothered to flirt with me.

Leo introduced me to his wife, who had one of their kids asleep in her lap and seemed as nice as could be. I settled onto one of the logs as the fire glowed and Tilly fixed me a s'more. Gratefully, I accepted the cider Chase handed me.

"To old friends," he said, and we all clinked drinks.

"Where's your man?" Tilly asked, putting chocolate on a graham cracker square. "I want to meet him."

"He gets up with the sun," I said. "Before, really."

"Well, I sleep late." Saxon gave me a charming smile. "Every day."

"That's called a hangover," Tilly's husband cracked, and we all laughed.

Tilly handed me the s'more. The marshmallow and chocolate melted in my mouth, gooey and sweet. It was the best thing I'd eaten in ages.

"So, catch me up," I said. "Tell me everything. Let's stay here until dawn."

"We always tried to do that, didn't we?" Chase said.

"Yep." Tilly giggled. "Our parents never let us."

"It's weird to think we're finally adults." Leo stabbed a marshmallow onto a stick. "We could actually stay up all night."

His wife snorted. "You wouldn't miss a full night's sleep if someone paid you."

"Saxon would." Tilly nudged him with her foot. "Depending on the company."

He gave me a hopeful look and I held up my ring finger.

"Married," I said, and everyone laughed.

The conversation was easy and the jokes frequent. Our group talked for an hour straight, before Tilly's kids ran over to grab a few pieces of chocolate. They really did look like her, four little copies, three boys and one girl. I felt that familiar pang and was grateful that nobody asked whether or not I had children.

The guitarist began to sing 'Piano Man,' and one of the other groups applauded and joined in. Soon, everyone down the length of the beach was singing. We waved our bottles and belted out the words as the stars gleamed overhead.

It got late. Tilly left to put the kids to bed, as did Leo and his wife. Saxon, Chase, and I stayed as the fire turned to embers, lingering over the final moments of the night. Finally, Chase got to his feet and stretched.

"Sadly, I've once again failed to stay awake until dawn."

I laughed. "Me, too."

It would have been awkward to sit there with just Saxon, so I brushed the sand off my legs and stood up. The three of us walked through the woods together, the silence of the forest broken by our memories. The one memory I did not speak out loud was a walk just like this one, where Chase and I had kissed for the first time.

It had been a perfect, clear night. We were headed back to our cabins after a bonfire, when a white streak shot through the sky. Chase had pulled me behind a tree and kissed me, as the stars fell around us.

It was such a sweet memory and so funny to think that we were back here again, so many years later, under such different circumstances.

"Enjoy your five a.m. wake-up call," Saxon said, after I'd hugged them both goodbye.

"Shh." Chase pointed at the open windows. "Don't get her in trouble."

They laughed like kids.

"You guys are ridiculous," I said. "It was fun."

The bed shifted as I settled under the covers, and Tristan woke up. He raised himself on an arm and looked at the clock.

"It's one o'clock," he said. "Where have you been?"

"The campfires." I settled into the pillow, my voice hoarse from the smoke and the singing. "You should have come. It was the best time."

I wanted to tell him about the joy I'd felt for the first time in ages, but Tristan had already pulled a pillow over his head. Tugging the sheets close, I went to sleep.

The next morning, I headed straight for my mother's when I woke up. The nurse had come and she was dressed, sitting at the kitchen table. For a split second, I tricked my mind into thinking I was here for a fun weekend getaway until my mother tried to smile, seemed to realize that it didn't look the same as it used to, and instead, stared down at the floor.

"Good morning." I kissed her cheek. "Tristan sends his love. He went fishing to give us some time together."

My mother nodded, as if relieved. He had come to see her the day before but both Tristan and I could tell she was embarrassed, so he decided it would be best to not come today. I studied her, trying to figure out what I could do to make her feel better. Typically, at this time of day, my mother would be weeding the vegetable garden, planting flowers, or working in the kitchen at the lodge.

"Do you want to go outside?" I asked. "To the flower garden?"

Her eyes lit up. Eagerly, she nodded.

The wheelchair served as her chair at the table, so I undid the brake and wheeled her to the front porch. It felt like pushing a baby carriage. It didn't seem fair to think I was wheeling my mother around before I had even pushed my child in a stroller.

The situation made the world feel out of order, like things weren't happening as they should.

Once we'd made it down the ramp and across the grass to the flower garden, I used every ounce of strength I had to push the wheelchair through the mulched path that cut through the center of the garden.

"How was that for a joyride?" I asked, and she smiled.

We sat in silence, listening to the birds and letting the sun warm our faces. It felt strange to put my hands in the dirt, since it had been so long. The smell of the soil was so rich, like wet coffee grounds or the mud after a rainstorm. I scooped some up and placed it in my mother's right hand.

"You know me," she said.

I nodded, watching as she squeezed the dirt. It was hard not to feel angry that she had to deal with this. My mother had been the picture of health, so the idea that she'd had a stroke was not only unjust, it scared me. Would I go through the same thing at her age?

The first thought that came to mind was how long Tristan would put up with the challenge. I could imagine him setting up goal charts all over the house, to push me to recover at full efficiency. The thought made me shudder.

"What are you thinking about?" my mother asked.

"Butterflies," I said quickly. I pointed at the lilac wings fluttering against the bright flowers. "They've always reminded me of you."

My mother watched the butterflies, and a sense of peace settled over me. We sat in the garden for over an hour and when we went back, I was grateful for the time we'd had. I couldn't stand to think how long it might be until we'd have the chance to do something like that together again.

*

When it came time to leave the resort, Tristan and I loaded the bags in the car in the main parking lot, but I couldn't bring myself to open the passenger's side door.

Tristan rolled down the window. "It won't get easier."

It was early Wednesday morning and the sun had yet to rise. Crickets chirped while bugs darted back and forth in the headlights of our car. My mind lingered on the feeling of my mother's arms around me as we'd said goodbye the night before.

When would I be back? When could I see my family again? In three hours, I'd be sitting in the leather chair in my office, like nothing had changed.

Tristan cued up classical music. He was dressed in one of his many business suits, and looked completely out of place in the middle of the forest. I had planned to change at home, before racing into the office.

"Look, this whole visit has been a shock," he said. "You need time to process all of this. Come on. We have to go."

I reached for the door handle and then stopped. "I'm not coming." The moment I said the words, the tightness that had sat in my chest for days broke open. "I can't. I'm going to call my boss and see if I can take a leave of absence for the summer."

"You must be joking." When I didn't respond, Tristan gripped the steering wheel. "You could get fired. There's no reason for you to ruin your life because you think that your mother can't live without your help."

"I don't think that," I said. "But I'm not ready to leave her. It's time I started investing in the people that I care about."

He drew back at the words. "I see."

I couldn't believe he was trying to make this about him.

"Tristan, come on. I'm with you for life. You could even…" My pulse quickened, as the idea of summer at Wood Violet shaped into reality. "Tristan, you could work remotely. Stay here, have virtual meetings, and make the drive if you need a face-to-face."

"I'm not doing that."

"Why not?" I demanded.

"Because the in-person connection matters." Tristan leaned back against the leather seats as if discussing the issue exhausted him. "This won't work, Julie. Even if they agree to letting you take the time, which they won't, you wouldn't get paid."

I drew back. "It's a little insensitive to talk about money at a time like this."

"Spoken like someone born into privilege. Bills don't stop because you're going through a hard time. In my experience, the more bills, the harder the times."

It was rare that Tristan addressed his upbringing. I knew it was what drove him to be successful. Still, the topic irritated me because my sister and I both received monthly checks from a trust fund created by my grandparents during the years the resort was at its most successful. Yes, it was a privilege, but if I wanted to take some time off, the money was there to do it.

"Put my check from the trust towards my share of our expenses," I told him. "That will more than cover it."

Tristan drew back. "That money is for our retirement account."

"It's for whatever we decide it's for," I said. "It makes sense to let money coming directly from the resort to fund my time here helping at the resort, don't you think?"

For a second, it looked like he planned to argue. Instead, he glanced at the clock on the dashboard. "The international markets are open. I need to get to work." When I didn't make a move to get into the car, he got my suitcase out of the trunk. "Do you want me to walk you back?"

"I'll be fine."

It was nearly light out. Besides, I didn't want him to spend the next ten minutes trying to talk me out of this.

I stepped forward to hug him, and we stood in silence. The birds had started to chatter.

"There's nothing I can say to convince you that this is a bad idea?" he asked.

I peered up at him, trying to read his expression. "This wasn't an easy decision, Tristan, but it's the right one."

"The right one for you," he said. "There's no point in me being here. You barely spent time with me this weekend. It's not like that would change."

"Because my mother is sick," I said, in disbelief. "I'm sorry that you didn't get my undivided attention. Sometimes, other people matter, too."

Our eyes locked. So much anger had simmered between us for the last few months. Petty moments, topics too difficult to address.

It was hard to admit it, but time apart might be the best thing. We could figure out where we could bend because at the moment, it felt as if we pushed too hard, we might break.

"I'm going to go," he said.

Tristan got in the car without even looking at me. It was a good thing the parking lot was paved, or I had no doubt a cloud of dust would have billowed up behind him as he drove away.

CHAPTER SIX

My father looked over the rims of his reading glasses when I walked into his office. Surprise registered on his face, followed by hope. "I thought you'd be on the road by now. Did you leave something in the cabin?"

"Nah." I set down my bag. "I decided it was time to take a summer vacation. Do you have a vacancy through September?"

My father rushed forward to hug me tight. "We could have done it without you, Julie." His voice was gruff. "I'm going to tell you something, though: we didn't want to."

My eyes misted as he bustled to the coffee bar next to his desk to make me a cup. Tristan and I had planned to get coffee on the drive home. I wondered if he'd already grabbed a double espresso and was back on the road.

"I want to help out with Mom and the resort as much as possible," I said. "So, think of some tasks to give me. Whatever you need, starting today, I'm happy to do it. Also, I'll need somewhere to stay."

He handed me a steaming mug of coffee.

"Normally, I'd want to stay with you guys, but I've been thinking about it, and I don't want to be in the way."

My parents were under too much stress to add a houseguest to the list. I'd be happy to cook and clean, but they needed things to stay as normal as possible.

My father nodded. "If there's not a couple's cabin available, we can put the two of you in one of the family cabins. Maybe it will inspire you to start your family." My father pulled out a carton of creamer from the mini fridge. "But the—"

"Tristan's not staying." The smooth liquid swirled into the cup and I returned the carton, ignoring the comment about kids. "He's headed back."

My father paused. "Julie, that's not the best idea. If you don't make your marriage a priority, it won't last." The wooden desk chair creaked as he sat back down. "You committed to forever. So did he."

It must have been more obvious than I thought that Tristan and I weren't at our best, but I didn't want to discuss it at seven o'clock in the morning or any time, really. My father had enough to worry about.

"This has nothing to do with my marriage," I told him. "It has everything to do with the fact that I almost lost my mother." Sitting in the chair across from his desk, I set the coffee on a piece of paper. "Did you know she called me a week before the stroke? I had planned to call her back but never got to it."

"You're busy." He clicked through his emails. "She knows that."

"Right, but…" Shame swept through me. "Then, there was back in March. She asked me to come for Mother's Day. I couldn't find the time, even though I had over two months to plan it."

"Julie." He sent an email, then looked at me. "Don't put yourself through this. Our job as parents is to raise you to have your own life and move on. It's part of becoming a grown-up."

I put my hand on his. "Then let me live my life. If my marriage falls apart, I'll fix it. That's part of being a grown-up, too."

My father went back to his email, responded to a few, and even wrote himself a few Post-it notes. I could tell he was trying to decide whether or not to tell me to go back home to my husband. Eventually, he nodded.

"I'll text your mother that you're staying," he said.

"She's awake?"

"She gets up at six."

"Don't text her," I said, getting to my feet. "I'll go tell her myself."

The visits with my mother over the weekend had been quick and simple. With the exception of the time in the flower garden, I had sat with her in her room, reading her books or telling her about my life. I had been careful to guard my heart, since it would be so hard to leave.

Now, when I stepped into my parents' house, I stood in the foyer and drank in the fact that it once again smelled like my childhood, that the chandelier in the dining room had never changed, and that even the sound of the front door closing sounded like home.

My mother sat in her wheelchair at the kitchen table, watching the nurse cook an egg. She looked small and fragile, with her slumped posture practically drowning in an oversized cardigan sweater. I snuck up behind her and wrapped my arms around her shoulders.

My mother jumped and then turned her head towards mine.

I pressed my cheek against hers, cherishing the warmth of her skin on mine. "Hope you like company," I said. "Because I'm going to be here every day for the rest of the summer."

Her eyes lit up. "You did?"

I knew she meant to say *You are?* and that small mistake was enough to break my heart. It didn't matter that I might fall behind at my job. Being with my mother, getting the chance to show her how much I loved her, mattered more than anything.

"How many eggs would you like?" the nurse asked. She was a heavyset woman with tightly curled brown hair and a friendly smile.

"Can I finish them up?" I asked.

The nurse handed me the silicone spatula. "I'll give the two of you some time," she said, and headed down the hall. The creak of the hallway closet indicated she was about to change the linens.

I sat down at the kitchen table. "One thing that's been on my mind lately is how sorry I am that I haven't been here," I told my mother. "I should have been here more."

She rested her hand on her cheek. "You are good."

"No, but I'm going to be," I told her. "If I've learned anything from what's happened to you, it's that I need to focus on what's important and that's you. I love you, Mom."

Her eyes misted. "Love you." She reached out her good hand and held mine. "I'm glad you're here."

I stayed with my mother until she had to take a nap. Then I headed out the front porch. With the bees buzzing around the flower beds, I left a voicemail for the partner I worked for, my boss, asking for permission to be out of the office until September.

"I realize I haven't been there long enough to request a formal leave," I said. "But this situation is unexpected, and I hope you'll understand. I'll work twenty-four seven starting the first week of September."

I settled in on the glider and the sun warmed my shoulders as I replied to work emails that were urgent, before setting up an out-of-office reply. Then I tried to call Tristan. He didn't pick up and my chest felt hollow. I didn't like how we'd left things but wished he could understand why I'd felt the need to stay.

I was by my mother's bedside with flowers fresh from the garden when she woke up from her nap. I helped her sit up against the pillows and handed her a lilac.

"Smell it," I suggested. "It's so fragrant today." She smelled it and smiled, and I passed her a pink rose, followed by a daisy.

My father dropped in when we were on the purple salvia. "My girls," he said, kissing us each on the head. "What do you think of all this?" he asked my mother.

She gave me her half-smile. "I love it."

"Me, too." My father ruffled my hair, then sent a quick email on his phone. "Nikki, our marketing director, is willing to share her office with you, and I'll send you daily tasks that need to be done, if that works. I've got the IT guys getting it all set up now."

"Perfect."

"The nurse typically bathes your mom before lunch. Why don't you come back to the office to meet Nikki, and then I have a field trip for you. I need you to check out the abandoned cabins by the river."

"Abandoned cabins?" I echoed.

"The ones that your grandmother wanted shut down, once she got older. I think she didn't want the guests back there, bothering her while she worked. It's time to decide whether to raze them or not."

"Sounds good." I squeezed my mother's hand. "I'll be back for dinner," I said, and she nodded.

My father and I walked together to the main office.

The sun glinted off the windows. The one that had been replaced the night of the break-in looked great, like nothing had happened at all.

"Have you thought more about installing a security system?" I asked.

"Yes, and it's a no. It would send the wrong message to our guests."

Before, I'd dropped the topic since I was only here for a short time. Now, the summer stretched before me. Keeping the resort safe and secure felt like a fair priority.

"Dad, it's lovely to keep Wood Violet quaint and simple but this is the modern world. People have cameras all over their homes. They have cameras in their doorbells. Heck, I think you can even buy a drone to circle your house. It's almost weird to not have security at a place like this."

"Julie, we have a whole team of people."

"Right, but you don't have electronic security," I said. "From a legal perspective, you want that extra layer of protection. The option to review videos, if something happens. If you protect the resort, you protect the guests. It's that simple."

"It doesn't make sense for us," he said.

Having security made sense on so many levels, so I still wasn't quite sure why he was pushing back.

"Dad, what's the real issue here?" I asked. "I'm confused to be fighting over something so simple."

"It's an investment, and it's important to take that into consideration when we've been fine for years." He brushed away a mosquito. "You can research some options, but I can't make any promises."

We walked into the building in silence. The thick navy carpet was soft against my sandals as we walked down the hallway to an office door. My father rapped on it, before walking in.

"Good morning, Nikki," he sang. "I'd like you to meet my daughter, Julie."

"Oh, it's nice to see you, Nikki," I said, delighted. "Dad, we went to school together."

Nikki was two years younger so I didn't know her well, but I'd always liked her. She was one of those naturally beautiful Midwestern girls with shiny brown hair and simple features, the type who looked great in a baseball cap. I'd always admired her ability to get along with anyone.

"Julie!" Hopping up from her desk, she gave me a warm hug. "I'm so sorry about your mother. I'm glad to hear you'll be here for the summer. We can use your help."

My father got me a skeleton key for the cabins and described how to find them. "There's the bird-watching event right now, and they'll be on the path, so I'm not worried about you being back there alone. But if you want security, tell me and I'll send someone."

"I'll be fine." I stopped at the door. "This sure beats what I'd be doing if I were back in Chicago."

My father smiled. "I'm glad to hear it."

I was about halfway into the woods when it hit me that I didn't need to rush, I had all the time in the world. I came to a stop in the middle of the forest and took in a deep breath.

The trees were thick overhead, and delicate shadows stretched across the path. Other than a vague rumble of thunder somewhere off in the distance, the only sound was the wildlife going about their business.

I walked in silence for at least a mile before encountering the bird-watchers. They were scattered across the path, with their faces pressed into the binoculars. Squeezing by a small group, I noticed Chase. He looked like something out of an Indiana Jones movie, dressed in a pair of khaki tearaway pants, a white T-shirt, and a safari hat. He had a pair of binoculars around his neck and turned them my way.

"What are you still doing here?" he called, his voice echoing through the forest.

I half-expected one of the bird-watchers to shush him but no one paid a bit of attention.

"Hey," I said, walking up to him. "I didn't peg you for the bird-watching type."

"Tilly roped me into it. She said it was life-changing to watch the birds in their natural habitat. Clearly, she lied. Not even a white lie, more of a, *No, I swear you look like a male model in your safari hat* lie."

"That hat is rather stunning," I said, touching the floppy brim.

"Tilly's husband handed it to me like it some rite of passage." He tugged at the strings. "I had a choice: take the hat or look like a complete jerk. So, I took the hat and I still look like a complete jerk."

Tilly appeared out of a thicket of the ferns at the sound of my laughter, dressed in lime green shorts and a Lilly Pulitzer polo. Spotting me, her face brightened.

"I thought you'd left," she said, bustling towards us.

"I couldn't leave my mother," I said.

Chase got serious. "She's not doing well?"

The sky darkened, and I looked up, noticing that the day had started to look gray.

"No, she's the same," I said. "But I wasn't doing well at the idea of leaving her."

Tilly put her hand to her heart. "That's exactly why I had four kids. If I play my cards right, maybe one of them would do the same for me. If I buy them things and don't limit their screen time."

My watch buzzed and I hoped for a text from Tristan. It was just a reminder I had in my phone about a work meeting. My boss hadn't responded to the message I'd left but he typically dealt with emails and calls that weren't urgent after lunch. I wasn't worried about his silence quite yet.

"I'll leave you to bird-watching," I said. "My father asked me to evaluate some of the older cabins down by the river."

"Do you want company?" Tilly took a sip from a pink-enameled water bottle that matched her perfectly manicured nails. "The birds are being dull today."

"I would love that," I said.

"Consider this my resignation from bird-watching." Chase took off his hat and tried to hand it to Tilly. She waved it away, so he plunked it on my head. It smelled good, like lemongrass. "Let's go."

I texted my father that Tilly and Chase were with me, because the visit might take twice as long and I didn't want him to worry. I was happy with the company. Back when I was a kid, summer wasn't summer without Tilly Fisk.

"It's about half a mile," I said, pointing up the path. "Over the hill."

"I have to call my husband on the way," Tilly said. "Make sure the kids haven't locked him in a closet."

Taking in the lush pine trees and the feeling of the mulch on the path beneath my feet, I said to Chase, "It's strange to walk in the woods instead of sitting at a desk. It feels like I'm doing something wrong."

Chase laughed. "Did you take a leave from your firm?"

"I'm waiting to hear back," I said. "My boss knows I'm a hard worker, so I'm hoping it will be fine. It's the best I can do."

"Family comes first," Chase said. "That's the mindset at my company."

Two deer strolled across the path in front of us and Tilly pointed them out, before mouthing *Sorry* and indicating her phone. It was fine; I'd been wanting to talk to Chase about his move from tech to ice-cream ever since he mentioned it that first night at dinner.

"Was it always your plan to work at Moo-ya?" I asked. "Personally, if my family owned an ice-cream business, it would have been a life goal."

"No, it kind of snuck up on me, believe it or not," he said cheerfully. "My brother stepped into the VP role right out of college. He and my father were always discussing strategy and I liked the problem-solving aspect of it all. I'd just moved back from California when Garrett left Moo-ya to develop a healthy fast-food chain. My parents were about to sell, and I stepped in. It ended up being perfect for me. What about you and Wood Violet?"

"It wasn't an option," I admitted. "My parents wanted me and my sister to graduate from college and have five years' real-world experience first."

Chase raised his eyebrows. "Wow."

"Yeah. The idea that I'd have to wait half a decade seemed like a lifetime, so I turned my focus to a career in law. It was probably for the best."

Thunder rumbled, and Tilly ended her call. Sliding her phone into her bag, she said, "I keep hearing thunder. Is it supposed to rain?"

The sky was definitely darker than before. The birds had also gone silent, which was never a good sign.

"Maybe we should—"

Before the words could leave my mouth, raindrops tapped on the leaves above us, light and steady. Then a crack of thunder crashed and buckets of water dumped from the sky.

"Come on," Chase called, breaking into a run.

Tilly squealed as the three of us slipped, slid, and failed miserably at keeping water out of our faces. The cabins came into view over the crest of a hill. Chase rushed down to them and ducked under the eaves, Tilly right behind him.

In spite of the rain, I stopped to take a look. The roofs were caved in on three of the five cabins, and they were all covered in fallen nettles. The setting had potential to be pastoral, but it had been neglected for far too long.

I had good memories of being out here, catching frogs with my sister in the river or playing settlers when the resort had closed for the season. We'd swept the floors with this decrepit broom that used to lay around and had spent hours in this very spot.

"Julie, what are you doing?" Tilly beckoned. "You'll catch cold!"

I joined them, trying to squeeze the water from my clothes. Chase's curls were plastered to his forehead, while Tilly's nose was flushed with the chill. The safari hat must have been weatherproof, because my hair was inexplicably dry.

"Thanks for the hat," I told Chase. "I'm snug as a bug."

Tilly swooped her blonde hair into a ponytail and secured it with an elastic band. "My kids would love this. They have no concept of discomfort."

"I'll try to get us in," I said.

The skeleton key unlocked the old wooden door on the third try. We escaped into an empty cabin that reeked of dust and wet wood. The cabin really wasn't in too bad shape, though. It looked old and dirty, but the floor didn't feel rotten and the windows were only half-broken.

Chase peeled off his sun shirt and draped it over a door handle, and his T-shirt clung tightly to his upper body. He was as cut as Tristan, with strong arms and well-defined, broad shoulders. Tilly whacked him on the back, her silver bracelets clinking.

"Please talk to my husband about your workout program, buddy." She started opening closets. "Julie, how long has this place been vacant? Is there hope for a spare blanket?"

"I think twenty years," I said. "But if you find one, I have dibs. Resort property and all that."

Chase laughed and the three of us settled in on the floor. The wood was rough against my legs, but it felt so much cozier than the sterile tile of my luxury condo back home.

"I have snacks." Tilly rummaged through her gigantic shoulder bag. Chip packets, granola bars, gummies, crackers, and dried fruit tumbled to the floor. "Have at it."

"It's funny to be back here," Chase said, reaching for a granola bar. "My family stayed back here for years, because my brother and I were obsessed with the river. Your grandmother worked at her studio a lot. She was always sketching something or other."

"She was an amazing artist," I said.

My grandmother had asked to draw me when I was five years old. My father explained that it was a very big deal, that my grandmother did not do portraits of people. I'd sat on a wooden stool that overlooked the river for an hour at a time for months and remember taking breaks to splash in the water or chase after dragonflies.

The drawing was picture-perfect. My parents had it framed and hung it over the fireplace in their house. My sister was irritated for at least two years, until my grandmother asked to sketch her. It wasn't a measure of favoritism; my grandmother had found us engaging at different stages in life.

"Don't you have an artist-in-residence cabin in her honor?" Tilly asked, and I nodded.

"My parents choose one artist each year to live there. They didn't do it this year, because of what happened with my mom." Thunder crashed outside and I turned to Chase. "You really liked being so far back in the woods?"

"Heck, yes. My brother and I spent the whole summer in the river. There were different bugs than what you could find in the lake. Garrett even tried panning for gold. He found a huge nugget—"

"Of gold?" The story shocked me. "I didn't even know you could find gold around here."

Chase grinned. "I spent a whole day panning and getting burnt, turning red as a lobster, but I couldn't find anything. That night, Garrett left the gold inside my pillow and a note on top that said, *There's a reason they call it fool's gold.* He'd brought it from home for the sole purpose of pranking me. Man, he was such a jerk."

The last part was said with such pride that Tilly and I laughed.

"You miss him?" she asked.

"Every day," he said.

The rain pummeled the roof overhead, and I hugged my knees to my body.

"It's helped me to be here." Chase's eyes were dark in the dim light. "There are actual moments where I'll get to a certain turn in the path and think, oh, he's just up ahead."

The words made me tear up, and Tilly took my hand. "Garrett might not be around every corner but he's alive in your memory, Chase. He always will be."

Chase crumpled up his wrapper. "Part of the reason I wanted to stay here this summer was because we buried one of those memory boxes together. Do you remember those?"

"The memory boxes," I breathed. "I haven't thought about those in ages."

There were several years where my grandparents picked a theme for each summer. Back when I was twelve, it was *Making Memories*. My grandmother had commissioned an artist friend to create etched steel boxes that were gifted to each family. The objective was to return home with a box full of memories from the summer.

It was the same year Chase and I had our summer of puppy love. I was not about to tell him, but my memory box had been filled with his letters. It had sat on my dresser for years, and I'd pined over its contents more times than I could count.

My grandmother would have been horrified to know that Chase and his brother had buried one of those beautiful boxes but under the circumstances, I was excited to hear it.

"Do you know where you hid it?" I asked.

Chase frowned. "It was in a bunch of different spots because we had to dig it up a couple of times. My mother kept asking where it was every time she wanted to add a picture."

"Chase," Tilly scolded.

He grinned. "Garrett and I made a pact that we'd come back one day and find it."

The three of us sat in silence, lost in our own thoughts, when Tilly looked up at the ceiling. Hopping to her feet, she spread her arms wide. "It stopped."

I pushed open the door. The storm was over. Light filled the sky above the branches and the birds tentatively chattered.

"Do you guys mind if I check out the other cabins before we take off?" I asked.

"That's why we're here," Chase said.

The second and third cabin were in worse shape than the first one, with leaks in the roof and some rotten patches of floor, but it wouldn't take much to repair them. The door to the fourth was broken at its hinges, so we walked right in.

Chase stopped short. Tilly and I bumped into him like something out of a comedy skit.

He turned to me with a worried expression.

"What's wrong?" I asked.

"Someone is living in here."

CHAPTER SEVEN

"Someone's living here?" I peered over his shoulder and spotted a sleeping bag and a few camping supplies. My heart started pounding.

The forest was silent, the light from the sun sneaking through the dirty panes of glass on the window, making it feel like the storm had never happened. The three of us hovered in the doorway, as if staring at the objects would somehow explain their presence. It was impossible to tell how long the person had been there, or anything about them, other than the fact that they played guitar.

It was a beaten-up acoustic, with deep brown wood that had hints of red, and simple black accents on the bridge and tuning keys. The strings were still intact and a small pearl inlay circled the hole in the middle. There wasn't a case anywhere in sight, and the guitar rested on top of a navy blue sleeping bag.

The image brought to mind the street performers in Chicago, the ones that played near the L train stops in the hope of getting a few dollars to buy some food. I kept spare dollar bills in the pocket of my coat for the purpose of giving money without taking out my wallet. That caution was part of living in the city but I never would have expected to feel scared at Wood Violet twice in four days.

"I'll call security." I pulled out my phone and dialed, but it wouldn't connect. "Tilly, try yours."

Tilly's face was frantic as she punched away at the keys. "Nothing."

Chase tried his at the same time, shaking his head. "Let's get out of here. We'll notify security when we get back." He looked at me. "It won't be an issue."

I appreciated his effort to downplay the situation, but it was already an issue. The idea of a homeless person hiding in the woods did not match what Wood Violet was selling. The fact that Tilly and Chase had seen it was a problem, but I couldn't exactly ask them to sign a non-disclosure agreement.

I could ask them to keep it quiet, of course, but there was no such thing as a secret. The news would get around to our group of friends first, make its way to other guests, and it wouldn't take long before people would question their safety. The idea that my father had let this slip through the cracks had me almost as worried as the threat of the person who could return to find us in the cabin.

I followed Chase and Tilly outside. The sun was hot on my shoulders and we'd only made it a few feet when I heard the rhythmic, rushing sound of someone wading through the river. Chase must have heard it too, because he beckoned us to follow him to the cluster of trees between the second and third cabins.

Chase pulled his bird-watching binoculars out of the case around his neck, peering in the direction of the water. Tilly looked pale and the wet pine needles on the ground jabbed into my knees. There had only been one sleeping bag in the cabin, but there could be more than one person. There was no telling what—

"I see someone," Chase whispered.

I held my breath and he said, "Oh, I wasn't expecting that."

It was the girl I'd met in the forest the other day. She wore a pair of ragged jean shorts, a navy T-shirt, and her hair fell in wet strings around her shoulders. The same backpack was slung across her thin shoulders, and she gave a furtive look around before stepping onto the embankment and making her way to the cabin.

"I saw that girl in the woods a few days ago," I said, in a low voice. "She smelled like she hadn't showered, but I figured it was some teenage phase. I can't believe she's been living out here the whole time."

"I can't believe she got caught in that storm." The perky tone in Tilly's voice had returned. "Poor little thing."

Poor little thing? Hardly. The girl was probably the one who had broken into the office. She could have been looking for food, but she probably wanted money. Either way, I didn't feel an ounce of sympathy. She had no business being here at all.

I got to my feet. "Let's head back and I'll report this."

"Well, I don't know," Tilly said. "She's a young girl, alone in the woods. It doesn't seem right to leave her here."

Chase capped his binoculars. "Julie's right. Security will know how to help her. We don't."

The shadows of the branches looked like worry lines on Tilly's face.

"Look, I have four kids. They say it takes a village and I'm telling you, that's not a joke. If one of my kids was hiding in an abandoned cabin somewhere, I would hope someone would help them out."

"I hear that." Chase's gaze met mine before returning to Tilly. "But because you have four kids, it's probably even more important to leave this to the experts. We don't know what this person is capable of and just because she's young doesn't mean she's not dangerous. Your kids need you and your husband would be mad about giving me the safari hat if anything happened to you, I can guarantee that."

I was about to tell Chase that he would have made a good lawyer when the slow strum of a guitar started to play, followed by one of the sweetest and most haunting voices I had ever heard. I couldn't make out the words but the music was slow and jazzy, gliding through the early afternoon like a bird.

The three of us turned towards the cabin and stared.

"Is she really singing?" Chase said, and Tilly shushed him.

I don't know how long we listened to the girl play her guitar, but when she stopped, we looked at each other in shock.

Chase's face was settled in a frown. "Well, huh."

"Her voice is incredible." Tilly rose to her feet. "I'm going to talk to her."

My leg had started to cramp, and I had to kick it out as I followed. "Tilly, wait," I whispered, but she held up her hands.

"I get that there's a risk here." Her pretty face was intent. "But life is full of risk. There are moments you have to dismiss that and make a choice about what's right. I think it's right to find out if this girl needs help, and that's what I'm going to do."

Even though I did not want to deal with this girl face to face, I didn't want anything to happen to Tilly. I followed her. Chase must have had the same mindset, because he tried to come, too, but Tilly waved him away.

"Three's too many," she whispered. "Wait out here. We'll be fine."

Chase didn't look pleased but he stood next to the porch, once again trying to get reception on his phone. "Be careful," he said quietly. "We don't know anything about her. Or if she has friends on the way."

The words made my heart beat a little faster. We walked quietly up the old steps, the sound like drums to my ears. Tilly pushed open the door and we stepped into the dim interior.

The girl sat on the sleeping bag, her eyes closed and her head thrown back as she played. Tilly took a step and the floorboard creaked. The girl's eyes opened and, spotting us, she scrambled to her feet.

"Get out of here," she shouted, holding out the guitar like a weapon.

"Honey, we're here to help," Tilly said. "My name's Tilly Fisk."

"Julie Scott," I said. "We've met." From the girl's expression, I knew she recognized me from that day in the woods. "I'm aware that you don't have permission to stay here—"

"But we want to figure it out together," Tilly said quickly.

The girl's eyes were wild, as if thinking a hundred miles a minute. Lowering her guitar, she said, "Let's go outside."

Good. A lot less attitude than the last time we met.

We stepped onto the porch and I pointed at some stumps next to the creek that looked like a good place to sit and talk. The girl shot me a vicious look, and ran for the forest.

Chase sprinted past her, blocking the way. "Wait." His voice was firm. "We just want to talk. You shouldn't be out here alone."

The girl turned to run back to the cabin but Tilly and I were behind her.

Once she realized she was surrounded, she let out a furious cry, and grabbed the low-hanging branches of the nearest tree. She yanked on one with all of her might, as if trying to rip off a stick. Nothing broke free, so she shook the branch, screaming out swear words as water rained down.

The girl collapsed onto the ground and started sobbing, curling her body into a tight ball. Tilly watched with her hand to her mouth and Chase looked stunned. Every part of my body felt tense and I wished more than anything that my father had already issued me one of those radios that the main staff carried around.

I knelt by the girl, ready to leap back if I needed to. "Hey." I tried to not wince at the smell of her wet, dirty hair. "It's alright. Let us help you."

"No one cares. No one cares. No one cares," she repeated, like a chant.

"We care." Chase joined me on the ground, Tilly hovering behind him.

"What can we do to help?" Tilly asked. "Do you need food?"

The girl went silent. Then she nodded, her arms still wrapped tightly around her body.

"When you're ready, let's have something to eat and talk," I said. "Or just something to eat. Alright?"

The crying slowed to gasps and finally silence. The girl sat with her head buried in her knees for what felt like ages, then she dried her face on her shirt and looked up. Her skin was blotchy from the tears.

Once Tilly had dumped out the collection of snacks on one of the stumps, the girl headed over to them and ripped into the packages, barely taking time to breathe between bites. I had no idea how long she'd been out here, but I was grateful Tilly had something for her to eat.

After she'd had two granola bars and had started in on a bag of chips, I said, "What's your name?"

She focused on the food. "Margaret."

"Tell us why you're here," I said.

A shadow crossed her face. "Not a chance."

"We're trying to help," I said. "It would be great if you'd drop the attitude."

The girl's red-rimmed eyes met mine. They were a haunting ice-blue, like two full moons hanging over the horizon. Then, she looked back down at the food.

"Our goal is to help you find a place that's safe, warm, and dry," I said. "You don't need to tell us anything if you don't want to, but sometimes it helps to talk things through."

"Yup." Chase gave her a friendly smile. "Like, how did you end up here, of all places?"

The girl reached for a package of gummies. "I used to come to this resort when I was little. Seemed like as good a place as any."

"Do your parents know where you are, Margaret?" Tilly asked.

The girl's shoulders stiffened. "My mother…"

Tilly gave an encouraging nod. "She knows?"

"No, she kicked me out." The girl pulled her arms close again. "My stepdad lost his job and started drinking a lot. One night, I talked back and he punched me in the face."

My stomach dropped. I don't know what I'd expected to hear—maybe that the girl was backpacking across the country and this had seemed like as good a place as any to stop—but I wasn't expecting that.

"He lied about it to my mom. Told her I got hit in the face with a soccer ball. When I tried to tell her what really happened, he said if I was going to make trouble, my mom could choose between him or me. She chose him."

I swallowed hard, trying to fight the tightness in my throat. No wonder the girl was angry at the world.

"I'm so sorry that happened to you," I said.

"Me, too." Chase's voice was gruff.

The girl looked down at her hands.

The wind blew, scattering mist over us. I brushed it from my cheeks, hard-pressed to imagine what it would feel like to have anything less than my mother's complete love and protection. It would be a trauma.

Tilly touched her arm. "Honey, how old are you?"

Margaret drew back. "I turned eighteen in March. Why?"

"Well…" Tilly gave her a big smile. "I think it would do you good to stay at a cabin here at the resort. Would you like that?"

I nearly choked. This girl might have a sad story but that didn't mean we should bring her around the other guests. She could be dangerous, and her meltdown had been nothing short of disturbing.

Chase must have felt the same. "Hey, Tilly?" He got to his feet. "Let's have a chat."

Margaret gave a bitter laugh. "No cabin for me." She pointed at his belt, where he had attached a black water bottle with a carabiner. "Is that water?"

Tilly pulled out a Gatorade. "Drink this." She handed her the red sports drink. "You need the electrolytes."

The silence between the three of us was intense as we walked a few steps away, close enough so that Margaret wouldn't try to run but far enough that she would have to strain to hear what we had to say. She glared at me between mouthfuls of food, as if the fact that we were discussing her was my fault.

"Look," Tilly said, in a low tone. "I know you're worried but there's something special about this girl. Her talent, for one. She's been through it and needs time to process her pain. I'm happy to get her a cabin so she can do all of that."

Leave it to Tilly to try to save the day. Back when we were kids, she made the boys put fish back in the water, played cards with the widows, and even had her mother take a bird with a broken wing to the vet. Helping a runaway was probably a regular day for her.

To me, the situation was full of problems. Yes, this girl was clearly in pain, but that didn't mean she wasn't also a threat. She could be up to no good. I was here to protect my parents, but I also couldn't afford to upset Tilly.

Her family owned one of the biggest pharmaceutical companies in the Midwest. The Fisks had been coming here for years and had sent countless referrals. The risk that this runaway could cause trouble was high, but it might do more damage to alienate the Fisks.

Taking a deep breath, I faced Tilly. "It's wonderful that you want to help. Still, we don't know a thing about this girl. She could be on drugs. Or…" Inspiration struck. "She could be lying about her age. If she's a minor, we're obligated to report her."

"We'll find out," Tilly said. "Listen, that story crushed me. The poor girl has dealt with so much. I can't in good conscience leave her here."

"I agree that she's been through a lot," I said carefully. "It's just—"

"Wait!" Tilly grabbed my hands, her diamond rings flashing in the sun. "Your parents have that artist-in-residence cabin. Tell them you found the perfect candidate! Her music was unbelievable."

"Tilly, let's take a breath." The sun was bright and Chase put on a pair of mirrored aviators. "Let's find her a place to stay in town. That way, we're helping but not putting her in the center of the resort."

I gave Chase a grateful look. "Excellent idea."

"No." Tilly frowned. "It is not appropriate for a young girl to be in a strange town all alone. We'll ask Julie's father to put her in the artist cabin. If he won't, I'll book her a cabin for the summer. That's that."

Before we could argue, Tilly flounced back over to the girl.

"Did she just say 'for the summer'?" I echoed.

It was stressful enough to think Margaret might stay for the week.

Chase took a sip from his water bottle. "Tilly thinks with her heart, not her head. I'm sorry she's putting you in such a tough spot."

"Yeah." I wished I could tell him about the break-in at the office and my fear of alienating Tilly, but above all, he was a guest. I couldn't let him in on any of that. "Let's see what they're plotting."

"It's all decided," Tilly called, as we walked over. "Margaret wants to stay. She's going to show you her license, so you can confirm her age. Let's go find her a place."

Margaret glared at me with her big eyes. "Next time, trust a person instead of making them feel like a criminal." She held out her ID, her dirty thumb pressed over everything but the birthday. "I turned eighteen in March."

My head started to hurt at the liability behind housing someone so young. Most hotels had a 21-and-over policy but my parents had never gotten around to adopting that trend, because it was not an issue. This was a family place, so the only time young people were alone in the cabins was when the parents booked something for say, kids who had returned for college, and the parents had the cabin next door.

"The resort will need to make a copy of your license," I warned, since she'd made a point of hiding her name and address. "They will also check to make sure you're not giving them a fake ID and that you're not reported missing or wanted, so there's that, too."

Margaret chewed on her lip. "Whatever. We went on a school trip to Europe and they checked our passport at every hotel."

"Great!" Tilly clapped her hands. "Julie, let's go talk to your father."

It seemed like a good sign that Margaret wasn't scared off at the idea of having her ID verified, because it increased the odds that she was just a normal girl going through a hard time. Unfortunately, it also weakened my argument to turn her away. Every part of me wanted to scream *No, this is a bad idea* but there was nothing I could do.

"That's fine," I said. "On two conditions." I waited, then said, "You cannot tell my father you were trespassing. Otherwise, he will send you packing."

Margaret's expression darkened. "What's the second condition?"

"You have to take a shower before you meet him." I looked at Tilly. "Would you like to volunteer your cabin?"

Tilly's cheeks flushed. If she felt comfortable bringing Margaret into the center of life at the resort, she had best be willing to let Margaret into her life as well. If she wasn't… well, then maybe she would stop pushing so hard for this.

Margaret saved her from making the call. "Forget it. There's no way I'm taking a shower at some stranger's hotel room. Not a chance."

Tilly nodded. "Good for you, honey!" She held up her hands when Chase and I looked at her. "Hey, she doesn't know us."

"And we don't know her," Chase pointed out.

"Instead of the shower," Tilly suggested, "what if she stays out of sight until you've spoken with your father? She can meet him once she's cleaned up. I'm happy to buy her some clothes at the gift shop."

Margaret stared at the ground, chewing on her lip. "I'd do that. I mean, if that's the second condition."

I racked my brain trying to think of a place where she could hide until we had the keys to the cabin. Maybe the back deck at my grandparents' house. She could sit there with Chase and Tilly while I spoke with my father, and the path to the artist-in-residence cabin wasn't too far from there.

"Can you sit with her while I talk to my father?" I asked.

"Of course," Tilly said.

Chase adjusted his sunglasses and gave a reluctant nod. It was clear he did not think any of this was a good idea. I appreciated his grip on reality, and wished Tilly would show the same common sense.

"Being a part of the artist-in-residence cabin would mean you'd have to perform here and there, or do music lessons or something to be a part of life at the resort. I don't know how hard my father will push for that, if he says yes at all, but typically that's the way it goes. Are you okay with that?"

She hesitated. Finally, she nodded.

"Then let's go," I said.

"Let me get my stuff." Margaret rushed back into the cabin and returned with the guitar strapped over her shoulder, a rolled-up sleeping bag and her backpack.

Chase reached out to help and she snapped, "Don't touch that."

The hike back through the forest was not nearly as cheerful as it had been on the way to the cabins. Chase and I were silent, while Tilly tried to engage Margaret in conversation, without much luck.

The whole thing was so frustrating. I had enough to worry about without adding a surly teenager to the list. My boss could call back any time, my mother could barely function, and I was here to make sure the resort was doing well, not add to its problems. But Tilly was right; we couldn't just leave her there, especially after what she'd gone through.

"It's not too late to say no," Chase said. "Tilly is a force but she can listen to reason."

I shook my head. "I'm conflicted about this, but even if Tilly wasn't pushing so hard, I think I'd still help. The idea that her mother could betray her like that—I can't imagine. My mother would never…"

My throat tightened, and I looked out towards the trees. The water on the leaves sparkled, and everything smelled fresh from the rain. I turned back to Chase.

"Do you know what I mean?" I asked.

"Yeah." He fiddled with the binocular case. "I've dealt with so much this past year, but I have more than a decade on her. I can't imagine what it would be like to have something like that happen at her age." He paused. "It's good you want to help. The situation is stressful, but you'll still have the summer. If today is any indication, your time here won't be dull."

"It feels surreal," I admitted. "Especially now."

"Well, things happen the way they're supposed to." Chase thought for a moment. "We wouldn't have found her if you hadn't stayed. She seems like someone who needed to be found."

I watched Margaret walking. Her shoulders were hunched but her steps were sure.

"I don't trust her," I told Chase. "But I'll still do my best to help her."

His eyes met mine. "That seems more than fair to me."

CHAPTER EIGHT

The main office smelled like citrus pine, and it was soothing enough to calm my nerves as I geared up to talk to my father. Like I'd told Margaret, my father would not let her stay in the artist-in-residence cabin if he knew she'd trespassed on resort property. But if he said no, Tilly would be furious at the idea that we could turn our back on someone in need, which would not be good for our relationship with the Fisks.

My role this summer was to reduce my parents' stress. It pained me, but it would better serve the resort to just go along with the charade. I would keep a close eye on Margaret, and keep the situation under control.

One way to do that would be to enlist the help of the security team. Since Margaret was young, it wouldn't be unreasonable to ask them to keep close watch on her. I could also have the front desk run a background check, like I'd threatened. With those steps, I would have the chance to stay in front of this thing, instead of getting run over by it.

My father's office smelled like chicken curry when I walked in. He was buried in paperwork and a half-eaten wrap sat on his desk. Taking off his glasses, he gave me a warm smile, the one that made his dark eyes wrinkle at the corners.

"What did you think of the cabins?" he asked.

I perched in the chair across from his desk. "They're falling apart, no question, but I think it would be possible to remodel and reuse them. It's beautiful out there. But let's talk about all that tonight—I can see you're busy. I just need to run something by you."

"Go ahead," he said, while marking up a purchase order.

"So, Tilly Fisk has taken this girl—she's young, she just turned eighteen—under her wing. She plays guitar and sings, and needs a place to stay to work on her music. You'd mentioned you hadn't found anyone to fill the artist-in-residence cabin this year, and she might be a good fit."

I got up to grab a bottled water out of the mini fridge, since my mouth had gone dry. "Tilly's pushing for it. It's a long story but the girl's here with her at the moment. Tilly's willing to book her a private cabin if the artist cabin doesn't work out, but I don't want her to spend more money. Their family has been so good to us over the years."

"I agree." He studied me over the rims of his glasses. "Have you heard her play?"

"Yes. She's really good."

That part, at least, was completely true. Margaret had one of the best voices I'd ever heard. I could have sat in the forest listening to her sing for hours.

"Is there some sort of process?" I asked. "That the artist needs to go through?"

"Traditionally, they fill out an application and send a work sample," my father said. "We pick the top three, do phone interviews, and then make a decision. It's time-consuming, which is why we didn't get to it."

"Oh." I saw a way out. "So, it takes a few months or weeks to review the applicants, settle on the finalists, and make the decision. Well, no worries, then. I'll tell Tilly and she'll just have to—"

"Well, hold on." My father steepled his hands. "You know, this would have been the first year that cabin would have sat vacant. It's become tradition to have someone there." He smiled. "Key's at the front desk. You'll have to drop off a welcome basket, but the cabin should be clean and ready to go. Get her set up and I'll come meet her later. I'm swamped at the moment."

My heart sank. "Dad, if there's a process in place, we really should—"

"Nope." He waved at the stacks of papers on his desk. "I don't have time. If you think she has a beautiful voice, that's good enough for me."

"Well, great," I managed to say. "I hope it all works out."

Back in the hallway, I leaned against the wall. I'd made it through without lying but that didn't make me feel better. One problem was solved, but it felt like a hundred others were about to begin.

Tilly leapt up and hugged me tight when I shared the news. "Thank you."

Margaret sat on the porch swing that overlooked the lake, holding her backpack close. The guitar rested at her feet. "You know I don't have any money, right?" she said, eyeing us with suspicion.

"You don't need it," Tilly said. "Being an artist-in-residence is like winning an award, and with your voice, you deserve it. You can take this time to rest, practice your music, and work through what happened." She looked at her watch, then at me. "I really should get back. Julie, I placed a clothing order through the gift shop while you were talking to your dad. They're delivering it to her cabin. Is there anything else you need me to do right now?"

"Nope." I forced my voice to remain cheerful. "I'll talk to you later."

Tilly pecked both of my cheeks and headed down the stairs to the deck.

"Her husband called," Chase explained. "The kids were threatening mutiny." He put his aviators on top of his head, his blue eyes bright, and hopped up off his perch on a deck chair.

"I'll walk with you to her cabin and then head out." He picked up Margaret's guitar and started towards the stairs.

"Hey!" Margaret leapt to her feet. She snatched the guitar away with such force that Chase actually stumbled back in surprise. "I told you not to touch that."

"Excuse me." My voice was sharp. "Look, you get to stay here because Tilly is my friend but that invitation can and will change if you can't exercise basic courtesy. Got it?"

Margaret didn't answer, but pulled her backpack close. It dawned on me that she hadn't dropped it on the bench before going after her guitar, which made for a pretty bulky armful. There could be something dangerous that she was hiding, like a weapon.

I stepped forward. "Let me see inside your backpack and we'll go."

"No." Her face flushed. "Why?"

"I need to know that there's nothing in there that could get you or me in trouble."

The front desk had agreed to check her background but I could check what was right in front of me. If she had a weapon, drugs, or alcohol, she couldn't stay. It was that simple.

Since she just stood there, glaring at me, I pulled out my phone. "Chase, I'm going to text Tilly that I changed my mind."

"*Fine.* Geez." Margaret yanked open the zipper and displayed the contents inside.

The backpack cradled a bright pink folder, a dirty-looking tube of Chapstick, and a half-empty jar of hand sanitizer. She didn't open the front pocket until I pointed at it. I don't know why, but it surprised me to see normal travel items like toothpaste, a toothbrush, a cell phone and charger, and a plastic box for a retainer. The innocence of the items made the situation feel almost normal and I was a little embarrassed at being so insistent.

"Thank you." I straightened my shoulders. "Let's go."

*

Margaret's attitude improved once we walked into the cabin. It was a single, but fully equipped with a bedroom, living room and kitchenette. The bags Tilly had sent from the gift shop were already lined up on the bed in a neat row.

"I think those are the clothes Tilly ordered," I said.

Margaret hung back so I walked over and started pulling stuff out. There were five pairs of shorts and polo shirts, two pairs of linen pajamas, a dress for dinner, and even undergarments. Everything was in cute pastels and most items were embroidered with the Wood Violet symbol.

"That's incredible," I said, staring down at the haul.

"What's incredible?" Margaret's tone was dry. "That the most boring clothes in the world didn't fall asleep on the bed?"

My mouth dropped open. "Do you have any idea…" I was about to say *how much all this costs?* but didn't. The last thing I needed was Margaret trying to return the clothes back to the gift shop for cash. "There's other stuff in here, too." I pointed out the selection of candy, junk food, and entertainment magazines Tilly had included. "It was really thoughtful of her to do this."

"Do I really get to stay here?" Margaret's voice was cautious. "Or is this like, some trick to distract me while you wait for the police?"

I moved closer to the door that led to the main cabin, my body suddenly tense. "Why would I call the police?"

She glared at me. "Because I stayed in your stupid junkyard cabin without asking. Because if something's too good to be true, it probably is."

The pain in her voice startled me. "Well, I didn't call the police and yes, everything here really is for you."

The couch cushions in the living room needed fluffing, so I turned my attention to that, checked to make sure she had a decent display of books and board games, then showed her how to open the window.

"No one can climb into the cabin windows from the outside," I said, demonstrating how to open and close them. "It's impossible, so you'll be very safe."

The comment was meant to both comfort and warn. If she had considered breaking into the cabins, I hoped she got the message that it couldn't be done.

"Speaking of the police," I added, "I *am* going to tell security to watch over you. You're the youngest guest we've ever had stay alone and I do want to make sure you're protected."

Putting down her backpack, she settled into the couch. "I can't believe you guys are being so nice to me."

It would have been rude to tell her I couldn't believe it, either. It also would have been rude to tell her that I didn't want her on the furniture until she took a hot shower. But as I struggled to find a response, I realized she looked ready to fall asleep.

"Why don't you go lie down in the bed?" I said, heading for the door. "You're probably exhausted. The meal schedule is on the counter."

"Meal schedule?" she echoed.

"Breakfast, lunch and dinner are served in the dining hall. I'll send some food over for you tonight so you can have time to rest here and get cleaned up."

I was nearly out the door when she called, "Wait!" She sounded scared. "Leave your number. I'll call if I need anything."

"You can call the front desk from that phone," I suggested, pointing at the kitchen counter. "They'll find me."

"You don't have a cell phone?" she demanded. "Even I have a cell phone."

Even though I did not feel comfortable giving this girl my personal information, it didn't feel right to say no. She was so young. With a sigh, I jotted it down on the courtesy pad on the counter.

"Get some rest."

The door clicked behind me and I heard her mumble something, most likely something rude. Outside, I took in a deep breath, trying to understand how dealing with a teenage girl could be more stressful than an entire week at the office. The thought reminded me that I still hadn't heard from my boss, and I needed to follow up.

As I walked past the main window, I peeked into the living room. Margaret hadn't bothered to pull the shade or head back to the bedroom. She was lying on the couch with her muddy shoes on, her eyes closed.

For the first time since I'd met her, she looked happy.

CHAPTER NINE

Tristan ignored my calls and texts until late that night. It had just started to get dark and I had settled into bed with a pint of ice-cream from the gift shop when the phone rang. I stared down at the spoonful of blood orange sorbet, amazed at his timing.

Eating ice-cream in bed would not be an option if Tristan had been around. Not because he would have judged me—well, not openly—but because under his superfoods influence, I would have reached for the kale chips instead.

"Julie." The connection could have been from another country. "Can you hear me?"

I took a quick bite before answering. "Barely. Did you lose your phone?"

The question was a dig at the fact that he'd gone dark all day.

"Sorry." He sounded sheepish. "It was incredibly busy, I meant to respond, but I was pulled from one thing to another to another. Are your parents happy that you're staying?"

"Thrilled," I said. "I just had dinner with my mom and she was happier than she has been in days. I think the idea of me being here makes her feel less alone." There was shouting in the background and I paused. "Where are you?"

"Cubs game." Tristan described the private suite that one of his clients had given him, as I took a few sweet bites of the sorbet.

"It's big-time," he said. "You're missing out."

The bright lights against the green baseball field was something I'd always enjoyed, but I was hardly missing out. Here, a full moon had risen over the water and the trees scraped against the fading sky like something out of a painting.

"Did you talk to your boss?" he asked.

"I left him a voicemail this morning," I said. "He sent me an email around dinner saying he would discuss it with the partners. Hopefully, he'll come back with a plan tomorrow."

"Keep me posted," Tristan said. "I've been sweating it all day, trying to figure out what we'd do if you lost your job."

"Let's not focus on that until there's a need. There's enough going on here already," I said, and summarized the situation with Margaret.

The story was met with silence on his end of the phone.

"You there?" I hoped I hadn't been talking to empty air.

"Yes, I'm trying to wrap my mind around all this." Tristan sounded confused. "Why didn't you tell your father the truth?"

"I couldn't," I said. "Tilly really wants to help this girl and the Fisk family is a powerhouse. It would have been a disaster to say no."

"Tilly Fisk, as in, the pharmaceutical heir?" Tristan said. "I did not put that together when I met her."

"Yep." The trees waved in the breeze outside the window. "You know, you really could build a lot of relationships here, Tristan."

"I can also do that right here. Speaking of, I should go. I need to spend time with the new client."

"Wait," I said. "I need to get your take on one thing about this girl. She—"

"Julie, I really don't have the time to hear the woes of some teenage girl. Call you tomorrow, okay?" He'd hung up before I could answer.

I took a furious bite of sorbet. Yes, Tristan was working when he was out and about, but that would be the case all summer. His job relied on entertaining clients and he would be distracted every time we talked. Of course, a lack of communication had been our problem for too long.

Distance will only make it harder, unless you put in the effort.

It didn't seem fair that I had to be the one to put in the effort, though. My husband had once asked me to mourn the greatest grief of our lives on my own. The anger from that still lingered; I didn't know if it would be possible to let it go.

I had found out I was pregnant a year and a half ago, when Tristan and I were a week out from competing in a relay race. The event was sponsored by his financial firm, and it was an intense obstacle course that combined running, swimming, and cycling. I hadn't wanted to do it, because the expectations were tough and I didn't want to embarrass myself or, most importantly, him.

The Saturday before the race, I'd woken up woozy and with no energy. I'd thought it was dehydration at first but when the feeling persisted, I took a test. The idea that we were going to have a baby was the best news I could have imagined. Tristan and I celebrated, cried, and celebrated all day.

Sunday, we had a training session for the race. I planned to skip it, stay in bed, and research baby names. When it came time to go, Tristan walked into our bedroom and seemed surprised that I wasn't dressed in workout clothes.

"You need to train," he said. "Our team's counting on you."

I thought he was joking. "Should we sign up our extra teammate?"

He kissed me. "Yeah, I guess it is kind of cheating, having an extra player, but I'm okay with that. Come on, I'll get your water bottle ready."

The realization that he actually expected me to do the race made me nervous. "Tristan, I need to drop out. I need to take care of my body."

"Staying fit is taking care of your body," he said, with a confused look. "Listen, it's your choice, but women are strong. You're not an invalid because you're pregnant. Besides, think about how great it would be to tell our child that he completed a relay race before he was even born."

It took some convincing, but I finally agreed. It was important to stay fit and healthy, because I wanted to feel strong during delivery. So, I went with Tristan to the training session and pushed through the exhaustion.

The next night, Tristan surprised me with a vision board. It had all these pictures of pregnant women doing impressive physical feats, like carrying jugs of water on their heads or standing at the edge of a mountain. Looking at it, there did not seem to be a legitimate excuse to back out of the race and I actually felt excited about competing.

My sister, on the other hand, was furious at the idea.

"That's dangerous," she insisted. "Let your body rest. Tristan does not get to make this decision for you."

"It's my choice," I assured her. "Women all over the world are active while pregnant. It'll be fine."

"Julie." My sister's voice was full of warning. "I'm telling you now. Don't do this."

But I did.

Our two-month check-up was two weeks later. I'd felt especially stressed and exhausted since the race and I wanted to make sure that I hadn't caused any damage.

The nurse came in first to ask if there were any issues so I ran it by her. "It's been hard to bounce back after that," I said. "It's like it took all my energy and then some."

"That's a pretty intense thing to put your body through while pregnant."

Tristan looked irritated but kept quiet until she left the room. "Why did you ask that?"

It was hard to explain. I'd asked because I'd had a bad feeling ever since I'd slipped getting out of the boat during the race. Profound guilt coupled with panic.

The race had been a risk. I'd ignored my instincts, let Tristan push me too far, and now, I was scared to think I'd made such a stupid mistake. The nurse came back in to check for a heartbeat. It was there and tears rolled down my cheeks.

Tristan kept beaming at me. "You see?" he said. "You're Superwoman."

"Yes, she is Superwoman." The nurse's voice held the tiniest sense of warning. "But now's the time where she doesn't have to prove it."

The miscarriage happened at twelve weeks. Two of the cases at work closed on the same day and I had the rare luxury of taking a stroll along the water, before it got dark. I'd walked seven blocks along the lakeshore, the sun warm on my shoulders and the wind whipping my hair around my face.

Tristan and I had been looking forward to the weekend. It had been such a busy time, and I'd been fighting to stay awake. We'd planned to set up our gift registry and tell our parents the big news, something we'd been waiting on. The idea of a happy, peaceful weekend was exactly what I needed.

The cramping started about a block before I got home and once I was there, it was obvious there was a problem. Tristan was with a client so I took a cab to the hospital, where my OB-GYN's office was located. Two hours later, he met me in the lobby, the place I'd been sitting since I received the news, the announcements of the hospital loudspeaker numb in my ears.

The office was closed at that point, but Tristan called their after-hours line to ensure that he could do everything possible to take care of me that night.

Where was this care and attention, I wanted to scream, *when you pushed me to do that race?*

We went to see my OB-GYN the next morning. She had assured me the two things were not connected, that miscarriage was not uncommon, I had done my best, and I could try again soon. Still, I felt responsible and couldn't shake a sense of deep anger directed at Tristan, because he'd pushed me too hard.

I was careful to not say these things out loud. He was devastated, too, obviously. But the anger burned deep inside me.

The day the trophies were shipped to us, I set them down on his desk. "Hope it was worth it," I said, the first and only reference I ever made to the incident.

He shot up out of his chair. "What's that supposed to mean?"

I stared at him with such hate that he got the message. His face crumpled and he pulled me close.

"I'll take the blame, Julie," he said. "If that's what you need, I'll take the blame."

Of course, that made me feel terrible. I reassured him that no, I didn't blame him and that no, it wasn't his fault. The first trimester was full of risk and we would try again.

Deep in my heart, though, I could not forgive the vision board he'd put up on the wall—particularly, the image of the pregnant woman standing on a cliff—all to remind me that there were no excuses, I just needed to work a little bit harder to be strong.

The second miscarriage happened sooner than the first, just eight weeks into the pregnancy. Tristan had gone into his office and locked the door, most likely with plans to stay there for the rest of the night. I had sat on the couch, wrapped in a quilt, and staring out at the lights of the city.

It seemed so unfair. Tristan and I were in a position to raise a family and we wanted to love our children with our whole hearts. Yet my body kept betraying me.

It was one thing to blame it on the race, to think that I'd pushed myself too hard. This time, I had done everything right and I still wasn't able to accomplish the one thing that I'd wanted since I was a little girl, feeding my baby dolls and tucking them in at night.

I sat on the couch alone for as long as I could but finally, I needed to share the grief with my husband. I tried knocking on the office door and he didn't answer, so I used the key to go in. He sat at his desk, the skyline bright behind him in the window, the computer glowing on his face. He looked up and when my face crumpled, he gave me a blank stare.

"This could happen a lot," he said. "If it's all the same to you, I'd prefer to not emotionalize it."

The surprise I felt chilled my blood. "You mean, you'd prefer not to feel our feelings?"

The handsome lines of his face were set with determination. "It's hard. But maybe we are putting too much weight out into the universe. Let's not make it a big thing."

It seemed like a ridiculous way to avoid grief but I also understood it. Trying to get pregnant had proven to be a heartbreaking experience. If we gave into those feelings, we might stop trying altogether.

I went back out to the couch alone, watched a show, and pretended like nothing had happened. But as the weeks went by, it was impossible to push back my grief. I wanted support, to talk about it, and for him to be there for me but he was ready to move on.

"I gave myself forty-eight hours to be sad about it," he said, his voice firm. "That's all the energy I'm going to give it."

This removed approach worked for him but it didn't work for me. He didn't understand my "need to be gloomy" but he wasn't the one balancing on the edge of hormones and experiencing a loss and heartache that cut so deep that I wondered if I would ever fully recover. I needed to talk and work through these feelings, not goal-set my way out of them. Tristan was not capable of doing that; he shut down every time. Finally, I sat him down and said that I'd made the decision to take birth control.

"What?" His face was outraged. "How are we going to have a family?"

"We're not there yet," I said, simply. "I'm not going to have this keep happening and have to walk that road alone."

Tristan had slammed out of the condo and gone on a three-mile run. When he returned, he said, "Do what you need to do."

We hadn't discussed it since.

CHAPTER TEN

The next morning, my eyes fluttered open to see bright green leaves swaying from delicate branches, the golden rays of the sun shining down through them. The birds called to one another as the early morning breeze wafted in through the screen. I pulled the cozy, white duvet close, grateful that I finally had the space to slow down and breathe.

Out in the kitchen, I took my time making coffee. I ground the beans, picked out a pretty pottery mug, and added the perfect amount of cream. Then, I stood at the picture window, watching as swirls of mist rolled across the lake.

Taking a shower felt luxurious, like I had all the time in the world. I rubbed down my entire body with a lavender scrub, washed my hair with organic mint shampoo, and felt ready to face the day. That is, until it came time to pick up the phone and call Margaret.

Tilly had asked me to take Margaret to breakfast, and promised that she would take over after her kids were at their activities. It was irritating that I was the one slated with the task of entertaining her first, but at the same time it would give me the opportunity to delve deeper into her history.

I'd looked her up on social media before going to bed, and hadn't found a thing. Either she wasn't online, which was not likely, or she'd used an alias since she was so young. It would have made me feel more comfortable to know something about her life and, hopefully, I could learn that during breakfast.

Steeling myself for a barrage of attitude and insults, I dialed the artist-in-residence cabin. No one answered. I felt a brief flicker of hope that Margaret had jumped ship in the middle of the night but then, she picked up.

"Hello?" she practically whispered.

"Good morning," I said. "It's Julie."

"Excuse me, I was *asleep*." She sounded outraged. "Do you seriously have landlines at this place? I thought an air-raid siren was going off."

I counted to five. Then, I said, "I have to get to work but I'd like you to join me for breakfast. Can you be ready in ten minutes?"

"I'll be asleep in ten minutes."

"Look, you have to eat," I said. "I'm not going to have meals delivered to your door each time."

It wasn't the worst idea, actually. The idea of turning her loose at the resort, when she could do or say anything, was much worse. Still, if she didn't go to the meals, my father would have questions.

"I'll see you in a few minutes?" I asked.

She was silent for a long moment. Finally, she said, "It's a bit creepy how much you're trying to hang out with me."

"Thanks." My voice was thick with sarcasm. "Oh, wait. You're the one who's supposed to say that to me."

Margaret answered the door dressed in a pair of pale lilac shorts and a pink Wood Violet branded polo. Other than the scowl plastered on her face, she looked like a completely different person. Her dark brown hair fell just past her shoulders, her skin glowed, and her haunting eyes stared me down. I had to hand it to Tilly, she'd somehow managed to transform the girl into a Wood Violet guest.

"The clothes look nice," I said.

Margaret gave a huge sigh, as if making small talk with me was an indignity she had to endure to get her hands on a piece of bacon. "Let's go." She clutched her dirty backpack close and I shook my head.

"You can't bring that," I said, pointing at it.

The fabric was dark purple but it was so dirty that it looked black. There were patches sewn onto it that had, at one point, probably looked cool, but were now ragged and falling off. If the backpack was anything like the clothes she had on yesterday, the smell alone would clear the dining hall.

Margaret stuck out her lower chin. "It stays with me."

"It can't," I said, feeling my blood pressure start to rise. "People will know that you…"

I stopped myself from saying *don't belong here* because I didn't want to make the girl feel bad, but in reality, the majority of the teenage girls that stayed at Wood Violet wouldn't carry their garbage out in anything less than a designer bag.

"People will know that you haven't seen a washing machine in a while," I finished. "You can't bring it."

Margaret shrugged. "So I'll stay here." She turned on her heel and shut the door in my face.

I couldn't believe it. She had to be the rudest person I'd ever met.

The window was open and I leaned close enough to the screen to smell the dust. "Margaret," I said, in a furious whisper. "Get out here right now. I refuse to let you starve. Come to breakfast or you go home."

It was a complete bluff, and I wondered if she knew that. Tilly would never let me get away with sending her home. My heart pounded as I waited for her to respond.

Two minutes later, she hadn't said a word. I gripped the porch railing in frustration. What was the real issue here? Why did she want to keep her bag? It didn't have a medical kit or anything; I'd looked. Was she just worried that someone would take what little she had?

"Margaret." I pressed my face against the window, trying to see her. "Listen, no one can get into your cabin. Put the *Do Not Disturb* sign on the door and the cleaners will not come in. The moment breakfast is over, I'll buy you a backpack at the gift shop that won't make you stand out."

"Get me one now." I could hear her breathing and realized she was standing to the left of the window, by the door. "I'm not leaving my stuff."

"I *can't.* The gift shop is not open."

My frustration was mounting. The sun danced through the trees and I wanted to enjoy a walk to the dining hall, not deal with this nonsense.

Margaret came to the window. "You own the place, don't you? So, open it."

The look on her face was pure defiance but her eyes were full of pain. Then it hit me.

The backpack probably held something precious to her, like pictures or mementos from her mother. It made sense that she wouldn't want to lose those things, especially since she'd been forced to leave her behind.

"I can do that," I said quietly. "See you in a few."

The master key my father had given me let me into the gift shop with no trouble. I picked out a bag for Margaret and left a note on the cash register with my credit card information. I doubted the store would charge me, but the only backpacks sold by the gift shop were Dooney and Bourke, so I wanted to give them the option.

Back at the cabin, I waited for Margaret to answer the door, wondering if she would complain about what I'd picked out, the way that she did with the clothes Tilly had given to her.

She opened the door. "Did you really go get me a bag?"

"Yep." I handed it over.

The brown leather backpack was patterned with the letters of the brand, with a small gold plate on the back. It smelled like new leather and was really nice, but I braced myself for a put-down.

"You're serious right now?"

"Yes." I hesitated. "Do you… like it?"

"Yes." Margaret hugged it close. "Be right back."

She raced back into the cabin, shutting the door in my face again. I felt relieved, like I'd achieved the impossible. When she came out with it firmly slung over her shoulder, she gave me a shy look and I smiled.

"Let's go." The mulch on the path was quiet under our feet as we walked. "My father might be there at breakfast," I mentioned. "If he is, tell him about yourself and your music. He'll need to hear you play at some point, so he'll probably try to set up a time."

"I don't play in front of people."

"Why?" I said, and she rolled her eyes. "Margaret, you have a phenomenal voice. We heard you singing outside yesterday and I'm telling you, every single one of us was in awe."

She shrugged. "It's not that hard to sing."

"Well…" I thought of all the times I'd mumbled my way through 'Happy Birthday' and mouthed the words to 'Silent Night.' "Either way, you don't have to sing in front of him if you don't want to. He can sit out on the porch or something and you can play guitar in your living room. You'll have to let him hear you sing, though, or he'll get suspicious."

"About what?" she said.

"About whether you belong in the artist-in-residence cabin," I said. "I told you yesterday that you'll be expected to give lessons or perform or something, so you'll have to pick one."

She gave me a look that bordered on judgmental. "Don't you feel bad about lying to your dad?"

My skin prickled. "Yes," I said, slowly. "It makes me feel rotten. But sometimes in life, you have to decide what people are ready to hear and what information they can do without."

She sneered. "That's garbage. People should have the full story so they can make their own decisions. Not be fed a pack of lies." If she felt this way, there was a strong chance she would say something to my father just to prove a point. I forced my tone to remain steady, so that she didn't pick up on my fear.

"Margaret, I know you're young, but you have to trust me on this. Not everything is black and white."

Her eyes narrowed. "It has nothing to do with age. You can choose to tell the truth, or you can choose to lie."

"Or you can make the choice to present the information that best serves your case and leave out the rest unless it's absolutely necessary to share."

"What are you, a lawyer or something?"

"Yes, actually," I told her. "I am."

Margaret stopped in the middle of the path. Then, she started laughing. She laughed so hard that she had to hunch over to catch her breath, then she laughed some more. I stood there, not sure what to say, while a family walked past us and smiled, like we were a mother and daughter having the time of our life.

"What is so funny?" I demanded, once they were gone.

"It's just so perfect." She was still laughing. "Of *course* you're a lawyer. You twist the truth to make it suit you, and somehow find a way to justify it."

The words hurt. There had been too many times where I had helped insurance companies that were making a case too close to the right side of wrong, and yes, had found a way to justify it.

"You don't know what you're talking about," I said, fighting back the burn in my cheeks. "You know nothing about me, my life, or my family."

"I know that all grown-ups are liars," she said.

This girl was really starting to give me a headache.

"Margaret, I am not telling my father the whole story about you because he has too much to deal with right now. He doesn't need to deal with this mess, too. So, drop it."

"This mess?" Margaret jutted her chin out. "So, that's what you think of me."

"I didn't mean it like that," I said quickly.

She didn't say another word to me for the rest of the walk.

I headed to the main office building after breakfast to experience my first weekly staff meeting at Wood Violet.

On my walk there, I saw the guests milling about, dressed in their colorful resort wear, ready for a day of outdoor fun. A polite smile was fixed to my face but inside, my mind was on breakfast with Margaret. It had been painful.

She'd buried her nose in the entertainment section of a paper and ignored me with all her might, but still managed to eat every bite of her eggs, waffles and bacon. I'd tried to apologize to her a few times but it was a lost cause. I was glad Tilly planned to deal with her for the rest of the day because my patience was shot, and it wasn't even nine o'clock in the morning.

My law office called right as I reached the main door. Quickly, I headed to the edge of the building and sat on a shaded bench that overlooked the lake. Fishing boats lingered in the water, a few couples kayaked across the stillness, and the bright green of the golf course loomed large across the way.

Letting out a breath, I picked up the phone. "This is Julie."

It felt strange to use a formal tone while in such a serene setting. Thanks to Margaret, it made me feel like I was telling another lie.

"Good morning, Julie," boomed a deep voice. "Phil Reed."

My boss. I sat up straight.

"Phil, good morning." I ran my sweating palms over the smooth wood of the bench. "Thanks for taking the time to get back to me."

"It was the least I could do, given the circumstances. It's been a battle," he said, with a chuckle. "I'll be honest with you, Julie. Two members of our team have expressed disinterest in keeping you around, simply because they feared this incident could extend beyond the summer—or worse, that it could reoccur."

It frustrated me that Phil had referred to my mother's stroke as an 'incident,' but I said, "That's understandable, but this was unexpected. My family will be better equipped to find assistance in the future, as my father will have the time to adjust to the new reality of my mother's health."

The words were so clinical. They didn't convey the heartache that I felt every time I saw her try to speak, the humiliation in her eyes each time my father wiped food off her chin, or the sense that my mother might never be the same again.

"It's not an easy situation," I told him. "However, we'll find our way out of it."

"That's good to hear," Phillip said. "Unfortunately, I have concerns as well. You didn't return to work on the date we'd discussed and instead, informed me you'd be out for the next three months. We've only had you for eight. That makes it difficult for me to trust that you're willing to put our clients and our policies first."

The bench suddenly felt uncomfortable and I stood. "Phil, I sincerely apologize. You're right; I should have returned to Chicago, gone through the proper channels, and taken the time when and if it worked for the team."

My gut told me to offer to do that now, but I couldn't. Nothing could make me leave my mother.

Squeezing the phone tight, I took in a deep breath. "Phil, you mentioned that my departure was abrupt. Keep in mind, I waited ten days to get to my mother's bedside because I upheld my commitment to closing out a case. You can expect that type of commitment in the future."

The surface of the lake rippled in the wind, making the water look choppy in spite of the bright day.

"I do appreciate that," he said. "There's a quote that says something like, *If someone shows you who they are, believe them.* You've shown me that you are a strong person with a deep commitment to your family."

Before I could breathe a sigh of relief, he added, "However, I need that type of commitment to our business. It's my job to resolve issues before they happen and unfortunately, I can't see past a red flag. What's happening here does not match up with the plan we put in place when we agreed to work together. It's best to part ways now, before we run into further issues. The office manager will be in touch to discuss your severance package."

He seemed to wait for a response but my mouth had gone completely dry. I couldn't speak.

"Julie," he continued, "take care of your mother and take care of yourself. It's been a pleasure," he said, then hung up.

It took a full minute for the words to sink in. It had been a major decision to move to this new firm, and the door had shut in an instant. My legs shook and I sank back onto the bench.

I couldn't believe I had actually been fired. I'd spent countless late nights at the office, grinding to get the work done and do it well. I'd canceled birthday dinners, date nights, and had worked myself to a state of exhaustion so extreme that it often took a triple espresso to make it through the day. Phil had praised my work ethic so many times that I was certain he'd be willing to work with me on this, especially since he'd fought so hard to recruit me.

Tristan will be upset.

The image of his face, red with rage, loomed in my head. I'd told him he'd be the first to know what my boss had said but I couldn't bring myself to pick up the phone, tell him the news, and have him start shouting at me. I needed some time to process this before sharing it with anyone at all.

CHAPTER ELEVEN

Shoulders hunched, I headed into the office for the staff meeting at a clipped pace, hoping I didn't appear as embarrassed as I felt. Letting out a shaky breath, I pushed open the door to the large conference room. Nearly fifty members of our staff stood around, chatting in groups. I headed straight for the side tables with the donuts and settled in with a cinnamon roll in one hand and a coffee in the other as my father started the meeting.

"Good morning, everyone," he said. "I thought I'd kick us off by introducing my daughter. Julie, will you come up here?"

I set down my cinnamon roll and joined him at the front of the room, looking out over the sea of faces. Some members of the staff had been with us for years and I recognized them, but there were countless faces I didn't know.

"Julie is here this summer to be with Lilian and to help out. If you need anything at all, feel free to reach out to her. She's a lot smarter than me. I'm also delighted to share that Julie has already worked with one of our guests to help fill our beloved artist-in-residence cabin."

My smile wavered but I nodded as my father beamed at me. "Yes," I said, since he seemed to be waiting for me to fill in the blanks. "Margaret is a singer and guitar player, and she plans to use her time here to write songs and work on her musical development. She's still quite young and might feel out of place, so be sure to welcome her if you see her."

Once I was back in my seat, my father ran through updates on rules and regulations, dates for safety trainings, and then addressed the importance of security.

"If you notice anything unusual, report it right away," he said. "Wood Violet is an opportunity for our guests to step away from the harsh realities of the real world. That's what we're selling, to be sure. It's more important than ever to ensure we maintain that level of safety and security."

My stomach tightened to think that I'd been advocating for one of our main safety concerns only moments before. Tilly had met up with Margaret right after breakfast and planned to keep an eye on her but that didn't mean much. If Margaret was difficult, I was worried that Tilly would jump ship and focus on her family, instead. I had asked her to text me if that happened, but the whole thing still made me nervous.

"Moving on," my father continued, "I'd like to discuss an outstanding moment from this month." He smiled at Wilson, our concierge. "So, Wilson called a man about his fortieth wedding anniversary, to see if we could make the day special. Well, the husband had completely forgotten." The employees laughed. "Wilson arranged flowers and chocolates, as well as a candlelit dinner accompanied by our string quartet in the mosquito tent by the water. The husband can confess to the mishap when he's ninety but until then, bravo to Wilson. He has earned the Wooden Violet."

My father stepped forward with a small wooden flower in a vase. The vase was covered with sparkling beads and colorful glass stones. "Julie, your mother started this tradition about a decade ago and this is our most coveted prize," he said, holding it up to show me. "It gets passed around each month to the most deserving member of our staff, who then has the opportunity to add one decoration. It's become quite colorful over the years."

Wilson gave a speech that had everyone laughing, and accepted the trophy. The vase held a handful of gift cards to local restaurants and coffee shops. It was a sweet idea and the recognition seemed to mean as much to Wilson as the prize.

"Now that we've covered everything, I wanted to give you all an update on Lilian. Several of you have talked with me in passing but I wanted to be sure I told the entire team." My father gave a bright smile as the room fell silent. "Her spirits are good, and she's making progress every day. She sends love to each and every one of you and plans to be right back here with us in no time!"

The staff members applauded and the older woman next to me blinked back tears. Turning to me, she whispered, "I knew she wouldn't be out long."

I nodded, but couldn't meet her eyes.

What was my father doing? There was no need for false cheer. My mother would not be back anytime soon. I couldn't stand the sound of the applause, or the idea that my father felt it was necessary to pretend things were fine. It again made me think of what Margaret had said about all adults being liars.

He concluded the first part of the meeting and the majority of the staff headed out to get to work. Nikki and the office team stayed, refilling their coffees and grabbing another donut before my father went on to the final portion of the meeting.

"One last order of business," he said, once everyone had settled back into their chairs. "Nikki has been working on a presentation and she's ready for our input."

My father dimmed the lights and cued it up. I sat back and watched with interest. That interest faded to concern as I realized the theme of the presentation was 'Progress' and that the focus was on ways to update the resort.

"There are so many ways that Wood Violet is amazing," Nikki said, clicking to a picture of the formal dance night. "There are also so many ways Wood Violet has fallen behind."

I flinched as she showcased a photo of our spa, with its basic dry sauna and massage rooms, beside a photo of a luxury spa in Palm Springs.

"This presentation is designed to help us think of the ways we can grow and develop as a brand, while tapping into a new generation of guests."

I held my coffee cup tight as Nikki ran through a list of ten detailed changes designed to bring new business to the resort. The ideas were all in tune with high-end resorts, like hosting weddings or providing a butler, but they missed the mark. For me, it seemed that Nikki was invested in turning Wood Violet into something that it was not.

Our business model centered around family time outdoors, special events, and fine dining. I had liked a few things on the list, like installing a zip-line for our extreme sports trail, or creating a high-end games room for kids. Still, many of the ideas put Wood Violet at risk for becoming a cookie-cutter resort.

Once she reached number ten, Nikki gave the room a charming smile. "For years, our guests have asked a simple question." She clicked the controller to reveal a mock-up with a flat-screen television mounted in the living room at the cabin. "Where are the televisions?"

I nearly dropped my coffee as everyone started laughing. My father stood at the front of the room, nodding and smiling at the reaction from his staff.

"If we want to retain our guests and attract new ones, we must remain competitive." Nikki clicked to an image of a happy family watching a movie together in their cabin. "These are my suggestions on what we can do to build our business. I welcome your feedback and would like to know if you see these improvements becoming a part of what makes Wood Violet so special. Thank you."

My father flipped back on the lights and Nikki took her seat, as the small group of employees clapped once again.

"Nikki, these are all strong ideas," my father said. "We stand for tradition, but we can't become a dinosaur. Does anyone have any feedback on what we've seen?"

I sat in silence as the office staff discussed a few of the options, surprised to hear that the wine bar idea was gaining traction, along with upgrading the spa.

"Julie, do you have any thoughts?" my father asked.

The room fell silent as the staff members turned to me. Uncomfortable to be put on the spot, I got to my feet. "Yes, and I'd love to share them, but I need to get to the dining hall for the food delivery."

Everyone laughed and Nikki gave me the thumbs-up sign.

Outside, I leaned against the wood of the building. Maybe I was in a bad place but Nikki's presentation bothered me. Wood Violet was about tradition, like my father said. It concerned me that she wanted to change that.

Once I'd signed off on the food delivery, I texted Tilly to see if her time with Margaret was going any better than mine. Tilly's text surprised me.

She's great! Such a sweet girl.

Well, good. I was glad that Margaret wouldn't cause any trouble, at least for the time being.

I headed over to my parents' house and found my mother still in bed.

"She's tired today," the nurse warned when I walked in. "I'd keep your visit short."

"Mom, how are you?" I laid on the bed next to her and took her hand.

She didn't answer, but a single tear trickled down her cheek. "What is it?" I asked.

"Frustrated."

My jaw ached as I tried not to let her see how much the idea hurt me. "I know. It has to be so hard." We lay in silence and she closed her eyes. Her breathing didn't change, so I knew she wasn't asleep. "Mom, can I ask you something?"

The question had been weighing on me ever since my dad mentioned it that first day in the Hut.

"Dad said you were burning some papers about a week before you had the stroke," I said. "What were they?"

My mother opened her eyes, her face pained. "Why?"

"Because Dad seemed to think it was something that had upset you."

Lifting her good hand, she smoothed her hair into place. "I'm tired."

"Rest," I said. "I'll get back to work." The bed creaked as I stood up. Resting my hand on a bedpost, I said, "If there's something that's upsetting you, I want to know, okay?"

For a split second, it seemed like she wanted to tell me something. Then, her eyes closed and this time, her breathing changed. She was asleep.

The rest of the day flew by at a rapid-fire pace. I was just about to head back to my cabin and take a hot bath to deal with the aftermath of the day, when Chase sent out a group text.

Cheese and wine event by the lake?

The responses pinged back quickly, but the only number I recognized was Tilly's.

Can't. Promised the kids I'd go frog-catching with them. Already panicking.

I stood for a moment in the woods. The options were simple: head back to my cabin and wallow in my worries, or have a glass of wine, hang out, and hopefully, get my mind off of things. I dashed off a response before I could change my mind.

En route. See you in five.

The shore along the lake bustled with guests milling alongside the white covered tables set up for the tasting event. Bartenders poured generous glasses of wine and the food spread looked wonderful, with finger-bites like stuffed mushrooms, grilled vegetables, and of course, a robust selection of cheeses to pair with the wine. Cocktail waitresses circulated with trays to offer new drinks and whisk away the old, and Nikki bustled around, overseeing everything.

It was a relief to see that, in spite of her presentation, she was more than capable of doing her job. The event was lovely and, most importantly, the guests seemed happy. I waved at her and she smiled, before offering an older woman a glass of wine.

It took a moment to spot my friends, but then I saw Chase by the water with Saxon, Leo, and a pretty blonde in a bright pink dress. Leo nodded at me as I approached but turned away, his cell phone pressed to his ear. Saxon gave me a big grin, before sliding on a pair of blue Oakley sunglasses.

"Hi, Julie." He slid his arm around the blonde woman's waist. "Sorry to break your heart, but this is Peyton, and she appreciates the fact that I like long walks by the beach."

"Don't forget fireside chats," she told him, winking at me.

"You two want to join us?" Saxon asked.

"Nah, go ahead," Chase started to say, but they'd already headed off down the sand. Chase laughed and handed me a glass of wine. "Leo's stuck on a conference call, so for the moment, it's you and me." He tapped his glass against mine. "Cheers."

"Cheers," I said, taking a sip.

The wine was crisp, oaked, and had hints of green apple. Definitely high-end, as my parents were meticulous about the wine selections.

"Thanks for texting," I told Chase. "This is exactly what I needed today."

The surface of the lake was still in the late afternoon light and the trees along the edge of the shore gave the right amount of shade. We sat on a log overlooking the water. I took in the view, while breathing in the scent of the wine.

"How did it go last night with Margaret?" Chase asked. "I saw her out with Tilly today. They were off to take a painting class together. She looked like a normal girl, which surprised me, after everything yesterday."

"Tilly had me take her to breakfast this morning," I told him. "It was fine, but I can't figure her out. She was guarded but determined to put me down. Typical teen, in some ways, but I got glimpses of this shy, scared young girl. I'm questioning…"

Chase studied me. "What?"

"I wonder why she's really here," I admitted, taking another sip of wine.

"You don't buy it that she used to come here with her family?" he asked.

"No. I looked her up in our records and couldn't find her anywhere. Now, her parents might not have listed her as a guest or they could have just used an initial or something, but the big tell for me was the way she acted in the dining hall. Like she'd never seen it before."

"Hmm." Chase rubbed his hand against the stubble on his cheek. "Maybe she was too young to notice."

"True, but…" I balanced my wine glass in the sand.

"You think she's lying."

I nodded. "It's ironic, because she spent a lot of time telling me off for lying to my dad. This was before breakfast."

Chase cringed. "Nice way to start the day."

"Yeah." A seagull soared over the water and I watched it go by. "I don't know if I'm worried because of the way that we found her or what, but something doesn't feel right to me. I just wish I knew what it was."

"I should have stopped Tilly yesterday." Chase scooped up a handful of sand and let it run through his fingers. "I get it that you had to be diplomatic because of the business side of things, but I should have spoken up. This whole thing has you backed you into a corner with your dad, which isn't fair."

"True." I stared out at the water.

"What's on your mind?" Chase asked. "Seems like it's more than Margaret. Is your mom doing okay?"

"She's okay. I saw her today and she was struggling, but that's to be expected," I said. "I was also helping out with Wood Violet and it got me thinking about the resort. It's been interesting to get a glimpse into how it runs. It's just odd to watch other people make decisions about something I've always loved, especially decisions I don't agree with."

Chase rested his elbows on his knees. "Why, what's going on?"

I told him about the progress presentation. "It had so little to do with Wood Violet. We could have been talking about Any Resort, USA."

"For example?" he said, scooping up another handful of sand.

"Televisions in the cabins."

He cringed. "That wouldn't feel right here."

"Thank you." I ran my finger over the cool precipitation on my wine glass. "I was stunned by the suggestion but more than that, I was stunned that my father seemed to agree that it was a good idea."

Chase took a sip of wine. "You said in the forest that your parents wouldn't let you be a part of the business until you'd had five years of experience in the real world. Now that you have, would you work here?"

The thought made me laugh. "No; that ship has sailed. I have to focus on my life in Chicago. Marriage, job, that whole thing. Well, no job as of this morning, but…"

"What happened?" he asked.

"I haven't been there long enough to leave. So, they fired me."

It felt good to finally say it. The news was something I'd carried around all day, unable to tell my parents or Tristan for fear that it would make them feel bad. Chase wasn't invested either way, so he made the perfect sounding board.

He looked frustrated for me. "I would never do that to one of our employees. Family first. Maybe you're better off without them."

"Hard to tell," I said. "I've only been there for eight months, so in some ways, I think it's a fair decision. Now, the anxiety of working there has been replaced by anxiety that I should probably search for a new job right away, but I don't feel particularly motivated to do that. I chose to be here, so that's where I want to put my focus."

The whole thing was a headache. I didn't have time to update my résumé, reach out to contacts, and find a new place to take me on. More than that, I was not about to return to the city for interviews.

"Then put your focus here," Chase said. "I assume your husband will support that."

I made a noncommittal noise. "How long were you married?"

One of the cocktail waitresses walked by with a tray of white wine and she offered us another round. Chase tipped her, then handed me a glass. "Three years," he said, settling back into the log.

The wine made me bold enough to ask, "What happened?"

He gave me a sheepish grin. "I was twenty-two and didn't know any better. My wife—ex-wife—had a huge position with a tech company in California. We met at a convention and I thought it was love at first sight. So, I moved out West and got a good job at her company. It would have been perfect, except for the tiny detail that she was in love with another man."

"You're not serious."

Chase swirled his wine, and I caught a hint of oak. "It took me two years to figure it out. When I asked her why she'd married me, she said she'd needed to do something drastic to end that flirtation. Her boss moved to another company for her and now, they're married."

I put my hand to my heart. "That's horrible."

"Nah, it was a blessing in disguise. We weren't a match. Our marriage would have failed, whether we chose to remain in it or not."

I thought of the moment I'd felt relieved to see Tristan drive away. It wasn't because I was happy to see him go. It was because I was hurt that he didn't want to be here with me.

I thought about the remark he'd made before leaving, that there was little point in him staying since he hadn't seen me all weekend, anyway.

Tristan had come here expecting a cozy couple's weekend and I'd barely spent time with him at all. One would think he'd understand that I needed to spend time with my mom, but there had been opportunities that I'd passed on, like that morning he'd wanted me to get up with him to jog. I'd chosen the late-night bonfire instead. Then, there was that time he'd wanted to dance.

It had been sweet of him to ask but, instead of seeing that, I'd decided to get irritated that he'd tried to push me out of my comfort zone.

I hadn't considered the fact that Tristan was in a strange place with unwritten rules, and that he was out of his comfort zone, too.

"Sorry." Chase kicked at the sand. "Didn't mean to suck the fun out of tonight. Funny how a good divorce story can do that."

"I hear that," I said. "It got me thinking about my marriage."

The lake loomed in front of me, and for a moment, I could see the possibility of what Tristan and I could still be, in spite of all the hurt and heartache, and the mistakes we'd made on the way. I'd spent so much time blaming him for the lack of support he'd given me during our miscarriages that I'd forgotten what had brought us together in the first place.

It had been our compatibility and our companionship. The nights cooking in our condo, jogging together during the sunset, discussing personal and professional issues at our jobs. Being a couple, a partnership. We'd been so clouded by hurt these past fifteen months that all of that had fallen away.

"There've been a lot of ups and downs," I told Chase. "I've been putting so much emotional energy towards the things that have gone wrong, instead of rebuilding where we've found the cracks."

"It's easy to do," he said. "No one wants to admit that their relationship isn't perfect, because we're sold the idea that if it's love, it has to be perfect. But I've been in love a few times and some of my best relationships, the ones that helped me become a better person, were far from perfect."

I clinked my glass against his. "Lately, he and I haven't taken the time to invest in one another. I'm wondering if I should do some big, some grand gesture while I'm here, to show him what he means to me."

Chase slid off his shoes and put his feet in the sand. "What do you have in mind?"

"Do you want to take dance lessons with me?"

He laughed. "Dance lessons?"

"Yeah." My cheeks flushed. "I wouldn't dance with him at dinner because I don't know how."

Chase peered at me, as if waiting for the punchline. "What do you mean, you don't know how?"

"I don't," I said. "He'll come back to visit at some point. It's not like I'll be an expert by any means, but maybe if I took some lessons, I could surprise him."

Chase's chuckled. "Let's do it."

Even though I'd avoided dance lessons for years, this felt different. It would show Tristan that I cared enough to make an effort to rebuild our relationship. It wasn't like learning to dance had the power to solve any of our real problems, but it could serve as a symbol to him that I was willing to do what was necessary to make things work.

I knew our marriage would fail whether we chose to remain in it or not.

That wasn't what I wanted, so it was time for me to take the steps back towards my husband, before the distance between us became too great.

CHAPTER TWELVE

Chase invited me to come to dinner with him, Leo, and Leo's family, but we'd hit the appetizer table after the wine and I wasn't hungry. Instead, I decided to sit in the Hut and think. The wine had gone to my head, and I wanted to talk to Tristan, to let him know that I had plans to get our relationship back to the place it was before all the heartache and the loss.

With an ache in my throat, I called him. He picked up on the first ring.

"Julie, what is it?" he asked, when I started to cry.

"I need you to come stay here with me," I said. "Even if it's just for the weekends. There's no reason for us to be apart."

His voice was cold. "You're the one who made that decision."

"Please don't act like this." I watched the surface of the lake break open as a fish jumped. "My mother is sick. Try to see the logic behind that instead of acting like I've done something wrong. I don't want to spend the summer apart, so I will ask you again, please let's set some times that you'll be here with me."

"That's a little ridiculous," he said.

The complete irritation he showed at the idea made me want to drop it all together. The tears were hot on my cheek but I brushed them away.

If a person shows you who they are, believe them.

Lately, Tristan had shown a complete lack of interest in being there for me at all.

Should I believe it?

I closed my eyes. Thoughts like that would not bring us back together. Positive actions would, like spending time together. Simple things, baby steps, had the power to close this gap between us.

Tristan sighed. "I can move things around and try to make it there the weekend after this one."

"Thank you," I said, tearing up again. "I have to tell you all that's happened with that girl, and I want you to spend time with my friends, and—"

Most of all, I needed to talk to him about the fact that I no longer had a job, and I wanted to do that face to face.

"Julie, I said I'll try," he warned. "I might not be able to. Let me see."

I wiped my tears with the front of my T-shirt, the breeze gentle on my stomach. "I just want to see you."

His voice softened. "I miss you, too." We were both silent, then he said, "Alright, let me check into it and I'll call you tomorrow. Love you."

"Love you, too," I said, squeezing the phone tight.

Once we hung up, I moved from the bench to the edge of the dock and put my feet in the water. The phone call had not been what I'd hoped, but at least he was willing to come back to the resort. For now, it was the best we could do.

The dance lessons were held in the large ballroom that overlooked the lake. They were one of our most popular activities because, once people saw the fun of the formal dance nights, they wanted to improve their skills so they could be a part of it, too. The classes were always full.

The beginner's dance class was first thing in the morning. My nerves, coupled with the fact that I wasn't quite awake, made me want to run in the other direction. What was I thinking, doing this? I did not like to dance and, besides, it was not going to change a thing about my marriage. The idea was symbolic, so why put myself through the drama? I could tell Tristan I'd thought about it, because it was the thought that counts, right?

"It's not too late to call it a day and go get breakfast instead," said an amused voice.

Chase was headed down the path, dressed in workout clothes. His arms looked tanned and strong, and I remembered the purpose behind it all. Tristan. To show him that I loved him and wanted to make things work.

"Is it that obvious that I was about to walk away?" I asked. "I think it was the buzz of the wine talking yesterday, not common sense."

I had made Chase promise that he would not tell Tilly or the rest of our crew that I was learning to dance because I feared they would show up in a sign of solidarity. Of course, that would have sent me running for the hills.

"You know, I worked on a motivational speech the entire walk over here," Chase said. "Then I realized that I am not good at motivational speeches. That said, I know you'll have the courage to follow through, even if I step on your toes."

I rolled my eyes. Chase had been a good dancer ever since we were kids. His mother used to have him dance with her friends, which embarrassed him more than the bow tie.

"Thank you for being here," I said. "I hate this. But I'm staying."

"That's right." Chase grinned. "Nobody puts Julie in the corner."

The dance instructor, Tomas, greeted me warmly at the door. We'd met at the staff meeting and he was a vibrant, good-spirited person who walked like he was balancing a plate on his head at all times.

"It is such an honor to have you here." He squeezed both of my hands. "However, this is the class for beginners."

I gave him a sheepish smile. "I don't know how to dance. Can you believe that? Somehow I've avoided it all these years but it's time to learn. Please don't tell my father that I'm doing this. Or anyone, if you can help it. It's embarrassing."

Tomas gave me a spontaneous hug. "You have nothing to be embarrassed about, *cherie*. We all have dance in our heart, it is simply a matter of listening to the music that is inside." Tomas looked at Chase. "Are you a beginner, too?"

"Nah." Chase gave a sheepish smile. "I've listened to the music inside for a while, now." He gave a dorky dance move to prove it and we all laughed.

The room was starting to fill up with guests, so Tomas directed us over to the side to stretch and warm up. We did some basic running stretches while people walked in. There were older couples and younger couples, but they were all couples.

"I can't tell you how much I appreciate this," I told Chase, stretching my toes out in a patch of sun on the wooden floor.

"You're welcome." His eyes looked aquamarine from the reflection of the water outside the window. "It should be fun."

"It's all couples, though," I said.

He shrugged. "We used to be a couple. That should count for something." He rubbed the stubble on his cheek. "Do you know how much it crushed me when my parents made my brother and me go to that sailing camp instead of coming back here?"

Even though it had been a lifetime ago, my heart skipped a beat to think he'd felt the same. I had cried myself to sleep for weeks over the news, cradling each letter he'd sent me close. Such first-love angst, but it had meant everything at the time.

"I was heartbroken." My cheeks flushed at the confession. "Do you remember that necklace you sent me for Christmas? I wore that thing for like two years."

Chase laughed. "Yeah, my brother made fun of me for that. He said that you would hate it. I wish he was still here, just so I could say I told you so."

I leaned my torso over my legs, my body still tingling with embarrassment. "Have you had any luck searching for the memory box? Have you looked for it?"

Chase lifted his arms up over his head. "No luck. There's a couple places that I've looked but your security staff gave me strange looks when I was walking around with a shovel."

"Let me know if there's anything I can do to help," I said.

Tomas clapped his hands and walked to the center of the room. "Everyone, let's walk with our partner out to the dance floor."

The look I gave Chase was nothing short of terrified. "Julie, it's going to be a disaster. Embrace it."

I didn't know whether to feel insulted or laugh. "You think it's going to be a disaster?"

"Why wouldn't it be?" His cheerful grin made my fears fade away. "You're here to learn, not because you're an expert, so plan to fail for a while."

The words took the pressure off.

Most men had an expectation that I could dance a little bit or that their incredible prowess could get me there, even if I didn't know how. The fact that Chase embraced the situation for what it was allowed me to relax and listen to the instructor.

Tomas started off by showing us a simple step and asking us to count. Then, we spent the next half hour doing that simple step while counting but I kept trying to turn it into a dance. Finally, Tomas came around and took my hands from Chase.

He shook my arms and said, "Count."

I counted to three.

"Very good. Now, do the steps. Great. Now, do the steps and count." He ran me through that routine at least five times before sending me back to Chase, where we did it exactly the same way.

I was actually disappointed when Thomas clapped his hands, thanked us for coming and invited us to return the next morning. I wondered if I should try to do the class alone. It wouldn't be as much fun, but it was a big ask to have Chase come with me every day.

"Tomorrow, then?" Chase said, as we were leaving.

I came to a full stop. "You would do that?"

He winked. "I owe you for never coming back here that summer."

Tristan had called while I was in the dance lesson. I returned his call on my walk back to the cabin.

"I'm already making plans for next weekend," I said, smiling.

"Well, don't make them yet." His voice sounded irritated, and I imagined him in the office, looking out over the skyline and Lake Michigan. "There's a golf tournament I apparently committed to back in April. It's with one of our biggest clients. I promise I'll get there eventually, I just have to figure out when."

The news was disappointing, but it didn't impact me the way it might have the night before, when I was so emotional. He was back to real life, where it was normal for us to be busy for weeks at a time. There was a reason we'd never made it to Wood Violet together, and it wasn't like anything had changed.

"I get it," I said. "How's it going with work?"

Tristan told me about all the networking things he'd been doing in the past few days. "Nothing like summer in the city. What about the firm? Surely, they've responded with a plan for you by now."

I wanted to tell him I'd gotten fired but something held me back. Mainly, the fact that I didn't want to fight. It was so nice to just talk to him without having to defend the choices I had made.

"Yes, I talked to Phil," I said carefully.

"What did he say?" Tristan asked.

"He had to talk to the partners. Listen, I have to find my key to the cabin, so let me call you later."

Being evasive made my stomach tighten but I just needed a little more time to figure out how to best address the situation. I'd have to share the news eventually, whether it was comfortable or not. It wasn't as if the issue was going to just go away.

Back in the cabin, I changed out of my workout clothes, which were hot and sticky in the heat. I planned to take a fast shower and slip into a sundress before heading over to work at the office.

On the way there, I spotted my father walking through the main area with two men dressed in suits. One carried a briefcase and the other chatted and laughed with my father like an old friend. Something about it seemed odd. Maybe that their robust laughter seemed forced or…

The suits.

The humidity was high already and it would get sticky-hot within the next hour. Wearing a suit in the woods would be uncomfortable. It reminded me of the hottest days in the city when we'd have to dress for court, and how out of place we all looked breaking for lunch at one of the outdoor restaurants downtown.

Those men stood out in the same way, which made me wonder who they were and why they were here.

The office I shared with Nikki was empty when I walked in, but the coffee was brewing, so I knew she was here somewhere. I was nervous to see her, because I still didn't know quite what to say about her presentation.

The IT team had hooked up the necessary computer equipment and the set-up gave me access to the various programs that helped run the resort. I planned to help my father get caught up on all the minutia that had been pushed to the side, and when I logged on, nearly twenty new tasks were waiting for me. Each one had detailed instructions, probably once prepared for the operations manager that my father had planned to hire.

It was a lot but it was good, because it showed that my presence here was absolutely necessary. My father had been falling behind, and that was not good for the resort or for him. There was not a harder-working man that I knew, but there were only so many hours in the day.

I had just finished up my first task, responding to a backlog of time-off requests, when Nikki walked in. She looked as put-together as always in a tailored blue dress.

"Good morning," she chirped, filling her coffee mug. "Feel free to help yourself. I drink it like water, so I apologize in advance if the pot goes empty, but you're welcome to it."

"Thanks," I said. "Hey, do you know who my dad is meeting with this morning?"

Nikki's expression clouded. She hesitated for a moment, then walked over to the office door and shut it. "Developers," she whispered.

"Developers?" I echoed.

"Julie, this might be a conversation you should have with your dad."

My shoulders tensed. "What do you mean?"

Nikki sat in her desk chair and stirred her coffee. "Your father is in talks to sell off a part of the property. The unused acreage. No one knows."

"Sorry, what?" I said in disbelief.

"I know." She dropped the stirrer in the trash. "It was something he'd kept quiet but ever since your mother had a stroke, the meetings have been more frequent. I only know because I happened to walk in on one of them, and their literature was spread out on his desk. He asked me not to say anything."

"He can't sell the property, though," I said. "It's part of who we are. Besides, my grandfather owns it."

"Well, I think your grandfather has agreed to it, because it all sounded pretty serious."

I fiddled with the trackpad on my computer. What was it that had prompted my father to make this move? If he'd started talks before the stroke, something else must have been going on.

"Do you know what part he's thinking of selling?" I asked.

"The acreage in the woods that no one uses. The part that's wild." She read an email that popped up, then turned back to me. "If a developer buys it, they could build a competing resort, anything really. The partnership has to be the right one, or there could be real consequences."

"There shouldn't be a partnership at all," I said.

The office was air-conditioned, but it felt too hot. I flipped on the overhead fan and leaned against the wall. "Do you know how close he is to following through on this?"

"No clue."

It was something I'd have to look into, and find a way to do it without breaking Nikki's confidence.

"Nice job on your presentation," I said, to change the subject. "Sorry I haven't had the chance to tell you that, yet."

Her face brightened. "Thank you. I was worried you didn't like anything that I'd said, since you didn't comment at the meeting."

The coffee smelled good and I poured myself a mug. "It's not that I didn't like it. There were just a few parts that called for a bigger discussion."

"I'd love to hear your thoughts now," Nikki said hopefully. "I'm trying to decide which improvements to pursue, so any input helps."

"Well, that's the thing." I added some creamer. "Why the big push for change?"

Nikki gave a sharp nod. "To remain competitive. We're a staple in this industry, but that won't last forever. It's important to offer the same value to a new generation."

"But my grandparents started Wood Violet in the seventies," I said. "The generations didn't move on, they brought their children and their children's children. We have the new generation."

"For now," she warned. "There's a lot of competition."

"Yes," I said. "Brightly colored waterparks and massive modern hotels, and they get crowds from all over the world, which is great. Wood Violet, however, is a quiet, lazy, retreat designed to help families reconnect with nature and each other." I gave a rueful smile. "That might have been straight from the brochure, my mother would be proud."

Nikki smiled. "I wrote that."

"Well, it's a great line," I said, happy that we were connecting on a real level. "So, why force anything?"

"Because business has been dying out over the past few years. Your father might not talk about it, but it's happening."

The words gave me pause. "Do you think that's why he's trying to sell?"

Nikki glanced up at me and quickly, back down at her hands. "Yeah."

Really, it wouldn't be a huge shock if the resort had taken a hit in the past few years. The travel industry had slowed down. The numbers couldn't be anything extreme, though, because my parents would have told me that.

Wouldn't they?

My father was big on character and he was an honest man. He also had that bad habit of holding back information for fear of upsetting us. It would be a simple thing to research, to compare the numbers from the past ten years. I would just have to come to the office when no one else was here, so I could get a true read on the situation.

"Thank you for sharing the information," I said. "I'll look into it and do what I can to help. The one thing I do have to say is, just because we might be experiencing a downturn at the moment doesn't mean it will be forever. There are people who cherish the idea of spending time at a slower pace. The opportunity to recharge and refresh. I think we would do better to think in that direction. Families want the opportunity to be together without the distractions of daily life. That's what we have to offer, and it has always served us well."

"I understand." She smoothed back her hair. "I promise you, I'm not trying to change what makes Wood Violet great. I'm trying to figure out what we can do to grow further in that direction, so that we can keep offering the quality that our guests expect."

"Thank you," I said quietly.

Nikki nodded and turned her attention to a spreadsheet. I watched her work for a moment. There was a stack of neatly labeled folders on her desk, which was spotless, with a couple of framed pictures of her husband, kids, and their dog.

It was clear that she loved her job and was happy here; she just wanted to make a difference. I wanted to support her, but I didn't want her to push my father to make changes he might regret at a time he was grasping for solutions. Before any big changes were made, I wanted to know exactly what was going on with the financials, and determine if my father was seriously thinking about selling off a piece of the resort.

CHAPTER THIRTEEN

Tilly had wanted us to spend time with Margaret together, so she'd set up a time to visit her cabin Saturday afternoon. I met Tilly in the main area to walk over after she'd dropped the kids at a Capture the Flag game. She looked rested and relaxed, in a designer sundress that billowed around her ankles.

"You make motherhood look easy," I said, kissing both of her cheeks. "How is it possible you look so refreshed?"

Tilly looked surprised. "Because my kids do not require a thing from me here. They have food, friends, and endless entertainment. They're happy, so I'm happy."

I raised my eyebrows. "And *I'm* happy to hear you say that."

"Thanks for coming with me to see Margaret," Tilly said. "It's important that we work with her now to set up plans for the fall. Once the summer's over, she'll be left out in the cold unless we can help her enroll in college or find a job or maybe a musical internship. I'm thinking we can kind of hint at the topic today, see how she reacts, and then start pushing her to think about these things in a week or so."

Tilly's tone was bright but by the furrow in her brow, I could tell she was serious about helping Margaret get her life back on track.

"I'll do what I can to help," I promised.

We walked in silence for a moment, then I said, "I'm thinking about what you just said, about your kids being happy here. Question for you: Do you see areas where the resort feels a little outdated? I'm sure you guys have traveled all over the place, and since I'm only here for the summer, I want to get as much input as I can to help out my parents as they move forward."

Tilly ran her hands through her necklaces. They were a mixture of art-fair wooden beads and Chanel chains that looked effortlessly cool blended together. "I don't know," she mused, as we strolled towards the path to Margaret's cabin. "My kids are at the age where the outdoors is a magical place. They love the scavenger hunts and the outdoor art classes. They grumbled at first about the lack of electronics—I do think a games room would be a strong addition for rainy days—but they love getting dirty. Being kids. There isn't enough of that these days."

"Do you think other parents feel the same?" I asked. "That we're still competitive?"

Tilly came to a full stop in the middle of the path. "Julie, you know what's funny? I've never thought of it like that. We come here because I've come here since I was a little girl. I want my kids to have the same type of summers I did. Safe, outdoors, surrounded by other kids."

The words were nice to hear but didn't instill me with confidence that we would be able to attract new guests. "I'm glad your time here meant that much to you."

"It means even more, now that I'm older," she said. "Seasoned? Maybe I should say seasoned. I don't age."

I grinned and we walked in silence for a moment.

"You know, Wood Violet is an important place," she said. "It has a perfect reputation and everyone knows its name, so as long as you keep the quality and the charm, people will always come."

Our talk gave me a sense of peace. That is, until we approached Margaret's cabin. I still did not know what to expect from the girl, but I certainly didn't want her to call me a liar again in front of Tilly.

"Hello, hello," Tilly called, rapping on the front door. "We're here."

Margaret peeked out the window and waved. She wore another round of pastel shorts and a polo from the Tilly contribution. Her cheeks were pink, like she'd spent the morning out on the water, and she actually smiled at Tilly.

"I had so much fun painting with you again yesterday," Tilly chirped, as we walked in. "I'm officially moving to Rome to live as an artist. I'll make a fortune."

Margaret snorted. "You might make a dollar if you don't have change. Mine, on the other hand…" She gestured at a copy of *Starry Night* leaning up against the wall. It was well done, with bright colors and sure strokes. "It inspires."

"Then, it's decided," Tilly said. "We'll sell your paintings and you'll buy me pizzas."

The two laughed and I hung back, confused at their easy connection. It was like they were best friends, while I couldn't even make it through a walk to breakfast without letting Margaret get under my skin. Maybe it was because I was still angry at the pressure her presence put on me, or the fact that I hadn't been able to shake my suspicion that she was lying about why she was here. Either way, I needed to try harder to accept the situation and offer support.

"Good afternoon," I said. "It's good to see you."

"Hi," she mumbled, smearing on some lip balm.

"Well, I brought snacks." Tilly pulled out a bag stuffed with treats that she would surely leave behind for Margaret. "Let me put these together and you two pick out the board game." She headed to the kitchen cupboards and put together a display of rainbow-colored candy-coated popcorn, while I considered the options Margaret had pulled out of the closet.

"Oh, I love Risk," I said, brushing my fingers against the box. "That used to be one of my favorite games. My sister and I had massive wars."

The thought of Kate reminded me that I hadn't called her and I needed to. I'd texted her that I'd decided to stay for the summer, which had resulted in several delighted emojis on her end, but I wanted to set up a video chat with her and Mom. I knew my mother would love to see her, and a call like that might help to keep her spirits up.

"Risk?" Margaret glanced at me. Today, she wore sparkling gold eyeliner that made her look ethereal. "Who won?"

"Me," I said, surprised she'd even responded. "Every time."

Margaret gave me a knowing look and picked up the box. "Well, I always win. So this should be interesting."

"Please. I'll crush you both like bugs," Tilly chirped, pouring sparkling water into glasses. She brought it all into the dining area and set it on the table. "Shall we?"

It took nearly two hours, but Margaret managed to defeat us both.

"Ha!" She swooped up the last of the pieces, her face gleeful. "I rule the world!"

Tilly peered over the rim of her pale pink reading glasses, as if still searching for her lost men. "My kids would be so ashamed of me." Her phone chimed. "Speaking of, they are nearly done with Capture the Flag. I should head out."

"Don't go." Margaret twisted her thick, dark hair up into a bun, and suddenly looked very young.

"Sorry, honey," Tilly said. "I've got to get back to my kids. Julie might be able to stay."

It hit me that Margaret was probably drawn to Tilly because Tilly seemed like a perfect mother. I still hadn't had the chance to be a perfect mother, or a mother at all, but if that was what Margaret was looking for, it wouldn't hurt to make a better effort to be someone for her to lean on.

"I can stay if you want me to," I said.

Margaret fiddled with the collar of her shirt. "Do you mind? I'm bored alone in here."

"Not at all," I said.

We'd had fun playing the board game together but I figured she was only being nice to me because Tilly was around. I never would have expected her to actually want to spend time with me, after our disastrous breakfast.

"I'll wave to you all at dinner." Tilly air-kissed my cheeks. "See you soon!"

Tilly's sandals tapped down the front steps, and Margaret went silent. She chewed on her lip for a moment and I could tell she had something on her mind. Suddenly, she blurted out, "I don't really need to hang out or anything but I did want to talk to you. I'm sorry for those things I said to you."

I set down the board-game pieces I'd been putting away. "Wow… I did not expect that. Thank you. For your apology. That means a lot."

Margaret sank into the couch and buried her head in her hands. For a tense moment, I thought she was about to cry. Then, she sat up and regarded me with her big eyes.

"I have to admit it," she said. "I don't know what I'm doing here."

I sat on the chair next to the couch. "Well, you've been through a lot," I said carefully. Now that she was talking to me, I didn't want to say anything that would set her off. "It can't be easy to be here all alone."

"It's not." She rubbed her eyes. "Things weren't perfect, but I miss my…"

The cozy cabin felt cold as I waited to hear that she missed her mother. It wasn't a conversation I wanted to have. The topic brought up feelings I didn't want to address because I felt the same, in a very different way.

Instead of saying *mother*, though, she said, "My life. The way things were before."

I could relate to that, too. So much had changed in such a short period of time. I'd lost my job, I was away from my husband, my home, and thanks to what had happened to my mother, it felt like nothing would ever be the same again.

"It's a hard time," I said. "You just graduated, right? Do you have plans to go to college or anything?"

She picked at the strings on a couch cushion. "I'm not planning on staying here forever, if that's what you're asking."

I held up my hands. "That's not what I meant. I'm curious about your life, that's all."

Margaret's cell phone rang. It rested on the distressed wooden trunk in front of the couch, and she glanced at it. "I have to take this. Hold on."

She darted back to the bedroom and I sat there, wondering who had called. Five minutes passed and then, ten. I still had a ton to do at the office and I planned to visit my mother later this afternoon, so I decided to leave and check back in later.

As I stood, I noticed the Dooney and Bourke backpack I'd bought for her resting on the floor by the couch. The bag was open and the edge of the pink folder I'd seen that first day stuck out of the top of the main compartment. Margaret's muffled voice chatted away in the bedroom and I hesitated.

It wasn't that I wanted to violate her privacy, but I needed information. I still couldn't find her online, I was pretty certain she'd lied about coming here in the past, and it would help me to have a glimpse into her life. My job was to protect my parents and the resort, so the fact that we were housing her for free felt like a fair exchange for a quick bag check.

I perched on the edge of the wooden trunk with a clear view of the bedroom door and pulled out my phone, cueing it up so it would look like I was scrolling if Margaret walked out. Then I pulled out the pink folder and opened it.

I don't know what I'd expected to find. Pictures of her mother, maybe, or a special locket in a plastic bag… something. Instead, the only thing in the folder was a photocopy of a legal document. My breath came fast as I read the first few sentences.

These are adoption papers. For Margaret.

I had started to look into adoption after the two failed pregnancies. I didn't know much about the process, but I knew enough to recognize that this was a private adoption, completed through a law firm rather than an agency. It also meant that the mother who had sided with the stepdad and kicked her out was not her birth mother.

There was a shout of laughter from the bedroom. It sounded like the phone call was wrapping up. Quickly, I snapped some photos of the document with my phone. My hand froze when I reached the last page and saw the signature of the birth mother, and the address listed below.

So, that's why she's here.

The address beneath the signature was Wood Violet. I had no idea why or how the resort's name was on Margaret's adoption papers, but there it was, plain as day. There was a sound at the bedroom door and quick as a flash, I moved to put the papers back in the folder. There was something else in there, tucked in between two thin, white pieces of cardboard.

Willing the bedroom door to stay shut, I pulled out the cardboard and the piece of paper inside.

It was a sketch of a pregnant woman. She sat by a river with her feet resting in the water. Looking over her shoulder as if at the lens of a camera, she gave a smile as bright as the sun. The date at the bottom was roughly eighteen years ago and I would have recognized the signature of the artist anywhere.

The portrait had been drawn by my grandmother.

CHAPTER FOURTEEN

I had just slid all of the papers back into the pink folder, and tucked it safely into the backpack, when Margaret emerged from the bedroom. She seemed surprised to see me, as if she'd assumed I would ignore her request to stay. I stretched and made a big deal out of clicking off my phone, like if I'd been on it for ages and needed a break.

"One of these days I'll just leave this in my cabin." I tucked it into my pocket, hoping it wasn't obvious that my hands were shaking. "Then maybe I could spend my time looking at the trees instead of scrolling through the news."

My acting skills must have been better than I thought, because Margaret flopped back onto the couch and folded her legs beneath her, as if settling in for a chat. "Pinterest," she said, nodding. "I spend hours looking at cakes. I don't know why."

I laughed, but it sounded nervous. More than anything, I wanted to race out of the cabin and read that document. There had to be some explanation as to why our address was on there, and I wanted to find out what it was as soon as possible.

There was, of course, the option of telling Margaret what I'd found. Then she could explain what she knew about her birth mother and why she was here, so that I didn't have to worry this would somehow impact the resort. But no doubt she would flip out at me for invading her privacy.

"That was a long phone call," I said, instead. "Who were you talking to?"

Margaret picked at the couch cushion. "My best friend, Lindsey. She's taking a cross-country road trip with our group of friends, so she was telling me all about it."

"Oh." The image of a car full of teenagers descending on the resort made me wince. "Where are they headed?"

"They're not coming here. They just went to Nashville and saw the Country Music Hall of Fame, and they're going to check out some live music before heading west."

"You'd probably enjoy that." Nashville had to be attractive to someone who played the guitar and sang. "Taking a road trip with your friends is something you'd never forget."

"Well, duh." Her eyes flashed. "I've been planning it with them all year. But plans change."

"Yeah." I thought of Tristan, and the look on his face when I'd decided to stay. He'd probably had our whole summer planned out, too. "Do your friends know where you are?"

Margaret pulled her knees to her chest. "Who do you think dropped me off at the edge of the forest?" The image sounded ominous. I was glad that we'd found her, no matter how difficult she could be. "I tell my friends everything. We're friends for life."

I was glad Margaret had a close group to support her. For some reason, Tilly and Chase jumped to mind. Even though we'd lost touch for so long, I felt closer to the two of them than I did to the friends I'd made in Chicago. It was the shared history, the sense that they knew me in ways that other people never would. I considered them friends for life.

"What's that weepy look?" Margaret asked. "Please don't cry or anything weird. This is supposed to be about me."

"I'm thinking about the importance of good friends. Margaret, you're so young. You should be spending your summer with them. I could help you find a way to meet up. Doing something fun might make it easier to process everything."

"Nope." She shrugged a skinny shoulder. "The road trip would be a big mistake."

"Why?" I asked.

Letting out a hearty sigh, she said, "There are boys on that trip, Julie."

The words were said with such gravity that I almost laughed. "That's a bad thing?"

Margaret chewed on her nails. "Yes. I dated one of the guys for like, six months. It's not wise to fall in love right now, so I told him we'd have to be friends. Now he's in all the pictures with this girl, Kelly. It's okay if they're together, I just don't want to be around it."

"Oh." I paused. "Why isn't it wise to fall in love right now? Because you're already dealing with so much?"

Margaret gave me one of her best *duh* looks. "No, because we're both going off to college. It was doomed from the start. I want to have good memories of my first love. Didn't you?"

I had so many good memories with Chase. Holding his hand as we watched movies in the lodge, sharing ice-cream cones on walks, tackling each other while swimming in the lake. It had been a summer of innocence, and even now, the memories warmed my heart.

"Yes, I have some good memories." The topic made me feel disloyal to Tristan, so I changed the subject. "So, you're going to college? That's great. Where?"

"I might not." Margaret grabbed her guitar. "Things are too weird right now."

I sat in silence, watching her fingers move over the frets. She strummed quietly at first but then began to hum along with the tune she was playing. Even her humming sounded better than anything I'd ever be able to do.

"Well, I'll let you play in peace," I said, getting to my feet. "I should head out."

The pictures I'd snapped flashed through my head. I hoped they weren't blurry but more than that, I hoped they'd give me some answers.

Margaret didn't look up. Instead, she focused on playing her guitar. I watched her for a moment, thinking of all that she'd given up to be here, and what she wished to find.

The poor girl had been through so much. I wanted to help her, but I wanted to understand the situation first. That way, there was less risk that it could all go wrong.

The moment I was on the path leading away from her cabin, I called Chase. His voice sounded distracted, like he was in the middle of something.

"Sorry to bother you. Do you have a few minutes?" I asked, brushing mist out of my eyes. It had started to rain again but it was light. "I was at Margaret's. I think I know why she's here."

"Is everything okay with her?" Chase asked.

It was so like him to wonder about Margaret's well-being first and the intrigue second. "Yes," I said. "She seems good, but she has no clue I know."

"Stop by," he said. "327. Fair warning, though: I've been writing tech jargon for three hours straight, so my head might actually explode."

I switched directions on the path and headed his way. It had started to rain in earnest by the time I arrived, and I was soaking wet when he answered the door.

"This is getting to be my thing," I said, indicating my wet hair and the rain dripping down my face.

Chase's hair was curly in the humidity and he looked relaxed in a pair of gray sweatpants and a Green Bay Packers T-shirt. Laughing, he said, "Come on in."

His cabin was warm and cozy, and it smelled like aftershave and coffee.

"Let me get you some dry clothes."

He emerged from the bedroom with a royal blue sweatshirt and a pair of green and blue flannel pajama pants. "These are clean, I promise. Unless you'd rather have a robe?"

My cheeks flushed at either idea, but I couldn't exactly stand there, drenched. "Perfect. Thanks."

I headed back through the bedroom to the bathroom to change. It felt like such a time warp to walk by Chase's bed. There had been a period in my life when the very thought would have sent me into a swoon.

The bathroom smelled like him, and I realized the origin was an open jar of lemongrass-scented hair pomade. It took no time at all to change into the dry clothes and wrap a towel around my wet hair but when I glanced in the mirror, the look seemed a little too intimate. So I took off the towel and used the blow-dryer instead.

Chase had poured us coffee by the time I made it back out to the living room. The table in the kitchen was covered with what looked like notepads of research for his book, so we settled in on the couch. Once I'd briefed him, he whistled.

"Can I see the pictures?" he asked.

"Yes." I scooted over to him and opened my phone. "Here."

Chase peered at the small print of the adoption papers, then shook his head. "This is why I hire lawyers," he said. "I have no idea what this says."

"Basically, it's a closed adoption through a private law firm." I recognized the name of the firm, as it was based in Chicago. "Closed means that the identity of the mother is not available. The name is blacked out but the address is here, so I think that's why Margaret came to Wood Violet. She's trying to find a connection to her birth mother."

Chase raised his eyebrows. "Because she's mad at her mother."

"Maybe that's how she's dealing with the pain." I considered the document. "The thing that scares me about what I'm reading is that if the adoption is closed, there's a good chance the mother doesn't want to be found. It's going to cause a lot of heartache if Margaret figures out who she is and reaches out to her, and she doesn't want to be a part of her life. Two rejections like that would be a lot to take."

"How would she find her?" Chase asked.

"That, I don't know, and it gets even more complicated." I hesitated, then opened the picture of the drawing. "My grandmother drew that. They might have been friends but really, I'm wondering if my grandmother was involved as some sort of a cover-up for one of the guests."

"Cover-up meaning…?"

I took a sip of coffee. "Like the father might have been one of the married guests or something. The mother's not that young, based on this drawing, so it's not like she's some teenager who didn't know what to do. It's odd. Don't you think?"

Chase ran his hand through his hair, deep in thought. My leg felt warm and suddenly, I realized our thighs were touching. Embarrassed, I shifted my position so that Chase could still see the phone, but so that we weren't as close.

"That wouldn't be great for the resort," he admitted. "It's the type of thing that the older crowd would not get behind, if the story got out. I mean, this happened a long time ago, but if your grandmother actually organized a hidden adoption for a guest, the more conservative folks might wonder…"

He stopped talking.

"What?" I asked. "Say it."

"They might wonder what other accommodations she made over the years. I don't think that, which is why I hesitated. But I know that crowd and the way they think."

"They wouldn't still care, would they?" I asked. "Like you said, it was a long time ago."

"Eighteen years is not that long when you're in your sixties and seventies," he said. "My mom says she remembers bringing me and Garrett home from the hospital like it was yesterday, and that was over thirty years ago. Still, there's not much chance word would get around about all this. Unless Margaret starts broadcasting it or something, no one would know."

I set down my mug on a coaster on the coffee table. "I hate it that there's another opportunity for her to cause trouble. She was great today, but…"

Her apology had seemed sincere but it could have been calculated, now that I knew how strong her motivation was to stay here.

"I'll just have to find out the truth before she does," I said. "That way, I can control the narrative. I could also find out whether or not her birth mother wants to meet her, to keep Margaret from getting hurt again. I don't know if that girl can take much more."

Chase nodded. "Any ideas how to find all this?"

"Two things." I ran my hands through my hair. It was still damp, but not soaked, thanks to the hair-dryer. "I have a contact at the law firm listed on the document. I can email her and see if Margaret's mother maybe changed her mind about leaving the adoption closed and left a letter for Margaret or anything. I don't know if that type of thing is even permissible, as I don't know anything about adoptions, but it never hurts to ask if there is anything she's allowed to tell me."

Chase finished his coffee. "Like the name of Margaret's mother?"

"No, she wouldn't be able to tell me that. But she might have some sort of detail she would be able to mention that could send us in the right direction." I zoomed in on the drawing, to better see the woman's face. My grandmother had done a beautiful job. The sketch was so real it could have been a photograph.

"I think she looks like Margaret. It's in the shape of the eyes."

Chase leaned in and we almost bumped heads. Laughing awkwardly, I handed him the phone so he could study it.

"The attitude, too," he said. "The look that she's giving your grandmother is confident but cautious, with something behind the eyes that's holding her back. Look at the drawing of the nose, too." He pointed at the bridge, and the way it slanted into pert nostrils.

"It's Margaret's nose," I agreed.

Chase handed me the phone. "Could you show this to your parents?" he said, after a moment. "Ask if they remember having her here as a guest?"

Outside, the rain had stopped, but the sky was still gray. A butterfly flew past the window, its colors bright against the gloom.

The drawing seemed to stare up at me and I clicked my phone closed. "I don't know. I'm nervous that would bring up too many questions. They don't need to have a new round of worries, especially with something that's not necessarily a threat."

"We could talk to the staff members that have been here a while," Chase suggested. "Someone might recognize the woman in the drawing."

We had a few people who had been on staff forever. It would take them about two seconds to tell me whether or not they recognized the woman.

"Yes," I said, nodding. "That could work. Let me put my wet clothes back on, I'll run back to my cabin and change, and then I'll ask around. Do you want to come?"

I'd assumed Chase would have to get back to work, but he got up and headed towards the door.

"Intrigue is much more interesting than data storage," he said. "I'm in."

*

Claude Moriarty had been at the resort since the beginning of time. Four feet nine, with wiry red hair, and built in the shape of a box, Claude gave the impression that she'd invented the hospital corner on bedsheets but had a smile that could stop anyone in their tracks. We found her cleaning one of the cabins on her afternoon route, scrubbing the floors like they'd said a bad word.

"Claude, you are incredible." I stood on the porch at the edge of the door. "Because of that, I need your help with something."

"You best not be asking me to pick up one of your messes." She leaned back on her heels and squinted at me. "I've got my hands full."

"It's not a mess," I promised.

"In theory," Chase whispered, from his spot behind me on the porch.

Claude pushed up her sleeves, revealing full, pale arms that had hauled around jugs of water and cleaning supplies for the past forty years. Then, she assessed Chase with a look. "Ever since Miss Julie got married she's tried to pretend like she never needed no one to raise her, but I changed that girl's diapers and put iodine on her knees. She better not be telling you different."

I shot Claude a warning look I might have given my sister for making that type of comment about marriage, and she shot me a look right back. Clearly, she didn't approve of me standing within six feet of anyone other than my husband. Instead of coming over to talk to me, she went right back to scrubbing the floors.

"Claude," I pressed. "I need the advice of someone with vast intelligence. If I'm in the wrong spot, please let me know."

"Well, keep talking," she said with a chuckle.

I zoomed in on the face in the drawing, a move that helped hide the fact that the woman was pregnant. "This was one of my grandmother's old drawings. Do you know who it is?"

Claude took my phone and her eyebrows shot up. "Your grandmother had a gift. That could be a photograph."

"You know who it is?" My voice sounded too excited, so I toned it down. "That's helpful. The drawing was in some papers and I want to surprise my family with it, maybe get it framed, but it would help to have some context."

Claude zoomed out before I could take my phone back. She studied the picture for a moment, then handed it back to me. "Time for a break." She headed down the steps and pulled out a Capri-Sun out from her cleaning cart. Claude drank about five Capri-Suns a day. My grandparents had kept her well stocked back in their day and now, my parents made sure to supply them.

Sitting down on the front stoop of the cabin, she stabbed the straw into the foil, took a long drink, then sighed. "Why did you come to talk to me about this?"

I met her gaze. "I just want to know her story."

Claude studied me as the fir trees rustled in the wind. Then she went back to her drink. "That's Ivelisse. She was from Colombia. Bit of a handful, never stopped talking. She wanted everyone to know that she spoke English and was well educated. The guests loved her and so did your grandparents, at first. She was older than the rest of us, even me, if you can believe that. They gave her jobs where she could interact with the guests, which didn't sit well with some of the workers who had been here for a while. Like, the memory boxes we did that one year—do you remember those?"

Chase and I exchanged a smile.

"Yes," I said. "I do."

Claude adjusted her position on the steps, as if settling in for a long chat. "Well, the other workers were furious because Ivelisse got to give them to each guest."

"Why would anyone care about that?" I asked.

"Tips, honey." Claude took a drag on her juice box. "You hand-deliver something nice, you're not walking away with just a dollar."

"Oh."

The sun suddenly felt hot on my cheeks. It had been a while since I'd considered one of the driving points of the hospitality business; that the staff weren't here because they loved Wood Violet with their every breath. It was because they wanted to make money, and working at a high-end resort was a great way to do that.

"Ivelisse almost made it through the summer. The season was just about finished when it all broke bad. She was here one day, gone the next." Claude rested her full arms on her legs, staring out at the woods. "It was a shame. She had a good heart."

"She got fired?" I said. "Why?"

"Your grandparents didn't like disruption." Claude squeezed the container of her drink, taking in the last drops. "Ivelisse was the definition of disruption."

"Meaning…?"

"I didn't know her all that well, because we were here to work, but she was my roommate and she did tell me a few things." Claude crinkled up the pouch of her drink. "I don't have much more to say about it all, but I do know this: Ivelisse might be pregnant in that drawing, but she certainly wasn't when she got here."

CHAPTER FIFTEEN

Chase and I walked to his cabin in silence. I sat on the porch and he brought us out ice-cold lemonade. We sipped at the tart sweetness while the afternoon bugs flitted around us in the heat.

I let out a loud sigh. "Do you think she got involved with one of the guests?"

"Claude made it sound like that."

"Margaret was born in March, so she probably got pregnant in June." I leaned my cheek against the cold glass. "I have a bad feeling about all this."

"Why?" he asked.

"I don't know."

I thought of the way Claude had looked at me when I first asked about Ivelisse. It was as if she was deciding how much to say, and I wasn't convinced she'd given us the whole story.

"This happened nearly twenty years ago," I said, "but it's still not a good look. Wood Violet is all about families and family values, so it probably wouldn't sit well with people if they learned my grandparents fired a pregnant girl."

"How would they know she was pregnant if she hadn't told them?" Chase said. "It's not their fault."

"True." I had been at nearly three months for my first pregnancy, and I had barely started to show. "Still, that wouldn't stop the uproar on social media if this came out now. Logic doesn't matter much there, but outrage does."

"Is that why you're not online?" Chase asked.

I paused. "What, did you look for me?"

"Yes, when Garrett died. I'm not on social media either, I only use it for work, but my parents had me shut down Garrett's accounts. He had kept up with a ton of people from back in the day. I sent messages to several of his contacts. I remember seeing your sister, but not you."

"Oh." The sun was bright and I put on my sunglasses, not sure what to say. The truth of the matter was that I'd looked for him once, back in college, because my roommate was online all the time. I was curious to see what had happened to him but it felt inappropriate, somehow, to admit that now. "I'm not on social media because I was always too busy with school and then, work. Besides, I didn't want the opposing counsel or any of the companies I represented to peek into my life and make assumptions about me."

Chase nodded. "Smart."

"This thing with Ivelisse…" I chewed on another piece of ice. "I feel like there's a chance people would be quick to judge my family if someone framed it the right way."

"Hold on a sec." Chase stepped inside the cabin and returned with his ballcap. Pulling it low over his eyes, he said, "I'm no expert but I'd say she's more than just a few months along in that drawing, don't you think?"

It was so hard to tell. "I'd agree. It wouldn't be that obvious if she was right at the beginning of her pregnancy, especially in a drawing."

"So, if she got fired in August," he continued, "it's very possible that she came back. Maybe your grandparents put her up for a while, if she was here long enough for your grandmother to make that sketch."

I gave him a grateful look. "You think so?"

"Definitely." He stretched out in the sun, leaning back against his elbows. "Your grandparents might have let her go but I don't think they turned their backs on her. There's nothing bad about that."

I took a sip of the lemonade and let an ice cube linger in my mouth. "I wonder why she'd ask them for help if they let her go."

"Claude said your grandparents loved her. Maybe Ivelisse knew that. She could have apologized for causing trouble and rebuilt that friendship. That's when your grandmother stepped in to help find a home for the baby."

I rested my hands on my stomach, grateful for a sudden breeze. "It's hard to think about all that," I admitted. "There had to be a reason she decided her daughter would be better off with someone else, but I can't imagine the grief that would come with that."

I wondered if it would upset Ivelisse if Margaret reached out to her, or if she would be happy to hear her daughter's voice.

"Her contact information has to be in our files somewhere," I said. "Do you think I owe it to Margaret to tell her what I know, to pass on the information? Or should I…" I stopped, as a terrible thought hit me. "Chase, what if Ivelisse came back to the resort because the father paid her off to put Margaret up for adoption? He could have gotten in touch with my grandmother and asked her to set it up."

"That's intense." He eyed me from beneath the rim of his ballcap. "But it's also completely hypothetical."

"It's where my mind is going with all this." I set down my glass, trying to imagine the potential scenarios that could play out. "I just keep thinking of all the ways this could turn into a PR nightmare. And it would be hard on Margaret. That girl's already been through a lot."

Chase studied me from beneath the rim of his hat. "You'd asked if it was right to have the information and keep it from her. What does your gut tell you?"

"It's hard to say. I'm here to help my parents, not to cause trouble. Getting involved with this feels like trouble."

Chase's eyes met mine. "Then maybe you should leave it alone."

"I don't know if I can," I admitted. "I think I'll just have to look into it as carefully and quietly as possible, figure out the whole story, and go from there. It seems premature to tell Margaret anything at this point, because I don't want to rush into anything that might hurt her or the resort."

"It's a hard choice," Chase said.

"Yeah." I looked out at the woods. "I hope I'm making the right one."

Nearly a week went by during which I was so busy helping out at the resort and spending time with my mother that I barely had time to look up. It was a good thing, because it kept me from having to make a decision about whether or not I should get involved with Margaret's search for her mother. I still hadn't heard back from my contact at the law firm that had handled the adoption, so it wasn't as if I had any new information to go on.

I had also been tempted several times to come right out and ask my father about his meeting with the investors and whether or not he planned to sell off a piece of the resort, but I wanted to review the financials first. That way, I could have a frame of reference in the event that he was willing to have a real discussion about the issue. My father had been at the office late every night, so there hadn't yet been a chance.

After a whirlwind Sunday, my father managed to make it home for dinner at home. My parents and I sat in the living room after dinner, while my father responded to emails and my mother watched television.

"I still haven't had a chance to hear the girl in the artist-in-residence cabin sing," he said. "I'd like to. Will you set something up?"

"Sure." Now that I knew that Margaret was here to try and find her mother, I doubted it would be a problem to get her to sing for my father. She knew it was a condition to her time here at the cabin.

I had been too busy to see her, but Tilly had kept me posted. Margaret had been making the most of her time, going to as many activities as possible. She was a regular at the pottery, painting, and stained-glass lessons, and she spent most of her afternoons swimming or sunbathing by the lake. I wondered what steps she had taken to try and find out the identity of her mother, or if she had no idea where to start.

"Yes, let me talk to her and find a good time for you to hear her sing," I said. "I'll take a look at your schedule and put it in."

"Thanks," he said, getting to his feet and giving me a kiss on the head.

My mother looked up from the television. "Are you going back?"

"No, thank goodness." My father yawned. "I've got some report-reading to do, so I'm going to finish that up in bed. You ready?"

My mother nodded and my father kissed her. It was a sweet moment and I hoped that one day, Tristan and I could get back to being that close. It was impossible to imagine at the moment, since we'd barely even had a chance to talk, but it was still something I wanted.

"Goodnight, Julie." My father wheeled my mother down the hall. "Lock the door behind you when you head out."

I let out a breath. I'd been waiting for a safe moment to search the records office for information on Ivelisse and review the financials of the resort for nearly a week, and the suspense had made me anxious. Now that my parents were headed to bed, I wouldn't have to worry about my father coming back to the office and I could do some research in peace.

On my walk over, I made a point to text the security detail on duty that I would be there, so that they wouldn't panic to see the lights on. My father had reviewed my research on security systems and had decided they were simply too expensive, so our security staff remained on high alert. I didn't know how late I'd be, or whether I'd find anything at all, but I wanted plenty of space to review the financials and see what I could discover about Margaret's birth mother.

It should be simple to find both. My grandparents had kept meticulous records, and my parents had continued the tradition.

Even though it had been almost twenty years, it was possible that Ivelisse's contact information was still the same. The thought that I might be able to reach out to her was exciting, but I wouldn't do that without Margaret's permission.

Besides, a big part of me kept telling me to stay out of it altogether. I didn't know a thing about this woman, other than the fact that she had gotten fired from Wood Violet. It was possible that she was still angry for losing a job at a time that she might have needed it to provide for her child, and contacting her would give her a reason to retaliate against the resort, by making the situation public.

I came to a stop in the middle of the path, the branches of the trees black against the night sky. The moon cast shadows on the ground around me that made me shiver. I still questioned whether I should let Margaret in on what I knew and let her call the shots, but at the same time, it might not be a good idea to let Margaret be involved at all.

Plus, there was also the simple fact that Ivelisse might not be interested in meeting her. The adoption was closed, after all. The odds were good that Ivelisse would want to leave this in the past, and that Margaret could face even more heartache and rejection if she tried to become a part of her life.

Not to mention the threat to the resort. It was very possible that the father was a high-profile guest—maybe even married—and that he would not want to be involved or identified. Plus, if word got out that my grandmother helped hide such a relationship, there might be questions about the integrity of my family and the resort.

In the end, I decided the best bet would be to gather as much information as possible and, once I had her last name, do an internet search on Ivelisse to make a judgment call. That way, I could have a better idea on who she actually was and whether or not it would be safe to connect her with Margaret. Taking in a deep breath, I headed towards the office to see what I could find.

Inside, with only moonlight streaming through the windows, it felt quiet and low lit. The place was vacant. It actually felt a little bit eerie.

The records closet was located down a back hallway that connected to my office. I headed to my office, flinching in the sudden brightness of the lights. I grabbed a notepad and was about to duck into the records room when I became curious about Nikki.

I'd made the assumption that I knew her since she'd been two grades behind me at school but really, I didn't know a thing about her. Walking over to her desk, I picked up one of her picture frames.

It was a picture of Nikki and her husband. He was tall and studious, with a warm smile. Nikki looked happy, with her arms wrapped around his waist.

The air conditioning clicked and I jumped, nearly dropping the frame. Quickly, I put it back on the desk and noticed a purchase order from the local electronics company sitting on the top of her paperwork. With a sinking sensation in my stomach, I picked it up and skimmed it. Flat-screen televisions, one for each cabin. The purchase order was signed by my father.

My stomach dropped. He and I had discussed the flat-screens one night at dinner, and he had agreed with me that it was not a good idea. Now, I realized my opinion did not carry as much weight as I thought it would simply for being a member of the family. In reality, I didn't work here and I hadn't been around much, so I could see why he hadn't taken my input into account. It was fine, I guess, but it stung a little. It also made me question whether or not I had the right to look at the finances. It might be overstepping in a big way. Even if I found something worth discussing, my father might be too angry at me for looking at the private paperwork of the resort to even listen to what I had to say. I hesitated, then placed the purchase order back on Nikki's desk.

Looking at the financials was a risk, but it was one worth taking. I had a stake in Wood Violet's success because it was a part of my past and I wanted to make sure it was a part of my future. The plan to install flat-screen televisions made me worry that some of the magic at Wood Violet was dying out, and the business needed to be solid enough to withstand those changes.

Inside the records room, I turned on the light and took it all in. It had been one of my favorite places as a child. The room was lined with shelves and stacked from floor to ceiling with forest green paper files dating back to the seventies. The room smelled like library books and if the day was humid, the faintest scent of damp cardboard. The years on the files were neatly labeled in my grandmother's precise penmanship and there were endless treasures inside each one, such as detailed notes on the likes and dislikes of the families that had kept the resort in business.

I'd loved going into the records room as a kid because it felt like a glimpse into what made my grandparents tick. They were so elusive to me, those larger than life figures that socialized with the guests, made the big decisions, and worked round the clock. The file room illustrated the scale at which my grandparents had built their business, from that very first year and the very first paper file. Now, it seemed archaic that my family had continued to use paper files for so long, but everything was so carefully organized that it was easy to find the section with the financial records. There was an entire area devoted to tax information, as well as the detailed annual reports. I selected the tax records, as they would be the most accurate. It only took ten minutes to see that the resort had experienced a significant downward decline in the past ten years, and had started to lose money in the past two years.

Sitting back on my heels, I took a minute to catch my breath. Then, I looked more closely at the numbers. The losses were significant, and if the trend continued for the next few years, the resort would not be able to survive.

I could only imagine how much this was hurting my parents. They worked so hard. They'd given everything to this place, but I could see how it had happened.

My father handled people, not business. Same with my mother. Her focus had always been on the guests, the garden, and the kitchen. My grandfather was the one who had managed the financial side of things, and without him at the helm, the business side had slowly come unraveled.

My parents must have figured that, as long as the financial sheets weren't in the red, things weren't that bad. Now, it wouldn't be long until my father had little choice but to sell off a piece of the land.

Slowly, I packed up the files. It wasn't as if this was a huge shock, given the information Nikki had shared, but it was upsetting. I was tempted to put off the search for Ivelisse's information until another night, but now it seemed more important than ever to avoid any problems that might be circling. I wanted to get to the bottom of that situation sooner rather than later, so that I could better understand what Margaret had hoped to accomplish by coming here.

It took almost an hour, but I finally found the employee records in the far corner of the closet, pretty much the last place that I looked. But once I was there, it only took a few minutes to find the section from the turn of the century, and a folder labeled

Ivelisse Kroll. It was late, but I called but I called Chase. "I found that worker's file," I said, when he picked up. "Her name's Ivelisse Kroll. I want you to open it with me. Ready? Here I—"

"Wait!" Chase seemed to hold his breath in anticipation. "Let me video-chat you."

I propped my phone up so my hands were free. Chase was seated at the table in his cabin, papers spread out all around his computer. His blond hair was tousled, probably from hours of running his hand through it while he worked.

"You ready?" I held up the folder. It was so old, it felt like wax paper in my hands. "Typically, the files hold a photo of the person, their contact information, and at least one pay stub."

Chase raised his eyebrows. "Already curious about the photo."

Letting out a breath, I opened the folder. Sure enough, there was a two-inch picture of Ivelisse stapled to the upper right-hand corner of the file. My grandmother had done a wonderful job drawing her, but in the photograph, her beauty was startling.

"Wow." I showed it to Chase. "No wonder the guys liked her."

Based on the records, Ivelisse had just turned forty during her time at the resort. Her face showed that life experience and character, with its high cheekbones, dark eyes, and the playful challenge in her smile. Her hair was raven black, a contrast to her pale skin, and there was a red flush to her cheeks and lips. In spite of her beauty, the shirt she wore was ill-fitting and worn, so it was clear that she'd needed the job.

"There's so much Margaret there," Chase said. "It's the same as the drawing. The shape of the eyes, and right around the bridge of her nose."

Quickly, I skimmed the information in her application. "She lived in Chicago." My pulse quickened. "There's a phone number and apartment address in Chicago." I stared down at the information. "I should hand this over to Margaret right now. But…"

Chase studied me. "You're worried."

"Yes." I pressed my hands into my temples. "I'm worried how this might affect Margaret but also about the resort. It sounds awful, but I'd like to know a little bit more about our role in all this before handing a teenager who's just gone through some pretty big life changes the reins. Maybe if I keep researching Ivelisse, I can get a hint to what type of person she might be."

"That's fair. Should we google her?"

"Yes, please," I said, leaning forward.

Chase typed in her name, but nothing came up.

"Try the social media platforms," I suggested. "She must be close to sixty at this point, and I doubt she lives under a rock."

"Like us?" Chase said, smiling. He checked on the main sites and shook his head. "Not here. What's the address on the apartment? It would be where she lived before she worked at Wood Violet, right?"

I told him and he pulled up a street view. It was an older building on Fullerton, and it looked pretty run-down. "She must have been struggling," I said. "She might not have had a choice about letting Margaret go."

The idea hurt my heart. The pain that I'd felt losing my pregnancies had been so intense. I couldn't imagine having a child out in the world without knowing where she was or what had happened to her. "I think we should call," I said. "What if she changed her mind and wants to see her daughter? They should be together."

"I don't know." Chase frowned. "I think the initial plan to find out more information was the better approach."

"She might be desperate to see her, though," I said. "Maybe she's even been keeping an eye out for her all of these years."

"It's a nice idea," Chase said carefully. "Or maybe she just chose to move on."

I sat back on my heels. "Sorry. It's just…"

He watched me closely. "What is it?"

"I can't imagine how that must feel." My eyes filled with tears and, frustrated, I brushed them away. "It has to hurt to be away from her child."

"Julie, not everyone wants to be a mother." His voice was gentle. "It's possible that she gave Margaret up for adoption because she wanted the freedom to live her life without being responsible for another person."

"That doesn't seem fair," I said. "Especially to people who want that so badly."

"To be a mother?" he asked.

I looked away from the camera.

"Julie, where are you right now?" he asked.

"The records closet in the office."

"See you in a minute."

I met him at the front door. Chase walked in, his hair still tousled, dressed in a pair of khaki shorts and a navy T-shirt. Without a word, I led him back to the records closet and showed him the folder.

Sinking down on the floor next to me, he studied the picture. He set it down and turned to me. "How are you doing?"

"Fine." My knees were pulled to my chest and my mouth dry. I was so embarrassed that he'd come over here to be with me. "Nothing's wrong. I should have told you to keep working."

Chase handed me a cold Sprite. "Look, my brother's wife went through a lot, trying to get pregnant. It was one of her biggest disappointments, one of the hardest parts of his death, that she and my brother had never had a child together."

"That's really hard." Fiddling with the tab on the can, I finally said, "I've lost two pregnancies. Supposedly, there's nothing wrong and I should be able to have children; it's just not happening. We've kind of given up for a little while."

The compassion on his face nearly made me cry again. "I'm really sorry."

"Yeah." It wasn't something I talked about, so the idea that I was sharing this with Chase, of all people, felt a little surreal. "I think that's the reason I am so invested in this thing with Margaret. The way that I felt when I was pregnant, the need to be with this being that I didn't even know, it was so strong. The idea that they were separated and she wants to make her way back to her mother…" My eyes went hot again. "But you're right. Ivelisse might not want that at all, and how will Margaret feel then?"

I sipped on the Sprite, the cold bubbles fizzing against my nose. The faded smell of lemon and lime reminded me of my childhood. My mother only gave me Sprite when I was sick, and I associated it with her, and the feeling of her arms around me.

"I think this is all affecting me because of the situation with my mother, too," I said. "The idea that we only have so much time with the people we love, if we're lucky enough to get that time at all."

"Yeah." Chase looked down at his hands. "I think about that every day."

Grief passed between the two of us. I was tempted to take his hand, but that wouldn't have been appropriate. Instead, I reached for the folder and stared blankly at the photo.

"There's nothing else in here that's helpful," I said, finally setting it back on the ground.

"When you finally do talk to Margaret about this, suggest a DNA search. I think there was a story in the news recently where a family was reunited because of one of those family tree companies. She could submit her DNA and see if anything comes back with a connection."

I looked at him with new respect. "Here I am in a closet full of dust, mold, and ancient paperwork, thinking it's hopeless, and you throw science into the equation. I could kiss you."

It was meant as a joke but the moment the words were out of my mouth, I regretted them. They had sounded flirty, which was not how I meant it at all. Quickly, I got to my feet.

"Listen, it's late. I should get some work done before bed, and I know I interrupted you in the midst of literary magic."

He chuckled. "Yeah. It was pure poetry over there."

The records closet must have been hot and stuffy because it was a relief to step into the much cooler space of the office. In the bright light of the office, I felt awkward about all that I had shared.

"Thank you for coming over here," I said. "I appreciate it."

"Of course." He shrugged. "I know what it feels like to go through a hard time."

"I'm going to stick around here," I said, indicating my computer. "Can I walk you out?"

Chase and I headed out to the main entrance in silence. The security cart was sitting back behind the trees, and I lifted my hand in greeting.

"You have good night vision," he said. "I didn't even know he was there. That makes me feel better about leaving you here."

The moon was out, and there was distant laughter down by the water, along with the smell of a campfire. In the woods, the fireflies danced back and forth, lighting the area like a meteor shower. We stood for a moment, looking at each other. Then Chase pulled his ballcap low over his eyes and headed back down the path towards home.

CHAPTER SIXTEEN

In the early morning, the loons called to one another across the lake, the sound mournful. It brought to mind the sense of gloom I'd felt the night before, searching for information on Margaret's mother and talking about the loss I'd faced with Chase. I still couldn't believe he'd made the effort to come over and check on me.

Chase was such a good person. He was one of those solid guys that would shovel snow for their neighbor, hand his coat to a person who didn't have one, or give up his seat on public transportation without being asked. I admired him for putting kindness above all else, and wished I could do something to help him get past the grief he felt for his brother.

That day in the woods when we'd all gotten stuck in the rain, he'd mentioned that he was here to find the memory box that they had hidden. I had been so caught up in everything that I'd only asked about it that one day, at our dance class, and I made a mental note to ask him again. Maybe Tilly and I could rally her kids, and we could all go hunt for it.

Pulling the duvet close, I looked at the clock. It wasn't quite six o'clock, so it was much too early to contact the property management company of the building Ivelisse had lived in. I'd try around nine, once I'd had time to find their number and come up with a reasonable story about why they should give me information about her.

I didn't feel hopeful that she still lived there, but it was worth a try. I could also bribe one of my friends in the city to visit the building and ask around in the lobby. Maybe they could check to see if her name was listed on the mailbox.

But the main thing I needed to deal with today was the conversation with my father about the financial status of the resort. The fact that Wood Violet was losing so much money was a major concern, especially since he was meeting with developers to resolve the issue. It was so far beyond the scope of what I'd thought I'd walked into this summer that I still didn't know quite what to think. The moment the clock blinked to six a.m., I sent him a text.

Can I set a meeting with you today?

He responded right away.

I'm slammed. Will after dinner work?

The thought of sitting with this until dinnertime made me feel more anxious, but I didn't want to spook him by making it sound urgent.

Sure. Come by at seven for coffee and peach pie.

Feeling better, I put my phone on my nightstand and started to think about what to say. I didn't want to upset him, or make a big deal out of the fact that business wasn't booming. I wanted to help, but before I could do that, I needed to know what was going on.

Chase was already on the floor of the dance studio, stretching, when I walked in later that morning. His hair was damp and his eyes looked tired, so I wondered if he'd stayed up late working after helping me. Once Tomas greeted us and moved onto the next group, Chase took a drink from his portable coffee mug and shook his head.

"You know, I've been thinking about the situation with Margaret all night. It really took some guts to come here with only the name of the resort and the address. What do you think she planned to do, to find her?"

"I don't know," I said, leaning down over my legs. My thighs burned with the effort. "Maybe see if she was actually here. See if she was a part of the resort or worked here or…"

My voice trailed off as it hit me that Margaret had almost certainly broken into the main office, because she'd been searching for information. She had been looking for the same thing we had, some lead on how to find her mother. Something must have scared her off that one night, and I had no doubt she planned to break in again soon. This time, though, security would be waiting.

"What is it?" Chase asked.

Even though I trusted him, it wasn't something I could talk about in dance class. Someone could overhear and that would be a problem.

"I'll tell you later," I said, leaning into another stretch.

Much as I wanted to help Margaret find her birth mother, I still had concerns about my grandmother's involvement in the situation. I needed to find some answers first to best manage the situation, so I'd have to find a way to warn Margaret about the main office in the meantime. Otherwise, I could see her breaking in, getting caught, and creating an even bigger scandal by getting arrested.

"I'm delighted to see all of your shining faces this morning," Tomas called. "On your feet and in the center of the room. Let's review our count and step."

"Every time I talk to my husband I want to tell him about this," I said, once we were in position in the center of the floor. "He's trying to figure out a good time to come visit but it's not looking good so far, so I'll have plenty of time to become a dance expert."

Chase gave me an innocent look. "I think you're already there."

I laughed. "Hardly. But it's helped me, doing this. I feel like I'm doing something for our marriage, even though we're not together. I know learning how to dance won't solve all our problems or anything but it makes me feel like I'm doing something at least." I looked out at the water. "I still haven't told him I got fired."

Chase's mouth dropped open. "Why?"

"I'm scared of his reaction," I said, holding my stretch. "He didn't want me to stay here this summer because he was afraid I'd lose my job and, since it actually happened, I know he's going to be upset and I'm afraid that..."

"What?" Chase asked, when I stopped talking.

"That he might insist that I come back and start looking for another job and if I won't, he won't come visit."

Chase furrowed his brow. "I'm sorry. That's a tough one."

"I know I should just suck it up and tell him, I just..." I gave an awkward laugh. "It's just easier to think that I'm solving things by learning to dance, instead. That's not true at all, I know. It's so surface."

"You're trying to take steps in the right direction," Chase said. "You'll get there."

"Thanks," I said quietly.

Tomas clapped his hands. "Before we get started, I'd like you to give a special welcome to Joe and LeAnne," he chirped, his hands on the shoulders of a smiling young couple. "They are learning to dance for their wedding and we are here for it." Tomas and his assistant led the group in applause, and the couple shared a shy kiss.

"Good for them," I said, as we headed out to the floor. "I wouldn't have been ready to get married that young."

"I sure wasn't," Chase said. "It feels like a hundred years ago. Sometimes, I wonder if I imagined it all and sometimes, I wish I had." He counted the steps with me for a moment, then said, "The idea that my marriage failed... it's embarrassing."

"I'm so sorry." My voice was quiet, as the other people moved around us. "It's a risk, to follow your heart."

He took in a deep breath. "Her family was heartbroken, probably more upset about it than we were."

"Because they loved you?" I asked.

He shook his head. "No. Because they paid for the wedding."

I laughed. No matter the situation, Chase always brought the humor. "Well, maybe you should send them some ice-cream."

"Excellent counting, people," Tomas called from the front of the room. He cued up a waltz, and said, "Let's try it now, to music."

Chase squeezed my hands. "You've got this." He guided me through the steps, counting like we'd learned. Once the music was no longer a distraction, he said, "What about you? Did you get married here at Wood Violet?"

"We don't do weddings," I said.

"Well, I figured your family would have made an exception for you."

There were moments Chase seemed to know me better than some of my closest friends. I had wanted to get married here, it was something I'd imagined my entire life, but Tristan wanted to get married in the city.

"Tristan wanted a Chicago wedding," I said. "He wanted it to start with an announcement in the paper and end with a splashy write-up. He got the write-up because he's good at making friends with the right people, not because we had any reason to be showcased."

The spread in the paper had embarrassed me. Two weeks after we were married, a reporter contacted me with a detailed questionnaire about our wedding. My answers had been short and to the point, while Tristan wanted to embellish and entertain. The whole thing led to our first big fight as a married couple.

"The article's a nice thing to have in our wedding book," I said, finally catching up to the music. "But it also felt invasive. Like, did the entire town of Chicago really need to know the name of the poem we read?"

"You are all doing fantastic," Tomas sang. He cued up another song, and I bit my lip, my brain fighting between memories of my wedding and trying to remember how to count.

"It sounds impressive," Chase said. "Why do you think it bothered you so much?"

We were at the side of the dance floor by my water bottle, so I stepped off for a minute to take a break. "Because it wasn't about him and me. You know? It felt more like an idea, a concept, rather than a celebration of our love. That sounds ungrateful. So many people would love to have a wedding like the one I had."

Chase shrugged. "And so many people wouldn't."

"Well, it wasn't the wedding of my dreams, but now I can have the marriage of my dreams, right?" I said wryly.

We waited for an older couple to move by and went back on the floor.

Chase took my hands and squinted at me. "What did you do about the couple's dance?"

"You wouldn't believe it if I told you." Then, because it illustrated the point, I said, "We had a flash mob. The dancers pretended to be guests, then hopped up and went into this whole routine with Tristan. I had to do a lot of mugging, like *Come get me, boy*. It was ridiculous."

"Probably a big part of the article."

I burst out laughing. Chase and I laughed so hard that we had to stop dancing again. Tomas sailed over and put his hands on his hips.

"Children, you must focus," he insisted. "One-two-three, one-two-three…"

I fought back the giggles and we went back to it. Of course, every time Chase and I made eye contact, we laughed again.

"Final five minutes," Tomas called, cueing up one last waltz. "Take everything you've learned, forget it and just enjoy the music."

The sweet strains of the song rang out, and the couples moved across the floor.

"Let's just focus on counting," Chase said. "Keep it at the basics."

I took his hands. "I feel like I've run a marathon," I admitted. "But I'm glad we're doing this. Life is short, why not try?"

Chase guided us across the floor, using the simple count. "That's how I've felt, ever since Garrett died. Maybe the thing with your mom is changing your perspective."

I had to look out the window so that he didn't see the pain in my eyes but of course, Chase noticed.

"Sorry," he said quietly. "I didn't mean to upset you."

Earlier in the week, my mother had broken down in tears when she dropped her fork at dinner and almost fell out of the wheelchair trying to pick it back up. My father was working, so I'd helped her back in the chair, holding her tight as she cried.

Out the window of the dance studio, the sun was bright on the lake and a bird soared across the water, the white clouds fluffy in the sky. It didn't seem right that the world could look so beautiful, when my mother had to struggle the way that she did.

Even though Chase and I had made it a habit to hold hands as we danced, I took a step closer and rested my head on his shoulder. He seemed surprised but then pulled me in and patted my back.

"It's okay," he said. "It's all going to be just fine."

*

Outside, the mood had passed and we settled in the shade beneath the fir trees to place the call about Ivelisse. Chase was sweating from dance class, and he lifted his T-shirt to wipe his face, accidentally showcasing his abs. Embarrassed, I looked away.

"Should we call?" Chase asked.

"Yes," I said, reaching for my phone. I'd found the management company that handled the apartment complex, and cued up the number. Then I hesitated.

"You call," I told Chase. "I think you'd be more convincing."

"I'm going to pretend to be a bill collector." He pulled his brows tightly together and snapped, "I think you are underestimating the seriousness of the situation."

"Brilliant," I said.

I picked up a fallen twig, running my hands over its pine needles while Chase placed the call. He put it on speaker, and said, "Good morning, I'm seeking to settle a financial issue with Ivelisse Kroll. Your office was listed as a contact. Can you put me in touch with her?"

There was a pause, followed by the sound of a computer clacking. "Ivelisse Kroll has not been a tenant here for years." The woman's voice was full of disapproval. "It seems she left debt here as well, and no forwarding information."

Chase and I exchanged a discouraged look. "I see. Thank you for your time." He hung up and ran his thumb over the dirt. "Didn't mean to hit that one so close to home," he said, looking embarrassed.

"Yeah." The call reinforced some of my earlier thoughts.

Ivelisse could have given up Margaret because she didn't have the means to keep her. It was sad, and it wasn't fair, but it made sense that she might have wanted to find a better life for her daughter.

"You know, I was thinking about what Claude said while she was sipping on that Capri-Sun," Chase mused. "She mentioned your grandparents. Your grandfather is still around. Could you ask if your grandmother was involved in an adoption? He might just say, *Yes, your grandmother helped this girl out and I just so happen to have her information right here."*

I fiddled with the stick. "We don't really text. I love him, but we don't have that type of relationship."

Back when I was growing up, my grandparents had been so busy with the resort that we couldn't spend much time together. The rare moment they took a break, my grandfather went to his workshop to build something, while my grandmother worked on her art. I did have several good memories of my grandfather taking me and my sister out on the boat, or my grandmother whisking us to town to buy a special dress for the holidays, but they would leave for the winter, so I never really had time to get to know them in the way I wanted to.

"It's the resort that makes me feel close to them," I said. "I would have liked to have gotten to know them better as I became an adult, but then I became busy. You know?"

"Well, if you want to make the connection, you have to start somewhere. Text him."

"Okay," I finally said. "Why not?"

I fired off a quick text.

> *Hi, Grandpa! Hope you're having fun on your travels. Random question—do you remember Grandma helping out with an adoption in any capacity? Long story, but wanted to ask. Thanks! Julie*

To my surprise, he answered within a few minutes.

"He already wrote back," I told Chase.

I read it out loud:

> *Your grandmother was always up to something good. I don't remember her trying to help a young mother set up an adoption*

but it wouldn't surprise me. You're welcome to look in her personal files in our home, and let me know if you find anything.

In the meantime, I'm sitting here having a pint in Kinsale. People talking, laughing, and living their life. Funny to be a whole world away and have it all be the same.

McGregor

My grandfather's note touched me. It was almost… chatty, and it showed such a different side to him.

"Do you think he sounds lonely?" I asked, reading it again.

Chase grinned. "I think he sounds happy to hear from you."

I wondered if I should answer. Finally, I dashed off a quick response.

I'd love to be in Kinsale, but I'm at Wood Violet for the summer and really, there is nowhere I would rather be. I wish you were having a pint with me here by the water, instead.

"That's perfect," Chase said.

I sent it before I could change my mind. Then, I waited, practically holding my breath. Two minutes passed, the squirrels chattering in the trees.

"I don't think he's going to write back," I said, disappointed.

My grandfather was on the other side of the world. Why would he—

There!

I clicked on the return response. My grandfather, my stoic, seventy-something grandfather, had sent me emojis. A flower, a picture of the water, and a heart.

Chase leaned in to see. "Good for him."

Lifting my head from my phone, I took in the sight of the trees, the lake, and the cabins that he had built from scratch. For a brief moment, I pressed my phone against my heart. Then, I looked at Chase.

"What are you doing right now?" I asked.

"Er… I was not about to go into the dining hall to eat a whole plate of bacon for breakfast. You in?"

The scent of bacon was wafting through the resort from the dining hall, and I'd been smelling it since the moment I'd walked out of my cabin. "Maybe we can squeeze in at Tilly's table. Then let's go see what we can find at my grandparents' house."

CHAPTER SEVENTEEN

My grandparents' house was located down the lane from my parents', in a secluded cluster of trees. It could only be seen from the lake, a rust-colored haven with windows as tall as a spire. Chase shielded his eyes from the sun and gave an approving nod.

"Perfect," he said. "I'd love to spend the rest of my life living in a place like that."

"Me, too. My grandfather has traveled all over but he always says the best thing he's ever seen is the sunrise from the chair in his living room."

Inside, it was neat and orderly, with a place for everything and everything in its place. Even though he'd been traveling for weeks now, I could still smell his cologne.

I walked through the house, noting the plentitude of family photos. There were countless pictures of me and my sister. Chase picked up a frame that held a picture of me when I was about twelve, right around the time he and I had started our summer of puppy love.

"I know this girl." He showed it to me. "Those French braids had me at hello."

My hair had been halfway down my back and because it took forever to dry, my mother got into the habit of French-braiding it into two pigtails after I'd taken a bath. The rare occasion that I took it down, it was crinkly with waves, and I had loved it.

"Thank you," I said. "I thought it was my braces that roped you in."

"The glint of metal was definitely your siren song."

I laughed, setting down a framed photo of me and my sister in matching jumpers, and we headed down the hall to the small home office.

Two hours later, I had searched through every personal file possible but had not found one reference to an adoption, the law firm that had helped, or any contact information for Ivelisse. I was tired, disappointed, and thinking about all the work piling up at the office that I really needed to get to. My cell rang just as we had started to put everything away.

"Hey," I said, picking up on the first ring. "Tristan, you wouldn't believe what—"

"You got fired?" The fury in his voice made my shoulders tense.

"Hold on." I signaled to Chase that I was going to step out. In the living room, I said, "Honey, I was going to—"

"When did you find out?" he demanded.

"Tristan, I'm so sorry." I slid open the glass door that led to the back porch. It overlooked the lake, which was bright in the late morning light. "I know you're upset."

"You humiliated me," he said. "I was talking to someone who told me information *about my wife* that I didn't know. What am I supposed to do with that?"

"I'm so sorry." My fingers traced the diamond-shaped pattern of the table that had sat on the porch for years. "I was waiting for the right time."

"The second you knew, *that* was the right time."

Tristan let loose on a tirade about our financial responsibilities, goals and commitments. It was hot in the sun, so I stepped back inside, shutting the door behind me.

Chase was sitting on the couch but he pointed at the front door. "I'll wait outside," he mouthed.

Sinking into the couch, I let Tristan work through his anger. My gaze shifted to a picture of my grandparents sitting on the mantle. My grandmother was leaning back in my grandfather's arms, as if it were the two of them against the world. When was the last time I'd felt like that with Tristan?

He stopped ranting and took a breath. Then, he said, "You need to start interviewing right away."

"No." I sat up straight. It felt surreal to be having the very conversation I'd worried about for days. "Tristan, my mother is sick. My focus is on this place. I do not have the interest or ability to job-hunt. I will do it in the fall, and contribute to our bills out of my trust, as we discussed."

"Must be nice." His voice was low. "To just take the summer off."

The words made me cringe. I refused to feel guilty about the fact that I had the option to be there for my mother and I couldn't help but resent his attitude about it, but that was how he'd always been about the trust. The first time I'd told him I had one, he was shocked, and then he'd spent at least thirty minutes joking about the fact that I made an income simply by being born.

I had joked about it then, too, because that seemed to be the best way to handle the topic. Still, it didn't seem fair that his jokes held a hint of jealousy and anger. It wasn't like I'd ever laid around, collecting money. I'd never understood why Tristan couldn't appreciate the fact that the trust was there to benefit us, not create a divide.

"Tristan, I love you." I fought against the tremor in my voice. "But I am not leaving Wood Violet until September."

"We're supposed to be a team." He sounded hurt. "The way you've been acting has made me wonder whether you feel that way at all."

"You have every right to be upset about this," I told him. "I should have said something, but I was scared."

"Of what?" he demanded.

"This. This entire conversation, of feeling like I did something wrong by choosing to support my family. I wanted to tell you in person so we could have the time to really talk about it, but you're right, I should have told you right away. That was my mistake, and I'm sorry."

He was silent.

I waited a moment, then said, "Tristan, I really do think it would help if we could see each other. I really want you to come here. I want to spend time together. Look on the bright side," I said, trying for levity. "When you do, I can't complain about my job anymore."

It might not have been the best choice to be flip but being here, in a house that had stood for over fifty years, helped me put this in perspective. Losing my job wasn't the end of the world. It might be a big deal now but in five or ten years, we would have a whole new set of problems to worry about.

"I'll have another job by October," I promised. "I'm sorry you heard it from someone else. That was not my plan. I'm sorry."

My hands were still shaking as we said our goodbyes and hung up. Clasping them tightly, I sat in silence, determined to let the cloud of heartbreak hovering over me pass right by.

"Everything good?" Chase asked, when I joined him outside.

The sun was bright and it was shaping up to be a hot summer day. There was a time when I would have spent hours at the swimming hole, and I missed those days. Life back then had seemed so much simpler.

I slid on my sunglasses. "It'll pass. Listen, I've got to head over to my mom's house. Thanks for searching with me."

"Of course," Chase said. "See you later."

I appreciated that he headed off down the path, instead of offering to walk me there. Chase had the ability to be supportive without being invasive. I walked along in silence, my breath shallow as I fought back tears.

I wondered if Chase could tell that I couldn't trust my emotions to remain under control. He was the one dealing with the loss of his brother but it wasn't like he was walking around like this live wire of pain, ready to cry at nearly anything. Yet here I was, almost losing it once again.

What was upsetting me so much? I didn't know if it was the fight with Tristan, the stress of watching my mother struggle, leftover heartache from the miscarriages, the guilt from losing my job, or the idea that this gorgeous life in the woods was only temporary. I'd wanted to share my struggles with the man that I married, but we were so far apart.

I didn't blame him for being upset to learn from someone other than me that I'd been fired. I should have said something a long time ago but the more time passed, the harder it had become. He had every right to be angry. I didn't understand, though, how he refused to accept the fact that I wanted to spend the summer with my mother as she recovered from a stroke. It was pretty obvious I was doing the right thing. Why couldn't he support me in that?

The past few days had left me feeling so raw. It was like all of the feelings I'd kept so carefully under control had bubbled to the surface, and I wanted to get them out before I saw my mother. I snuck into the downstairs bathroom at my parents' house and cried into a towel.

Once I'd got it all out, I washed my face. I felt better, but the sadness still lingered. I began putting together lunch in the kitchen, which gave me something to focus on other than my feelings.

There was a rotisserie chicken in the fridge along with a pint of mashed potatoes, and I heated that up, along with a package of frozen peas. By the time the meal was ready, I almost felt back to normal.

The nurse was reading to my mother when I rapped on the bedroom door, and my mother gave me a bright smile when I walked in. It was funny how quickly I'd become used to the way that her face drooped now, because I could still see the version of her that I knew in the light behind her eyes. Rushing over, I gave her a tight hug.

She smelled like lilac and baby powder, and she used her good arm to pull me in close. "How is my girl?" she asked, kissing me.

When she pulled back to look at me, a shadow crossed her face. I had no doubt she'd noticed that my eyes were puffy from crying.

"Lunch is ready," I said, turning away. "Do you want to come eat?"

The nurse helped to transfer her from the bed to the wheelchair and I pushed her through the thick carpet out into the hallway, doing my best to not bump against the wall. The wheelchair was impressive in its mobility, but I still hadn't gotten used to it and I definitely didn't like it.

We settled into the dining room, which had always been one of my favorite rooms in the house. The rustic, country table took up the majority of the space and was surrounded by the coziest chairs covered in deep burgundy fabric. Outside, the view was a sweeping expanse of the forest, along with my mother's collection of bird feeders.

No matter what time of day, my parents were guaranteed an impressive display of brightly colored birds passing through. Today, there was a group of goldfinches enjoying the seed I had set out the night before, and I had no doubt we'd see a few cardinals and blue jays. I had forgotten to fill the hummingbird feeder but that didn't stop a few birds from buzzing through, which delighted my mother.

She watched them out the window as I cut up the chicken into tiny squares, and then we sat down to eat.

I was quick with a napkin to wipe her face when she ate the mashed potatoes or to pick up pieces of food if they dropped out of her mouth, so that she didn't get frustrated. I was also careful to hide how upsetting it was to see her struggle to perform such a simple task.

Once she'd had a few bites, she said, "Tell me."

I took a small bite of peas, before pushing my plate away. Suddenly I didn't have much of an appetite.

My mother had always been the person I talked to about my relationships. She had such a big heart and the capability to see the good in people, but she did not shy away from the truth.

"It's Tristan," I said, and she nodded. "Sometimes, it feels like the person that I married and the person he is now are completely different. It's only been three years, he hasn't really changed, but…"

My mother nodded. "You have."

"Yeah." I blinked rapidly, determined not to cry again. "I lost my job," I said, running my finger around the edge of the flowered placemats. "He's mad about it." The placemats had always been cloth but the nurse had switched them with plastic ones, to make them easier to clean.

"Julie." My mother set down her fork. "Why?"

"Because I chose to stay here. And I'm happy with that decision," I said.

"Looks like it," she said slowly.

"Well, I'm not thrilled with the aftermath, but there has not been one moment when I have felt any form of regret. I had no idea how unhappy I was with my job, but I am so relieved that I will never have to walk back into that office and defend cases that I do not believe in again." The words tumbled out. "I feel free and I didn't even know I felt trapped. Now that I do, I would never go back."

I took a drink of water and hopped up to get some ice. "Tristan is furious," I said, pressing the cup into the dispenser on the fridge.

My mother dropped a piece of food and quickly I picked it up. "Why?" she asked.

"Because I didn't get a chance to tell him myself," I admitted, watching a goldfinch through the window. It hopped on the feeder and then darted away. "Someone else did."

My mother winced. "Ouch."

"Yeah." I sat back down. "I kept meaning to tell him, but I was scared. It was my mistake."

My mother finished eating a bite of chicken and then said, "The little things pass."

"Well, this is kind of big," I said. "It's not an argument about what sofa to pick out."

"Each fight matters that much," she said. "You grow." Her words came slowly, but they were becoming clearer each day. "Tristan is all about growth. He's impressive, Julie."

I thought of his intense motivation, the drive that made him get up each morning at five to tackle the day. He made goals, he met them, and there was no room for error. Yes, he was impressive, but there were days when I got tired of falling short.

"It's a patch," my mother said, watching me. "It will pass."

I hoped so because at this point, it felt like we'd never stop being angry at each other. The miscarriages, the lack of support, and now, this.

"Marriage is forever," she reminded me.

I swallowed hard. "I know. But these days, forever seems like an awfully long time."

CHAPTER EIGHTEEN

Once my mother had finished lunch and settled in for a nap, I headed to the office. Nikki was hard at work at her desk and I dug right in to an ever-multiplying list of tasks. There was so much to deal with, and whether it was a cleaning issue, updating the canoe licenses or scheduling events, it was all important. The day flew by and when it was time to meet with my father about the financials, I nearly canceled.

The peach pie I'd ordered sat in my small fridge along with raspberries and fresh cream, but I didn't know if I could handle another tough conversation. The day had been pretty intense already. But the problems with the resort were not going to fix themselves, and I needed to address them to better understand whether or not he really planned to sell off a piece of the land to manage it all.

I had just taken a quick shower and gotten dressed when his footsteps thumped up the wooden steps outside. "Hello, hello," he called, and I unlocked the door.

My father had gotten a haircut, and the silver strands blended nicely with the brown, making him look handsome and polished. My father was approaching sixty and age hadn't even begun to rob him of his good looks. If anything, he was one of those men that had become better looking with each year that passed.

"Now, did I imagine it or did you promise me a slice of pie?" He strode into the kitchen and looked in the small fridge. "A-ha! Where would you like to eat this little piece of magic?"

It was so typical of my father to swoop in and handle things even though I was supposed to be the one hosting. He had the coffee poured and the pie plated before I could even decide on an answer to his question. Finally, I pointed at the sofa.

I didn't broach the conversation I needed to have with him until we'd each had a slice of pie and were on our second cup of decaf. Then I shut the windows and turned on the fan, to keep the conversation firmly indoors. My father looked puzzled for a moment, then frowned.

"I figured there was a reason that you had me come here instead of talking with me at home," he said, setting his coffee cup onto a coaster.

"Yes." I hugged one of the throw pillows close. "This is not an easy topic. So, please trust that I'm on your side, here, and that I want to help."

My father raised his eyebrows. "Did something happen with your mother?"

Letting out a breath, I told him the information I'd seen in the tax returns. He listened without comment, his face becoming more serious with each word. Finally, he pulled out a piece of gum and started chewing, something he only did when he felt stressed.

"It concerns me," I said, "because it seems that you and Mom had this agreement to ignore the situation, as long as it didn't put the resort out of business. Things are overwhelming right now, I know, but I can help. My first thought is that we should request an audit. Bring in an outside, unbiased company to determine where we're losing money and missing opportunities."

My father folded his gum wrapper in a neat little square. "That costs money, Julie, and we don't have the capital to spare."

"Do we have debt on the property?" I asked.

My father dropped the wrapper into his mug, then gathered up the paper plates. Taking it all to the kitchen, he returned and kissed my head. "Julie, the pie was wonderful but this has been a long day. I hear your concern, and I promise, I will work to resolve things. For now, let's focus on your mother, and surviving the summer. We can revisit this another time."

"Dad." My voice was firm. "Who were the men you were walking around with that one day? The ones in the suits?"

"Julie, this is a much bigger conversation than I'm equipped to have tonight." He rubbed his eyes. "It means the world to me that you've loaned us a spare set of hands this summer, but that's where your involvement ends."

I couldn't believe that he was trying to dismiss me.

"Dad, tell me what I can do to help," I insisted.

"You can listen to what I'm telling you." His voice was firm. "I love you, goodnight."

My heart pounded as my father headed towards the door. If I let him go, there was a chance I would never address the other issue, the question that had nagged at me the entire time I'd been here.

"Why wouldn't you let me be a part of Wood Violet?" I blurted out. "Back when I wanted to make the resort my career?"

The words brought my father to a full stop. "Julie, what is all this about?"

"I wanted to be a part of the resort. I told you that back when I was in high school and you refused to give me a chance. Why?"

He tossed up his hands. "Because you needed to find what you were born for. Not what you were born into."

"This *is* what I was born for," I told him. "I have wanted to be a part of this place my entire life. Do you know how much it hurt that you wouldn't let me?"

The emotion of the day was getting the best of me, and I took a breath.

"You should have told me your reasons," I said, forcing my voice to remain steady. "Instead of insisting I should do something big out in the world. If I could do it over, I would have stayed right here. I would have picked the thing that made me happy, the thing that lit me upside. Not some grind that has nothing to do with who I am."

My father rested his hand against the door. "Julie, my father made me be a part of this place," he said quietly. "I wasn't given a choice. Did you know that?"

The words stunned me. "No."

He walked back to the couch and sat down. "My parents built Wood Violet from the ground up and wanted me to run it. Some people would see that as a golden ticket, but I wanted to make my own way in the world, create my own path. I wasn't given that chance. My parents refused to sign off on the forms I needed for college."

I blinked. "You're kidding."

"I wish I was," he said. "They wanted me to stay here, and join the business." His wrinkles were more pronounced in the light of the lamp from the end table. "I did what they asked, but for years I wondered who I might have been."

I couldn't believe my grandparents had refused to let him go to college. It showed me a side to them that I hadn't seen, but it didn't mean they hadn't cared about my father. They probably believed they had done the right thing, giving him a secure job and a comfortable life.

He looked at me. "I didn't want to push this place on you and your sister, the way my father pushed it on me. So maybe, instead, I pushed you away."

The coffee tasted sour in my mouth, and I set it down. "I had no idea."

"I'm grateful, now. I've had a wonderful life, even if it's not what I would have chosen."

"Dad, I'm sorry." Shame cut through me. "It's been one of those days, but I have no right to complain, and I know it. Wood Violet sent me to college, it gives me an income I've done nothing to earn, and it's all because you've given one hundred and ten percent of yourself, your entire life. I never would have guessed you didn't have a choice to be here."

"And I never would have guessed how badly you wanted to be here." He squinted at me. "Would you consider working here now? On a permanent basis?"

The idea of sipping on a steaming mug of coffee in the chill of the Wisconsin morning as I walked through the woods to work made my pulse race. Still, I shook my head. Tristan had our whole life planned out, and he would not be willing to make that change.

"It's too late." I stared down at my hands. They were getting freckled from the sun. "There was a time when I could have made this my everything but now…"

My father gave a sage nod. "You have a life. Well, I wish I had let you join the business back then. We'd be in a lot better shape, I have no doubt about that."

I found a tissue and blew my nose. "I know you're tired, but please sum it up. It scares me to think that everything's falling apart. Those men were developers."

"How did you know?" He tried to cover his surprise, but I could hear it in his voice.

I wasn't about to betray Nikki, so I said, "You gave me access to your calendar on Outlook. I noticed you all walking, they stood out, so I looked up the name of the company."

The development firm had been in business for years. Most likely, they would put up a resort right there on our land. It would be crowded, add a new level of competition, and ruin the aesthetic of our property.

"If we're in financial trouble, the solution has nothing to do with them," I said.

My father cracked his knuckles. "It was just a meeting."

"Do you want to sell?" I asked. "I mean, that's millions of dollars on the table. If you never wanted to be here in the first place…"

"No." He shook his head. "Like I said, I'm grateful for the path I've taken. I don't want to leave this place. It's a part of me."

I felt almost weak with relief. "That's good news."

"Tell you what, kid," he said. "I've got to get back to your mother, but we can talk all this through later this week. The long and short of it is that we don't have debt on the resort, but I've considered it many times. We're losing money. I'm borrowing from our savings to pay the team, the bills, and even my salary. Your mother has medical bills through the roof and it's not the time for us to worry about money. If I can't figure out a way to increase our revenue, it won't be about selling off a piece of the land. I'll have to sell the whole thing."

"Sell Wood Violet?" I whispered.

"I almost did it a few months ago but I had an obstacle. Your mother." He shook his head. "Let's just say she wouldn't let me sign the papers."

"There has to be a way to survive," I said. "First things first: the medical bills. There's plenty of money in the trust. We're paid out on interest. Take part of the principal."

He shook his head. "Your grandparents put that together for the two of you, not us."

"Then, we'll ask Grandpa," I said. "I know Kate would agree."

My father held up his hand. "We're not there yet, okay? We're trying to figure things out. That's why Nikki put together her presentation. I could tell you weren't impressed."

"I saw the purchase order for the televisions you signed off on. Dad, it's a waste of money and it's not what the guests are looking for. Trust me."

"Nothing is set in stone. Julie, let's talk this week. I need to get back to your mother. There's lots to think about, but things will look brighter in the morning."

My father headed down the steps and disappeared into the trees. I sat on the front porch, swatting away mosquitoes and thinking. I couldn't believe we were so close to losing Wood Violet. There had to be a solution to bring in more money, but I had no idea what it could be.

The next morning, I walked into the office determined to come up with a solution. The coffee was brewing and Nikki was in a meeting, so I settled at my desk and got to work on the weekly hospitality numbers. I was about halfway through when Nikki walked in.

"Morning," I said.

Nikki didn't answer. Instead, the door clicked shut and she walked over to the desk. "You're only here for a short time." She held her chin high. "May I request that if you have a problem with any of my suggestions that you bring the issue to me instead of your father?"

I was so surprised I didn't know what to say. "Nikki, I don't understand. What's wrong?"

"The email that I received last night at eleven o'clock, defunding the project that I've been coordinating for the past six months. That's what's wrong."

"The televisions?" I said.

She sucked in a sharp breath. "Your father informed me he'd received pushback. I can't believe it was from you! Julie, I have been open and honest with you from the moment you arrived. I can't believe this is how you repay me."

Nikki was obviously hurt. The orderly way that she kept her desk, the perfect outfits, and even the precise way that she made her coffee flashed through my head. She was so invested in being here. I hadn't meant to make her feel invalidated, I just didn't want my father to make the wrong choice for the resort.

"I'm sorry," I said. "Please don't take it personally. It was nothing against you, at all."

She pressed her hand against the top of the desk. "Julie, I appreciate that you are here to support your family. Since that's your function, can I request you focus on that instead of trying to do my job? I've done pretty well at it for the past five years. My suggestions come from careful market research, not personal preference. So, unless you have something constructive to add, please abstain from being destructive."

"I understand you're upset," I said, wondering what she'd say if she knew all the details about our financial status. "However, my father makes his own decisions and I believe this is the right one for the resort. There will be plenty of suggestions you bring to the table that will work—I know he's interested in several—but this wasn't one of them."

"Why do you think your opinion holds greater weight than research?" she demanded. "You're here for what, a minute? It might seem like a summer vacation to you, but to me, every decision matters."

Nikki stalked out of the office, shutting the door firmly behind her. I put my head in my hands.

A summer vacation?

My mother was battling her way back to normal, my husband wasn't speaking to me, and my father needed to improve our revenue stream or Wood Violet would have to close its doors. Not to mention the fact that Margaret's presence had complicated everything.

"Some summer vacation." I shook my head. "Everything is going to work out just fine," I said quietly. "It has to."

The words fell flat, maybe because I didn't believe them myself.

By the end of the week, my father still hadn't sat down to talk with me further about our finances, and I decided to meet up with Margaret to go on a canoe ride. I'd been so busy that I hadn't had a chance to see her since the day I discovered the adoption papers, and I wanted to check in. I had just about reached her cabin when my cell rang.

The number was out of Chicago but one I didn't recognize. I hadn't heard from Tristan since Monday, with the exception of a cursory text that said: *Need time to think.* He was obviously working through his anger, which I understood, but enough was enough. Perhaps something had happened to his phone and he was calling on a landline.

Stepping into a clearing in the woods, I picked up.

"Julie? Hi, it's Laura Wentz."

My stomach dropped. Laura was my friend from the law office listed on Margaret's adoption papers. "Laura, thank you so much for getting back to me."

"Sorry it took me a few days to respond," she said. "I've been swamped, but your email intrigued me."

I could imagine Laura sitting at her desk in the squat building in Wicker Park where her law firm was based. The firm was small, but it had a reputation for being a solid place with good lawyers. It was something to consider when the time came to start searching for a job in the fall.

The thought surprised me. Seeking out a position in Laura's office would mean transferring my specialty. No more work for insurance companies. It would be an opportunity to help children or families and I could actually wake up with a sense of purpose.

It was a potential solution. One that might not leave me feeling so trapped.

"So, I had a little time during lunch to do some digging," Laura said. "There wasn't anything on file that I can share with you, unfortunately, and the birth mother has not reached out to our office with anything to give her child. I wish I could be a greater help."

"Thanks for looking," I said. "I knew it was a long shot, but I wanted to check."

"Now, did I read your email correctly, that you're in Wisconsin for the summer?" she asked.

"Yes, I'm here with my mother. She had a stroke, so I'm planning to stay until September to care for her." I fiddled with the pendant on my necklace. "Laura, I wanted to ask you. I had to move on from my firm and I'm interested in perhaps pursuing family law. Do you know of any openings?"

"Oh, you'd be wonderful at that. I don't, but I will keep my ears open. I'm happy to help reach out to contacts whenever you're coming back. Just keep me posted."

"Thanks." My words felt lighter, now that I'd opened the door to a new possibility. "That really means a lot."

It was one step but it was a step in the right direction. I was glad that I'd had the nerve to take it.

Once Margaret and I had put on life jackets and were headed out on the water in a canoe, I was impressed at her ability to handle an oar.

"Where did you learn that?" I asked.

I'd accepted the idea that the canoe could very well go around in circles, but her steering was precise. She kept us moving forward in a straight line.

"Rowing team at school," she mumbled. "Oh, and by not being a moron."

The canoe sliced through the still water, keeping us moving quick enough that my hair actually blew around.

"Where did you go to school?" I asked.

She sighed. "Let's be quiet and look at the scenery. Okay?"

Fine by me. It was so peaceful being out on the water that I was happy for the silence. The sun was bright and sparkled off the surface of the lake. The rhythmic sound of the boat and the paddle was soothing, and I watched a group of young swimmers diving off one of the many covered rafts.

I glanced back at Margaret. She wore a pair of cat-shaped sunglasses, a pink linen swimsuit cover-up, and a ton of sunscreen. Noticing me, she lowered her sunglasses and studied me with her ice-blue eyes.

"You looked in my bag," she said.

I was so surprised that I nearly dropped the oar. Fumbling for it, I set it down in the boat and turned to face her. This didn't seem to be a conversation to have with my back turned.

We drifted slowly across the water. She didn't say anything else, just looked at me. Finally, I nodded.

"Yes," I said. "How did you know?"

"Like I'm going to tell you." She adjusted her sunglasses. "The drawing was upside down, okay? Why would you snoop through my stuff?"

"Because I wanted to know why you were here. I didn't believe you when you said you'd come here as a child. I could tell there was more to it."

"You can't just look in another person's bag," she said. "It's not right."

Her face had started to get red and I didn't like the way she was waving her oar.

"I'm sorry," I said. "I should have just asked you."

Margaret squinted at the shore. "What did you see?"

"The adoption papers," I said. "I know that you came here to find your birth mother."

It made me feel like a complete jerk to think that I knew her mother's name and even had a photograph of her, but that I couldn't say a word about it. I would have liked to hand the file over to Margaret and wish her luck on her journey, but until I understood my grandmother's involvement, I couldn't.

Besides, it was possible Margaret knew more about her mother than she'd let on.

"How's your search going?" I asked.

Margaret leaned back against the edge of the canoe, lazing her hand across the water. "I'm not getting anywhere. I came here because of the address but didn't exactly know where to look."

"That's fair," I said carefully. "But it's also important to make choices that won't get you into trouble. For example, taking your search to a place where you might want to break into places to access information is not a good idea, because breaking and entering is serious. Our security team is on high alert these days and I don't want you to get into trouble."

She glared at me. "What's that supposed to mean?"

"It means I know you broke into the main office trying to find out information about your mother."

Margaret went back to looking out at the water. "You don't know that."

"Do you have any leads?" I asked. "Other than the address of the resort and the sketch?"

"It's not like you care, so quit asking."

"I do care," I said. "That's why I'm asking."

"No, you don't," she said. "I've barely even seen you. You looked in my bag, violated my privacy, and then stayed away, probably because you were too scared of what I'd say to you. So forgive me for not believing that you care in the slightest. You don't want me here. You never did."

"Margaret, please." The sun was hot on my shoulders and her words hurt my heart. "I've been busy trying to help manage this place. It has nothing to do with you."

"Right." She dipped her hand in the water, splashing it across her chest. "You're so fake. It's obvious you just think I'm some dumb kid. As if you'd know anything about kids anyway."

I drew back. "Excuse me?"

"Tilly has four kids." Her face was full of fury. "You don't have any."

"I've lost two babies. Two." The words were so quiet, I wondered if I'd said them out loud. "I would give anything in this world to have a child. So don't you dare sit there and make assumptions about me. You have no idea."

I was so angry, I could hardly see. "Turn the boat," I said. "We're going back into shore."

When Margaret didn't move, I shoved my paddle into the water and tried to move without her help. The canoe went in a circle. Furious, I threw my oar into the bottom of the boat with a clatter.

I could easily swim back and I was not about to spend another second with her.

"I'll send someone to tow you in," I said, and moved to slide out of the canoe.

"Julie, wait," she pleaded, grabbing my leg. "I'm sorry. I didn't know. Truly. I had no idea, I was just mad you looked in my bag."

"So that gives you the right to say those things to me?" My breath was tight, and I was so upset I could hardly speak. "You know nothing about me or what I'm going through."

"I'm sorry." The words were small and tinny, and I could tell she was about to cry.

I dipped my hand in the water and splashed it on my face. It was fresh and cold, and I let out a deep breath. Did I even have a right to be angry at her, considering all that I was keeping from her? I didn't know anymore.

We sat in silence, looking anywhere but at each other. The sun was hot on my neck and I squeezed on some more sunscreen. It smelled like pineapple and coconut. It took a few minutes, but I finally turned to face her.

"It's fine," I said. "It's just been hard to go through all that. I am more than aware that Tilly has four children. My sister is pregnant and about to have her third. It seems like everyone has kids but me."

"I don't have any kids," Margaret said.

The comment was so sincere that I couldn't help but smile.

"So we have that in common," I said.

"I'm sorry I called you fake." She fiddled with her sunglasses. "You're not fake. Far from it. It's just that the stress of all this is getting to me. Some days, I'm not sure what I'm doing here at all. Please don't tell Tilly. I don't want anyone to know."

"I haven't said a word to her. Chase knows, because we talked the day I found the papers, but he's not going to say anything."

She considered that, then nodded. "Good."

"What steps are you taking to find your mother?" I asked.

"Tons of stuff. I've been trying to find a way to get my birth certificate, but I can't. I'm planning to take a day trip to the county clerk and see if they can tell me anything. Then, yesterday, I called the local hospitals, trying to find the one where I was born."

I felt bad, knowing that she was doing all that to find her mother's name, but at least she was on the right track. I wasn't ready to share what I knew, but I could encourage her in her search.

"Do you know for sure you were born in this area? The firm that handled your adoption is based in Chicago."

"I called the Chicago hospitals first," Margaret said. "I spent hours doing that last week, with no luck. I thought I was getting somewhere here because the person I talked to at Blue Spruce Hospital asked for my social security number, like she was about to look something up. Her tone changed when I said I didn't have it. I feel like I would have had better luck if I would have gone in person."

Blue Spruce was the hospital closest to the resort. It was the one my family had used for years. The sun was starting to burn my scalp, so I scooped up some water and pressed it into my hair.

"I also looked at the ancestry sites," Margaret continued, and I thought of the day in the records closet when Chase had suggested doing the same. "There wasn't anything there. Then, there were these other sites I looked at, too. Like this database that would connect us if she was looking for me, but I'm scared she's not interested in me at all."

"There's a lot of people who don't use the internet," I said. "Don't make assumptions based on that."

She drummed her fingers against the edge of the canoe. "That would also be so public, you know? My mother would be pretty upset if she somehow found out I was on there without talking to her first."

"Your adoptive mother?" I said.

Margaret looked down at her hands. "It's weird to call her that."

"I'm impressed that you're still taking her feelings into consideration, after everything that happened. That's true maturity, Margaret."

Her cheeks colored. "Or something."

The compliment seemed to end the conversation, because she made a move to pick up her oar.

"I hope that you find what you're looking for during your time here," I said. "Regardless of what it ends up being."

Margaret hesitated. "I'm sorry about what I said before. About kids? I think you're going to be a good mom."

The words caught me so off guard that my eyes stung with tears. Then, to my absolute surprise, Margaret dove in for a hug. The boat nearly tipped at the sudden movement, and we both screamed. Then we started laughing.

"I really do feel like I'm going to find her," Margaret said, after we'd settled back into our seats and slid our oars back in the water. "It's like, this sense that I have that led me here. Everything has a purpose."

It was pretty impressive that Margaret still believed the world was fair, good and right. Even after the way she'd been treated, she still believed that life had a navigation system that would take her where she needed to go. I liked her optimism.

"Do you want to go back?" she asked. "I'm starting to get hot."

"Sure. Let's go along the shore," I suggested. "We'll be in the shade."

As we paddled along the edge, I looked up at the trees. The once small buds had turned to perfect leaves, bright green in the sun. They rustled as we drifted past and along the shore. The sound of the bullfrogs was as hypnotic as the water.

"I'm sorry I looked in your bag," I said.

"Please." She snorted. "You're sorry you got caught."

"That's not true." I looked back at her. "I'm sorry about the way I've handled things with you. You're a good person, Margaret, and I'm glad you're here."

There was a pause in steering as she looked out over the lake. "Yeah," she finally said. "I'm glad I'm here, too."

CHAPTER NINETEEN

The week after my canoe ride with Margaret was so busy that it was practically a blur. It reminded me of working at the law office. There was one problem to fix after another and the mood in my small office had changed, as Nikki was angry that I'd put a stop to her plan about installing flat-screens. Still, there was nowhere I would rather be.

The time with my mother was so special. I read to her, we watched old movies, and we did a lot of baking. She sat in her wheelchair by the kitchen counter and told me exactly what to do. For the first time in my life, I took the time to learn how to whip up a frothy meringue, baked eclairs, and even made a chocolate souffle. She was finally smiling and there were moments my father seemed choked up to see us together.

Tristan called, and we had a long talk about transparency and how to best support each other. We made a point to talk several times after that and each call was awkward, but I apologized as often as he needed me to, and he made an extra effort to stay on the phone for a longer period of time. We were both trying.

I'd also made a point of investing more time with Margaret. We met for breakfast a few times, went fishing twice, and I worked with her to set up a sing-along for kids. She'd surprised me by being great with them. Neither one of us had made any progress on finding her mother, but it did start to feel like we might be becoming friends.

Once it got to the weekend, I was surprised to realize that I'd been at the resort for a month. It had felt like a minute, and I was grateful for every second of it that I'd had.

One of the resort nights that had seemed the most glamorous to me as a child was Casino Night. It was held the last weekend of each month, and the guests got dressed up in their cocktail best to attend a night of blackjack, poker and roulette. The jazz band set the tone for a swanky evening, and an impressive spread of appetizers and desserts made the mood nothing short of decadent.

I'd never been, and I was unreasonably excited on the night I finally had the opportunity to go.

The sky was clear and the stars were out as Tilly and I walked to the main building. Tilly's husband had met up with the other men for a drink, and she'd come to my cabin to get ready. Of course, she'd arrived with a split of champagne, so we were both bright and bubbly by the time we headed over to the main lodge.

"I have waited my whole life to go to a Casino Night," I said, smoothing the dress Tilly had loaned me.

I felt pretty for the first time in ages, wearing a cream-colored cocktail dress woven through with sequins. The pearls Tristan had bought for my latest birthday dangled from my ears and at the last minute I'd applied red lipstick to get into the whole jazz-scene vibe. The dress sparkled every time I moved, making me feel a little like Cinderella.

"In all these years, you've never been?" Tilly linked her arm in mine, her gold bracelets clinking. She wore an outrageous flapper-style dress complete with a feather train. It looked amazing, along with her dark eyeshadow and sparkling lips.

"Nope," I said. "By the time I was old enough, I was off to college and then, the city. I never made it back for Casino Night, which is a shame."

Tilly was quiet. "Julie, I haven't said it yet but I've been thinking it all summer. I'm so impressed by you."

"That's the champagne talking," I said, fidgeting with the bulbous pearl bracelet she'd loaned me.

"No, I mean it." Tilly's gaze was intense. "Sometimes, I regret not having a career. You've made something of yourself. You should be very proud."

The words stopped me on the path. "Tilly, what do you mean? Not to state the obvious, but you could have a bigger career than most people I know, any time that you choose. Is that something you're thinking about doing now?"

Tilly's perfect nose wrinkled. "Oh, please. Pharma is the last thing I'm interested in. My father has basically never forgiven me for that but…" She lifted her chin. "You branched out on your own, and that's impressive. I was too scared to do it back when I could, because I was afraid of all that I would lose."

I tried to decipher what she was saying. "What do you mean?"

"My parents didn't want me to go into another field," she said. "It would have been such a slap in my father's face, in the face of the business, if I had done something else. However, motherhood and charity work was considered acceptable, so that's what we silently agreed on."

It was the same story as the situation with my father. The expectation to do what you were born into, instead of what you were born to do.

"It all turned out fine, I guess." She stepped over on the path to make way for a well-dressed couple clearly headed to Casino Night. "How did a compliment to you turn into a pity party for me? I can't wait to hit the blackjack table. I seem to remember some tough dealers, but I can count cards, so they better watch out."

"What did you want to do?" I asked. "What career would you have had?"

Tilly frowned at me for a moment, as if irritated that I'd ignored her bravado. Then she waved her hand, which sparkled with jewels. "I wanted to be a vet." She giggled, leaning into me. "The time has passed. I'm too old."

"That's not true," I said. "If you didn't want to invest the time at this point—"

"Because I'm old—"

"Then you could find another way to help animals," I suggested.

"I'd love that," Tilly admitted, her face serious again. "It's not realistic, though."

We stepped out of the forest onto the main lawn. The lodge was lit up, and the warm, yellow light looked cozy and inviting.

"I can already smell the cigars," she said.

Back when I was a child, Casino Night had offered an indoor cigar room. The smell of the burnt tobacco with its hint of vanilla had wafted out of the main door all night. My sister and I were fascinated. One year, one of the boys stole a cigar from his dad and we all tried it out back. We inhaled, because we didn't know, and threw up for hours. That should have soured me on cigars, but I still loved the smell.

There was no longer a cigar room indoors but the tradition had lived on. Now, there was an open-air cigar tent. Tilly and I took a moment to breathe in the heady scent, listening to the jazz music singing from the open doors of the lodge.

Still, we hung back, caught up in the first one-on-one conversation we'd been able to have all summer.

"I think you should open a shelter or rehabilitation center or something," I said. "There are plenty of opportunities to do the same type of work you'd do as a vet."

The light in her face dimmed. "My husband wouldn't agree to that. He has the same attitude as my father. Expects me to raise the kids, be the perfect socialite, say and do the right things…

If I said I wanted to open up an animal shelter, my husband would find a hundred excuses why it wouldn't work. Ultimately, it would come down to the fact that it didn't match up with the image he wants us to project." She squeezed my hands, her skin cool and her eyes searching. "It's awful that I'm talking this way."

"The only thing that seems awful to me is that your husband is calling the shots when you're Tilly Fisk. Sorry, but that's a little outrageous."

The champagne must have affected me because otherwise, I would never have mentioned the money and prestige her name had brought to their marriage. I didn't know her husband's history but unless he was a Rockefeller, it wasn't like he'd brought more to the table than she had.

"The things we do for love," she said.

The statement frustrated me into silence. Mainly because it summed up my life over the past few years. It also made me wonder how many women gave up their power in the name of love. Tilly had wanted her husband to be happy, so she'd gone along with his vision for their future. I'd done the same with Tristan, for much too long.

In some ways, it seemed like the anger I felt towards Tristan was unjustified. I had always agreed with his choices instead of taking a stand, but it would help if he would give me the respect of an equal partnership. It shouldn't have been a battle for me to take the time to care for my mother, and the fact that it was indicated a much bigger problem between us.

"Should we go in?" Tilly asked.

"I'd rather get another split of champagne and stay out here, talking to you," I said, only half-joking.

"Me, too." Tilly looked up at the stars, her smile grand. "Thank you for listening. There's no friend like an old friend, you know?"

I squeezed her hand. "I really don't know who you're calling old."

*

Casino Night was as fun as I'd always imagined it would be.

Surrounded by the pretty dresses and dapper men, I spent the majority of the night at the blackjack table. True to her word, Tilly could count cards. We played side by side and she told me when to hit and when to pass, building my stack of chips into something impressive.

"I should stop you because you're absolutely fleecing the resort," I said cheerfully. "But this is too much fun."

I swept my latest win towards me, laughing at the intense expression on Tilly's face as she watched the dealer.

"Don't stop her," Leo's wife said, rooting for us from the side. "I want to see how much you guys can actually win."

Guests had to buy chips to play the games, so the stakes were high. The fervor with which our regulars competed to stack their chips was intense. At the end, guests took their winnings to the checkout table, where they were converted into credits towards the gift shop or their cabin charges.

Chase came up to the table with a fresh round of drinks for the group. "How's it going?"

"I'm clearly ready for Vegas." I waved at my stacks.

"That's it, folks," the dealer said, moving his hands back and forth like a professional. "I'd like to introduce Ward."

Ward stood about six foot five, had dark circles under his eyes, and an imposing stare. Tilly squealed and scooped up her chips like children. Ward expressed mock outrage and we ran off in our heels, giggling.

In moments like these, surrounded by the fun Wood Violet had to offer, I couldn't wrap my mind around the possibility of shutting down. I knew in my heart that we would find a solution; it was just a question of what it was going to be.

"What's next?" Leo's wife said.

"Roulette," Leo called, beckoning.

We all headed that way. I got swept up in the cheering of the crowd and the rhythm of the numbers but had no clue how to play. We kept picking numbers and Tilly, of course, ended up winning a bunch of times. Then Chase took my arm.

"Let's bet on eighteen," he told me. "It was Garrett's favorite number."

I slid my chips over, giving him a high five. We watched the wheel and as it slowed, my mouth dropped open.

Eighteen.

I turned to Chase, who seemed frozen in disbelief. Then, we jumped up and down, fist-bumping and screaming. Our friends shouted their support as the dealer slid over a massive amount of chips. It was the most fun I'd had in ages.

The music started around nine, once we'd all worked our way through a plateful of dessert. Tilly insisted on eating something off everyone's plate, as a drunken sign of friendship, and her husband kept kissing her. He asked her to dance, and she glided out to the floor, winking at me.

It was good to see that, even if they were facing problems, it didn't have to be the end of everything.

Everyone started to head out to the dance floor and Chase gave me a questioning look. "What do you say? Should we see if our lessons have a real-world application?"

I bit my lip. The answer would have been *absolutely not* only a few weeks ago. Now, I felt like I might be able to do it without making a complete fool of myself.

"No pressure," Chase said. "We could also stand here and eat these little chocolate cakes all night, either is good with me."

I held out my hand. "Let's try. With a complete right to back out."

Chase led me out to the dance floor. Our friends were in their own world, so no one even noticed us.

He squeezed my hands and I began counting. Slowly, we moved across the floor. It felt no different from dance class. Well, except for the fact that I was in a beautiful dress, the smell of chocolate permeated the air, and Chase smelled like the forest and spice.

"Did you put on cologne?" I asked, pulling at the lapels of his suit jacket.

"Yes." Chase grinned. "I wasn't sure if it said, *Hey, I'm a stick of cinnamon gum* or made me like, a really attractive man with a smoldering smile."

I laughed. "It smells good."

The jazz band covered old love songs. The step Tomas had taught us worked for everything. For the first time in my life, I was dancing and it felt great. I finally felt so comfortable that I stopped counting, and let the rhythm take over. Chase and I started talking, oblivious to everything until I felt a firm tap on my shoulder.

Chase took a step back. "I think he'd like to cut in."

I figured it was Saxon. Turning, I started to crack a joke, but stopped mid-sentence.

The man who wanted to dance with me was my husband.

"Tristan!" The word came out as a squawk.

It felt strange to see him after a few weeks apart. He looked handsome in a gray designer suit that showcased his broad shoulders but his lips looked mean, pressed so tightly together.

"What is this?" he demanded.

"Dancing." I tried to take his hands but he pulled away.

The expression on his face was pure disbelief. "You don't dance."

"Hey, man." Chase stepped forward. "She learned how to dance to surprise you. She's been working really hard."

The look Tristan gave him was nothing short of dangerous. "Get away from my wife," he said, in a low tone. Grabbing my arm, he led me to the exit.

My heart pounded, panicked that Tristan seemed so upset, but my mind instantly went to the importance of protecting the resort. It would not be a good look for me to have a fight with my husband in the middle of a major event. So I pasted a huge smile on my face and waved in the general direction of my friends, as if headed off for a grand night with the man that I loved.

Outside, crowds of people were talking, laughing, and smoking cigars off in the cigar tent. Tristan strode past all of them.

"Tristan." I forced him to a stop, once we were well out of sight of the party and on the path that led to the cabins. "What are you doing here?"

Tristan made a snorting sound. "I couldn't tell you."

"Look." I grabbed his hands. "I'm so happy to see you. I can't believe you're here. It's all I've wanted for weeks."

"Yeah, I can see that," he scoffed. "You wouldn't even dance with me at our *wedding*."

"Tristan, I'm learning how to dance for *you*," I insisted. "I planned to surprise you."

"Well, you did." He looked out at the trees. "Did that guy take lessons with you?"

This was going all wrong. He was missing the point.

"Honey, you're not hearing me. I took lessons for you. I learned to dance for *you*."

"Do you remember how many times I asked you to take dance classes with me?" Tristan's strong jaw clenched. "Before our wedding?"

"Yes." I fidgeted with the bracelet Tilly had loaned me. It had seemed so glamorous at the beginning of the night. Now, it felt clunky. "I wasn't ready. Being here has given me time to think. I want to be your partner in all things. I should have danced with you back then, but I get that and I'm ready to do it now. I will try harder and be better, because really, I just want to be with you."

The image of Tilly and her husband gliding happily across the floor flashed through my brain. Every marriage had problems. What mattered was the way that you dealt with them.

"You want to be my partner in all things," Tristan echoed. "Okay. So, would you go back home with me, to the city, tonight?"

Helplessness cut through me. I couldn't leave this behind, but I had made a promise to the person standing before me that we would be together, forever, and I could tell by the look on his face that my answer would impact everything.

"Yes," I said quietly. "I'd leave tonight."

Tristan stared at me. The anger in his face softened, and as the trees whispered around us, he leaned in for a kiss. The image of his lips thinned in anger passed through my mind but I put my arms around him and kissed him back.

"We'll stay," he murmured. "Because that's what you really want."

Tears ran down my cheeks, hot as steam. My mascara stung, and Tristan took my arm, leading me back to the cabin. My shoes were loud on the stairs and I remembered how, at the beginning of the night, I'd felt like Cinderella.

"Let's go to bed," Tristan said, peeling off his suit jacket. "We'll figure it out in the morning."

My head hurt from the alcohol, the tears, and the disappointment that the night had ended like this. The silence of the forest fell heavy around us as we settled into a bed that suddenly, felt much too small.

I woke up around six the next morning. The room smelled musky and I looked over at Tristan. He was already awake, of course, and he gently ran his finger over my lips.

"Morning." His voice was deep and scratchy. "Would you like coffee?"

The mornings I had spent here on my own, making the coffee while looking out at the lake, passed through my mind. "I'll come with you," I said, joining him in the kitchen.

The lake was covered in a thick layer of fog, making it look gray against the green of the pines. I stood back and let Tristan brew the coffee, as he had a certain way he liked it done. We didn't speak until we were seated on the couch, mugs in hand.

"This is cozy," Tristan said, smiling at me.

He'd added the perfect amount of cream, and I took a sip.

We sat in silence and then both spoke at once.

"Go ahead," he said.

"No, you."

We both did that awkward-laugh thing and I cringed. When had we gotten to that place, where we had to be polite in order to keep the tension out of the room?

"I'm so happy you're here." I smiled at him. "I have a couple of things I have to take care of in the office today, but then we can—"

Irritation crossed his face. "It's Saturday."

"This is a resort," I said. "It's twenty-four seven."

"Well, it can wait," he said. "I'm here."

I took a drink of coffee.

Yes, it meant a lot to me that Tristan was here, but at the same time it would have been nice to have some warning so I could have shifted things around. It was so typical that Tristan expected me to be available, simply because he was.

Stop. He's here.

I needed to make an effort, too.

"Let me make a few calls," I said. "Then I'm all yours."

Tristan and I took a walk to breakfast the moment it opened.

The forest smelled fresh, and drops of dew sparkled on the leaves. The air smelled like pine and something musty, maybe mushrooms. It was already starting to get hot and along the path, steam rose up from a cluster of ferns.

He took my hand and we walked along in silence. There were a hundred things I wanted to tell him about, but didn't know where to start.

"You'll meet Margaret," I finally said. "She's the girl living in the artist-in-residence cabin."

"The runaway?" Tristan said.

"No, she's…" The fact that Tristan still didn't know the whole story made me squeeze his hand tight. We hadn't been apart for that long but in some ways, it felt like an eternity. "It's complicated."

I told him the short version of the story as we walked and he frowned. "I can't believe you haven't told your dad what's going on."

"I will," I said, "but he has too much on his plate right now. It's fine; she's not causing trouble and it's going to upset him more to hear about the adoption if I can't find answers first."

Tristan shrugged. "It's not like you to be deceptive." His attitude irritated me because I knew he was right. Lying to my father had not been the right thing to do but for once, I wished Tristan could just support me.

They're his family too.

The thought made me stop in the middle of the path.

Tristan felt protective of my dad. I appreciated that, because it showed me how much he cared. Quickly, I kissed him on the nose.

He looked puzzled, but pleased. "What's that for?"

"For trying to protect my parents," I said.

We walked in silence for a moment, then he gave a little laugh. "You never fail to surprise me, Julie."

"Good." I squeezed his hand. "Then maybe we can make it for the long haul."

It was a joke, but not really. I was afraid he'd pull his hand away but instead, he squeezed mine back. It wasn't violins or harps playing but at least it was something, the two of us connecting on the fact that we had a long way to go.

Tristan was actually in the mood for pancakes, so we shared a stack of wholegrain, scrambled eggs, and a side of berries. The orange juice was particularly sweet and good, but I couldn't relax into the morning. It was like my mind was moving a hundred miles an hour, trying to adjust to bringing Tristan back into this world.

We were just finishing up our food when my father walked up to the table.

"Tristan!" He clapped him on the back, and gave me a big smile. "Good to see you, son."

Tristan got up and the two hugged. Once they'd chatted for a few minutes, my father turned to me.

"Nikki's looking for you," he said. "It's not urgent but she asked me to have you call her if I bumped into you."

"I'll give her a call later," I told him. "We're going to get out and enjoy the day."

My father popped a blueberry from our plate in his mouth. "Take out one of the boats," he suggested. "It's going to be beautiful."

The idea of putting around on a pontoon boat sounded great. I'd put my swimsuit on under my clothes, since I didn't know what the day would bring. We headed down to the beach. Laughing, Tristan pointed at one of the pedalboats.

"I haven't done that since I was a kid," I said.

"Me, neither," he told me. "Let's do it."

We climbed in, the boat shifting beneath our weight. Tristan started to pedal and he grinned. "This might actually serve as my morning workout." The water chugged beneath the pedals, the sound echoing against the water. The sun beat down and once we got to the middle of the lake, it was too deep to anchor the boat, so we took turns jumping in. Tristan pulled me out, happily chilled, and dove in. He came up, his smile as bright as the sun on the water.

This was what I had wanted. The two of us, here together, enjoying the simple things. When he climbed back in the boat, his skin damp, I pulled him in for a kiss. We kissed each other with an urgency that hadn't existed between us for months.

"Want to go back to the cabin?" he said, already turning the steering wheel.

Kissing him again, I said, "Thought you'd never ask."

It was such a comfort to feel his arms around me once again.

It was like we'd stepped back in time to a point when things were easy, and the moments of heartbreak had been erased. I buried my face in his shoulder and breathed him in, in love with the scent of his skin. It was hard to believe there had been a time a few months ago where I didn't even want to touch him, after he'd shut me out after the second miscarriage.

"What are you thinking about?" Tristan's voice was low and luxurious.

"You." I raised myself up on my elbow. "It's so nice to finally be together."

His thumb brushed my lower lip. "We took a detour, didn't we?"

I took his hand and kissed it to hide my emotion. There were so many times I'd wondered if Tristan had known how close I was to my breaking point and now, I knew. I could tell by the weight in his voice.

The sheets were soft against us and the scent of pine strong in the cabin, mingled with the scent of our bodies. He'd complained about the lack of air conditioning on his first visit but I couldn't imagine a more romantic setting, with the fan blowing a breeze that made the white curtains dance with the sun.

"I never thought we would have trouble," he said, staring up at the ceiling. "But we made our way out."

"That's a little premature." My voice held a warning tone. "We have a lot of things to work through, a lot of things to talk about."

"Right." He gave me a firm look. "But we made our way out because we're both willing to do that. That's how you build forever."

"Hey, I've got a question for you," I raised myself up on my elbow. "Want to dance?"

Tristan chuckled and took my hand. "Yeah," he said, kissing me. "But right here in this bed is just fine for me."

CHAPTER TWENTY

That night, Tristan agreed to go to a bonfire with Tilly, Chase, Saxon and Leo. I was delighted to have him spend time with my friends. I held tightly to his arm as we stepped onto the beach and spotted the crew down by a roaring fire.

Chase looked over as we walked towards the group, but instead of waving, went back to adding logs to the fire. Sparks flew up in front of him, scattering like stardust. He must have still been upset about the way Tristan had spoken to him, and I hoped Tristan would apologize.

"Hello, hello," Tilly called, skipping up to us. "Tristan, it is so nice to see you again. Julie, this man is absolutely *adorable.*" She pinched his cheeks and Tristan gave her his most charming smile.

"Ms. Fisk," he said. "I hear you have officially earned the title of the best mother in the world."

Tilly burst into peals of laughter. "You know what those little monsters had for dinner tonight?" she said. "Two bowls of soft-serve with toppings from the ice-cream bar. It wasn't worth the fight! So, if that makes me the best mother in the world, I'll take the title, and give them an extra helping of carrot juice in the morning." She grabbed Tristan's arm and pulled him towards her husband. "Come on, I want you to meet another Cubs fan."

I followed, enjoying the feeling of the sand between my toes, the heat from the fire, and the cool breeze off the lake. It was the perfect night, with stars stretched out as far as the eye could see. I snuggled up under the crook of Tristan's arm as he chatted with Tilly's husband and Saxon about everything from the World Series to extreme sports skiing.

Turning towards the fire, I saw Chase watching us. I caught his eye and smiled, but he looked down, poking at the flames with a stick.

"Be right back," I murmured to Tristan, and went over to sit by Chase. "Hey," I said. "I know he's going to come over and say it himself at some point, but Tristan feels awful about the way he acted last night. I'm sorry about all that."

"Not a problem," he said, taking a sip of beer.

"The dancing worked," I said, watching Tristan as he laughed at something Saxon said. "I think once he got over his surprise, he was touched."

"I'm sure." Chase's voice was wry. He didn't say anything else and when he looked up at me again, his blue eyes were bright. "Listen, I'm going to head out."

"Chase," I said, surprised. "What's going on?"

"Nothing." He shrugged. "I've got work to do, that's all. Sorry to miss his great homecoming but tonight's not the night."

He dropped the stick in the fire and headed up the sand towards the path in the woods. My face was flushed from the heat of the fire or embarrassment, and I got to my feet, trying to understand what had just happened. The great homecoming? Yes, Tristan had been rude but to be fair, he was my husband and, from his point of view, I was dancing with another guy. He didn't know the context of the situation, and he'd jumped to conclusions. I was really surprised that Chase wasn't going to give him a chance, and to be honest, I was a little hurt.

Chase was important to me, so I'd wanted him to spend time with me and Tristan. It was unfortunate the way things had happened last night, but I was irritated that Chase couldn't let it go. I'd expected more, since he'd proven to be such a great guy.

"He's in a mood," Leo told me, while heading to the cooler for another beer. "Heartache will do that to you."

It took a minute, but I got it.

Chase probably felt alone, watching all the couples together. It served as a reminder that he didn't have anyone, but he would, when he was ready. He was one of the best people I knew, and the woman who ended up with him would be incredibly lucky. It made me sad, though, to think that he was upset. I wished I could go find him and talk to him about it, but that wouldn't go over well with Tristan.

The group was headed over to the fire and Tristan winked at me as the guys gave him a beer and they kept talking sports. Tilly came over and sat with me.

"Margaret just texted," she said. "She's headed down to play."

"That's great!" I said.

Margaret had played for my father at the meeting I'd set up, and he'd been so impressed with her voice that he'd told me to try and get her to perform for the guests whenever possible. I'd texted her earlier because the regular guitar player had called in sick. It was a great opportunity but I figured she'd ignore me, in spite of how it had gone when she'd done the sing-a-long with the kids. I was delighted that she'd decided to perform.

"She told me you guys have been spending time together," Tilly said. "I'm glad you're feeling better about her. I keep trying to get her to talk about college, but she won't tell me much. I know she's enrolled somewhere, but I think she wants to take a year off. I'm wondering if there's any sort of music program we can get her into, because maybe she'd be more interested then."

Margaret walked down the sand, wearing a white dress that billowed around her like smoke. The beach was crowded and I could see her anxiety growing as she regarded the big crowd.

"I got her that dress," Tilly said. "Doesn't she look fabulous?"

"Really good," I said, getting to my feet. "I'm going to go say hi. Do you want to come?"

Tilly's husband called her over for something. "I'll catch up with her later," Tilly said, so I headed over on my own.

"Hey," I said, smiling at Margaret. "I can't wait to hear you play."

"I hate you for this." She looked frightened behind the mock-anger.

"You don't have to do it," I said. "But I'm going to tell you something. There is not a person on this beach who has even an ounce of your talent. You are giving us a gift by letting us hear you. So, have fun, enjoy the beautiful night, and while you play, think about the fact that there are people here who are going to wake up in the middle of the night with your music in their head."

Margaret swallowed hard but didn't look as angry. "This better not end up on YouTube," she muttered. "I have to go find out where I'm supposed to be." She headed over to the event planner and I watched her go with a sense of pride.

I sat back down by the fire and Tristan came to join me. He was just about to say something when Margaret started to sing. Melodic and enigmatic, her soft, sweet voice rang out as gentle as the wind. The chatter died down and I could feel the crowd transition from their conversations to listening to her play.

I laid my head against Tristan's shoulder, watching as Tilly snuggled up to her husband, and Leo with his wife. Even the blonde girl was there with Saxon, and we all listened to Margaret sing as the fire popped and crackled. It was a perfect night and I was so glad Tristan was there to experience it.

"Chase is really missing out," Tilly said, at one point.

Leo looked at me. "Yeah," he said. "I think he'd agree with you on that one."

*

The weekend with Tristan had been so healing. Somehow, we managed to cram an entire summer into two days. We'd biked, hiked, fished, camped, rafted, and made the most of every moment together.

It had been perfect, but the thing that nagged at the back of my mind was the idea that we hadn't dealt with any of our real issues. Tristan and I needed to sit down and discuss some of the more difficult topics that we'd been avoiding, like the fact that we needed to figure out how to support one another during the hard times instead of pulling away.

The short time I'd spent at Wood Violet had already reminded me that I was strong and self-sufficient, and I deserved to be treated that way. It was a conversation I did not look forward to having, because it had felt so great to let all that go and just enjoy having him here, without going too deep. There was a moment I almost brought up our issues but then I changed my mind. What was the point? We'd agreed that we were going to work to make things better. Rather than revisiting the past, wouldn't it be better to keep moving forward?

Monday morning, I returned to work with bleary eyes and a sense of peace. I brought Nikki a pastry from breakfast as a peace offering for not calling her when my father had asked me to. It had completely slipped my mind.

Setting an enormous cinnamon roll on her desk, I said, "I'm so sorry that I didn't call. My husband came to town unexpectedly and is staying through the fourth of July, so it's been busy."

"Julie, thank you," she said, touching the plate with the pastry. Then, she reached into a desk drawer and pulled out a large portfolio. "It wasn't urgent. I'd just wanted to give you this. It's my portfolio. I brought this in because I thought that if you could see a timeline of my work, it might help you see where we've been and where I'd like to take us. No rush, but it might help."

I was so surprised that I just stood there, holding the large folder.

"This is your home and your family's resort," she said. "I'll always be on the outside. But if you see some of the things that I've done, you might have a better understanding of what I can do."

"It's not necessary," I said, embarrassed. "But thank you. I'll take a look at it tonight."

It had been almost a week since she'd confronted me about the issue with the flat-screens. The fact that she was upset enough to hand me her professional history was a concern. I knew that Nikki had done so many great things for my family and for the resort, because my father had told me. I didn't want her to feel like she had to prove it to me, especially since I would only be at Wood Violet for a short time.

"Hey," I said, after I'd returned to my desk and we'd worked a couple of minutes in silence. "I've been thinking a lot about your idea about weddings. Do you have a half hour or so to come look at something with me? I was thinking that the area by the abandoned cabins might be a good spot for a venue, and I wanted to get your take."

"Let's get a golf cart," she said, her voice suddenly cheerful. "Business casual and humidity don't mix."

I drove the golf cart over the bumpy path, and Nikki hung onto the bar on the side, the breeze blowing back her hair.

"I'm so happy that you're considering weddings," she said. "The revenue potential is incredible. I have so many charts and statistics that go in depth about it, but if we were to open ourselves up to the industry, it would also be a ridiculous amount of free advertising. People post their pictures and link to the site and even if someone wasn't planning a wedding, it will build an awareness of Wood Violet. I can't think of one negative thing when it comes to stepping into this industry."

"I can think of a lot," I said. "We haven't done it before because wedding parties are so high maintenance and the stays are short. Plus, they'll crowd out our main area—and did I mention high maintenance…"

"But by putting the venue back here, we could eliminate the crowding." Nikki nodded. "That's smart."

We crested the hill and she sucked in a breath. "It's unbelievable back here. I haven't been here in years."

The squirrels chattered in the trees and the birds tweeted. It was like they all knew they were on display. With the beautiful canopy of trees and the gentle rush of the river, it really was an ideal spot and the type of place I would have loved to have said forever. Maybe one day, I could convince Tristan to come here to renew our vows.

Nikki slid on a pair of sunglasses and clucked her tongue, looking at the cabins. "Those two on the end are in good shape." She pointed at my grandmother's studio and the cabin Margaret had been hiding out in. "It would be a quick project to knock down those three, and in their place build a rustic, outdoor structure to allow for the ceremony. Open-air, but I'm sure we could do it so there's something lovely to pull down on the sides if it rains."

"What about the receptions?" I asked.

Nikki gave me an apologetic look. "They would have to be in the main area. Unless we built a separate storage area out of view to make it easy to transport the tables, chairs and sound equipment. Then there's the issue of the food, keeping out the bugs and mosquitoes, bathrooms…" She thought for a minute. "Unless…"

"What?" I asked, because her face had a tiny smile.

"Let's knock down a few trees. Build a small lodge for the reception."

Nikki pointed at an area by the edge of the river where the clearing stopped and the forest started. For a split second, I could imagine the whole thing. Couples exchanging vows at sunset by the river, and a small building that would light up at night like a cathedral. It could be the perfect oasis in the forest, to celebrate the newlyweds.

"I have chills," I said, showing her the goosebumps on my arms.

Nikki clasped her hands. "This might be the answer." There was an extra swing in her step as we returned to the golf cart. "It's remote enough that weddings wouldn't disrupt anything on site, but it would be a magical setting. The biggest problem I see is pest control."

"Let's talk to a mosquito company. Spray often," I suggested. "That would do it, I think."

"Julie, I have to tell you, I am so excited. Weddings at Wood Violet is a concept I've been thinking about for ages and I think it would be a dream. Let's talk to your father and see what he says." Before she turned the key in the golf cart, she gave me a sidelong look. "I'm really sorry about the way I acted."

"Don't be," I told her. "I completely understand."

Even though I wouldn't be here for long, it was nice to feel like I had a voice at the resort. It would help immensely if Nikki and I were on the same page, and I could help move forward the projects that would lead to the greater good. Knowing that things were on the right track, that the place I loved most in the world had the ability to thrive, would make it so much easier when it was time to go back to my real life.

High on the success of our site visit, I flipped through Nikki's portfolio later that night. Tristan had fallen asleep, since he planned to get up and run at five. I intended to join him, not because I wanted to but because I wanted to be a supportive partner. Still, I wanted to take a few minutes to look at her work because I wanted to give her that respect.

The social media section in her portfolio was interesting, mainly because she was responsible for building Wood Violet an online platform that hadn't existed before she came on board. I read through the presentation with interest, sipping on red wine. When I got to the section where Nikki had highlighted a campaign that had gone viral, I nearly dropped my glass.

I stared at the words for nearly a full minute before they fully sank in.

Did you leave your memories at Wood Violet? Locked memory box discovered beneath the floorboards of a cabin.

The resort had run a three-month campaign trying to find the owner of a memory box. There had been thousands of likes and interactions, and several discussions about what people had put in their memory boxes the year my grandmother had handed them out, as well as photographs of the people that had hung onto them. My grandmother would have been so pleased, but all I could think about was the Chase connection.

What if it was his box?

Chase and I had missed the entire thing since we weren't on social media back when this had happened. Tilly wouldn't have known to pay any attention. But there was the discovery, plain as day. He could finally get the opportunity to have one final, tangible moment with the pieces of history that he and his brother had selected to leave in the box and maybe, as a result, the chance to heal. I took a long drink of my wine, the redcurrant sharp on my tongue.

It had been a few years since the viral post and it was possible Nikki had thrown the box away, but I imagined she would have taken the step to break open the lock and see what was inside, before giving up on it entirely. She would have posted the contents online, and made that part of the topic, but since she didn't, I was willing to bet it was still in storage.

I went out into the living room and called her. It was a few minutes before ten, so I assumed she'd put my call to voicemail. Instead, she picked right up.

"This is Nikki." Her tone was as professional as it was in the office.

"It's Julie," I said. "Sorry to call so late, but I've been sitting here looking at your portfolio and there are several things that I found so impressive but one thing really stood out. I wanted to ask you, do you still have the memory box listed in your viral campaign?"

I held my breath, waiting for her answer.

"Oh gosh." The warmth in her voice made me feel like we'd officially moved past the issue with the flat-screens, and were headed back towards being friends. "I'm sure we still have it. I don't know where; I'd have to look."

"You don't think it got thrown away?" I asked.

"Doubt it. Why?" Her tone was curious. "Did you think we should do something further with that? It was a big campaign. It got a lot of attention, so we might be able to get traction on it again, if we took a new angle."

I looked out the window at the lake. The moon was high, a small crescent above the water. "No, it's not that. I think I know who it belongs to. I'm hopeful, at least."

"You do?" She let out a little shriek of excitement. "Julie, we searched for the owner like crazy. Everyone wanted to open it, but I was like, no. It has to be opened by the person who took the time to hide it in the cabin. I can't believe this. Whose is it?"

I thought of how depressed Chase had looked at the bonfire. I couldn't stand the idea of seeing him upset like that again, so I wanted to be cautious with this.

"Let me ask you something—do you know which cabin it was found in?" I asked. "There were so many memory boxes handed out. Really, it could have belonged to anyone."

"I do know." Her voice was confident. "It was hidden in one of the cabins in the woods by the river. Right where we were looking at the wedding site."

It had to be the box Chase and Garrett had hidden. Those cabins had been shut down by the turn of the century, other than the one my grandmother had used as her studio, and Chase had mentioned how much time he and his brother had spent back there.

"Then yes, I think I do know," I said, heart pounding. "I'll have to check in with him, but I wanted to get the information, first."

"Check in with who?" she practically squealed. "Tell me who it is!"

Nikki's excitement unnerved me. It made sense that she was delighted to see this through but to her, it was a successful PR campaign. To me, it was something beautiful, painful, but most of all, private.

"I'll tell you, but I need you to keep it quiet. It's one of guests who came here for years when he was younger. Chase Gibbs? He's the owner of…"

"Yes, of course." I could practically hear her nod. "People will love this story. The young, handsome ice-cream heir, returning to his roots. Do you think his brother can make it in to look through it with him?"

"No." I ran my hand over the back of the couch, the fabric rough against my skin. "His brother died last year."

Nikki was silent. "That is so tragic," she said quietly.

I moved to the kitchen and put my glass in the sink. "It will be important to let Chase have this moment. It's a delicate situation and he won't want it splashed all over our social media pages."

"That seems like a wasted opportunity," Nikki said. "This could make the local news, even statewide; the story's so good. It would be positive PR for his ice-cream company, too."

"No." The word came out firm. "This is his life, not a PR opportunity."

"I hear you." She sounded disappointed. "Well, I'll see if I can find it, okay?"

"Thank you. Hey, and Nikki?" I thought of her portfolio, and all of the things it showed that she'd done for the resort. "I wanted to say thank you for everything that you've done for my family. It was fun seeing all that in your portfolio and I wanted to let you know that I appreciate you."

"Thank you." I could hear the smile in her voice. "That means a lot."

I wished her a good night and we hung up. Heading back to the bedroom, I crawled into the bed with Tristan, watching him shift and turn over at the movement. I squeezed my pillow tight and said a quick prayer that the memory box hadn't been lost, and that it would be everything Chase was looking for.

Every part of me wanted to call him to share the good news, but I wanted to make sure it hadn't been tossed out, first. Like with Margaret, the disappointment would be too great if things didn't go according to plan. Still, I had high hopes that Chase would finally get reunited with his memories and find the closure he'd been looking for.

I wished I could do the same for Margaret. Now that I had gotten to know her, it was clear that she had come for information, and nothing more. I wanted to find a way to contact Ivelisse and, if I did, I planned to tell Margaret everything. Then, she'd have the information she needed to decide whether or not to make the choice to pursue the past.

CHAPTER TWENTY-ONE

The next morning, Tristan picked up food from the dining hall on the way back from his run. I'd meant to run with him but had been so cozy in bed that I couldn't bring myself to get up.

"If this makes me a terrible wife, please tell me," I had said, from beneath one of the pillows. "I'll get up and go."

Tristan had just laughed, so I went back to sleep. When I woke up, he'd brought me coffee and an egg sandwich with avocado.

"So, I saw that girl." He settled back into the bed with a plate of egg whites and a fruit smoothie. "The one who was singing on the beach? She was having breakfast."

"Margaret," I said, wiping salt onto a napkin. "Did you talk to her?"

"No." He took a drink of water. "She's talented. What do you know about her?"

"Not much," I admitted. "The things I told you about the rocky relationship with her stepdad and that her mother kicked her out. I can't find her online, even though I have her driver's license information, probably because she doesn't use her real name on her social media accounts."

"Did you google her mother?" Tristan asked. "That might give you some insight into her family, what her life has been like."

"I don't know her name."

Tristan grimaced. "Why didn't you ask?"

"There's no way Margaret would tell me."

He sighed. "This doesn't sit well with me, Julie. You've got a homeless girl living in the midst of a high-end resort. You're spending time with her alone. It makes me nervous. There's no accountability there."

"She's harmless," I said.

He gave me a look. "How do you know that?"

I thought back to that first day, the way she'd lost it in the forest, pulling on the tree branches and screaming. I had no doubt it was a result of hunger, fear, and frustration, but it did add weight to Tristan's concerns. That, coupled with the fact that I was positive she'd broken into the main office. But I trusted my instincts, and I knew Margaret was a good person.

Tristan was silent. Then, he said, "Let me see a copy of her ID."

I pulled up the picture of her license on my phone and showed him.

He typed something into the search engine, then held up his phone. "*Voilà.* Property value, listed by address. It includes the name of the homeowners, so here are the names of Margaret's parents."

"I'm… impressed," I said, typing in her mother's name. She popped right up on social media, a small blonde with a neat pageboy haircut. Tristan clicked through the pictures. "There's your girl," he said, pointing.

Margaret stood with her guitar over her shoulder, smiling at the camera in front of a small coffee shop. The caption read, *So proud to hear her play.*

"That's sad," I said. "It sounds like she was so supportive before the stepdad showed up."

Tristan kept searching, then laughed. "Yeah. Well, take a look at this."

He handed me the phone.

He'd found a photo of Margaret's mother, decked out in a sparkling white dress and holding hands with a kind-looking, bespectacled man. The two stood beaming in front of a dazzling cake lit with candles.

I frowned. "Is that their wedding?"

"Nope. This picture was taken two weeks ago," he said. "It's their anniversary party. Funny thing, though…" Tristan zoomed in on the cake. In ornate fondant, it read: *Happy 25th Anniversary.* "The cruel 'stepdad' might be sad to learn his new bride is already married. Or maybe not, considering he doesn't exist."

I marched up the steps at Margaret's house and banged on the door with every ounce of fury I had in me. Her face was etched in attitude when she opened the door, but her expression turned fearful when she saw me.

"What's wrong with you?" she asked. "Who's that guy?"

Tristan stood at the bottom of the steps, his arms crossed. "I'm her husband."

Even though I was stunned by what we'd found online, I'd made Tristan promise to let me talk to Margaret alone. He'd agreed on the condition that he could stand outside in case she got aggressive at the confrontation, and I needed his help.

"Start talking," I said, walking past her and taking a seat on the couch. "I want the whole story. The real story."

Margaret's neck went blotchy. "What do you mean?"

"You know what I mean." I glared at her. "You told me your stepdad punched you in the face and your mother kicked you out. So, how is it possible that I just found a social media site with pictures of your perfectly delightful parents, who recently celebrated their twenty-fifth wedding anniversary, and can't wait for you to return home from the road trip of a lifetime?"

Margaret's face flushed. "Please don't be mad at me."

"I'm not mad," I told her. "I'm scared."

This was the exact thing I'd been afraid of, that day when we'd found her camped out in the cabins. Being conned. When she didn't respond, I headed for the door, which made Margaret burst into sobs again.

"Don't go." She pulled at my arm. "Please, Julie."

It was the *please* that got me. Margaret would never say it unless she really meant it. Still, I rested my hand on the doorknob and refused to budge.

"Start talking," I said. "Now."

Margaret sat down on the couch and stared down at her hands for a full minute. Then, in a low tone, she said, "I was raised by the best parents in the world. Not a stepdad; my parents have been married for years."

"Yes, they looked very happy at their anniversary party," I said.

"Please just listen." Her voice shook, but she kept talking. "I had a great childhood. I had birthday parties, bicycle rides, and the opportunity to make lots of friends. My life was pretty much charmed up until six months ago when…" She bit her lip. "I needed my social security card to complete this scholarship application. My mom was out playing tennis, my dad was still at work, and I couldn't find it anywhere. So, I went into the files she keeps in her room and I found…" Her eyes filled with tears and the realization hit me.

"The adoption papers," I said.

She nodded, tears rolling down her cheeks. I hesitated, but finally went to join her on the couch.

"You didn't know?" I asked quietly.

"No clue." She blew her nose. "People have told me my entire life that I have my dad's smile, or my mom's sense of humor. There has never been one moment, not one, that I'd even considered the idea."

"So you ran away?" I guessed.

I didn't agree with the decision her parents had made to keep the adoption a secret but at the same time, I was surprised Margaret chose to run. She seemed so much braver than that, willing to look a problem in the eye and solve it. Or, at least, be incredibly rude to it.

"No, I didn't run away." She tugged at a small tangle in her hair. "My parents think I'm on the road trip. My friends are actually forwarding me their scenery pictures so that I can send them to my parents and it's…" Her voice went cold. "It's as easy to deceive them as it was for them to deceive me. I want to find my biological parents for the purpose of finding that piece of my history, I guess. I don't know. Wood Violet seemed like a good place to start and, really, it's been a nice place to be, as I've adjusted to the fact that I've spent every day of my life being lied to."

I didn't know what to say. There was the obvious response that her parents must have had their reasons and that she should still consider them her parents, since they raised her. At the same time, I couldn't imagine what it would feel like to think that you were someone's biological daughter only to learn it wasn't true.

I had so many questions about the situation that I could only imagine the scenarios that had run through Margaret's head.

"I came here hoping to find some sort of an answer," Margaret said, rubbing her eyes. "Instead, I've spent my time lying to you. I told you that story about my stepdad because I was tired, I was hungry, I was scared. You would have kicked me out, but I needed to be here, and besides, I didn't have anywhere else to go. I had no idea you would give me all this." She gestured at the cabin. "By then, it was too late to tell the truth. I'm really sorry."

"Did you break into the main office?" I asked. "Looking for information?"

"I thought I could find something about my birth mother. It was stupid, and if you want me to pay for the window, I will."

The fact that Margaret not only confessed but offered to pay impressed me.

"Thank you. But no, you don't have to do that," I told her. "I do want you to understand the seriousness of the lie that you told, though. Margaret, I know women who have gone through abuse and then suffered repercussions for speaking up. It's hard for me to take it lightly that you lied about something so serious."

"I didn't mean to," she said. "It was in this book I'd just read and I just blurted it out." She looked down at the floor. "It was wrong. I'm really sorry."

"You don't have to apologize to me," I said. "I think we've said sorry to each other enough, don't you?"

She gave me a watery smile. "Yeah. This place saved me." The catch in her voice made me fear she might burst out crying again. "Thank you."

"What can I do to help you from here?" I asked.

"Let me stay." She pulled her hair up, sending the scent of grape-scented hair spray in my direction. "It's helped me so much, to get over some of the anger I felt about the fact that they'd lied to me. I've been journaling and writing songs, and I'm just…" She squeezed her hands. "I'm still so mad about it, you know?"

"I'd be furious," I admitted. "You seem pretty calm, really."

My watch lit up. Tristan.

"Hold on. It's my husband."

"I thought that other guy was your husband," she said. "Chase.'"

"No." My cheeks went hot. "Why did you think that?"

"I don't know," she said. "It's the way that he looks at you."

I really hoped Tristan wasn't listening at the window.

"We're friends," I said, my voice firm.

Now that Chase was on my mind, I wished I could tell him about what had happened with Margaret, but he hadn't answered his phone the last few times I'd called. I hoped he hadn't fallen into a depression about his brother or I feared that he actually was angry with me about the way Tristan had acted. Either way, I planned to stop by his cabin to check on him if I didn't hear back soon.

"Now, are you going to tell your parents you're searching for your birth mother?"

She stretched her feet out. They were ensconced in thick, white socks that looked cozy. "Not yet. It's too awkward. My parents built their life around me. I'm really going to come at them and be like, oh, you're so terrible because you didn't tell me I'm adopted and now I'm looking for my mother?" She looked down and for a second, I was worried she might start to cry again. "I feel like I shouldn't be so mad at them, but I am."

"You have every right to feel your feelings," I said. "I'd be pretty upset to discover that the story of my family was more complicated than I was led to believe." I fiddled with my wedding ring. "Sometimes, though, you've got to listen to your gut. Something made you come here. You should see it through."

She lifted her chin. "You're going to let me stay?"

"I'd hate to see you go," I said, and she tackled me in a tight hug.

"Thank you," she said. "You don't know how much this means to me."

"Can I make one request?" I asked. "I'd like to continue to keep this between you and me, for now. It's odd that your birth mother listed Wood Violet as her address. I want to know what that means before we start broadcasting it, in order to protect the business."

I was still struggling with the idea that I had been searching for her mother without her, but I still wasn't ready to tell her. The fact that she had lied about her adoptive mother served as a reminder that she was still so young. I wasn't confident that Margaret could handle it if I found Ivelisse and it turned out that she was not interested in getting to know her at all.

"No problem," Margaret said. "I'm still so confused about it all that I'd rather people didn't know."

"I'm sorry all this happened to you," I finally said. "The good news is that it brought you here, and I had a chance to meet you."

Margaret rolled her eyes. "You have such a gift for making things awkward."

But when she thought I wasn't looking, she smiled.

Tristan couldn't believe I'd let her stay. He grumbled and complained the entire walk back to our cabin. "It's reckless." He walked so fast it was hard to keep up. "She's going to cause nothing but trouble."

"I disagree," I said. "I'm less afraid of her now than I have been this entire time. I don't think she's here to cause trouble, I think she's here because she wants to find her birth mother but has no idea how to do that."

The day was bright and cheerful, with dragonflies flitting about and bullfrogs calling down by the water. I was relieved to know that Margaret had finally shared the whole story but I could see why Tristan was concerned. Her lie had been so convincing and really, she probably would have kept it going if she hadn't been caught. I just needed to keep a close watch on her, and go from there.

"I think she's fine," I told Tristan. "Otherwise, I wouldn't let her stay."

"Your father deserves to know the risk," Tristan said.

"I've been dealing with Margaret this whole time. Now that I know the whole story, I really do think she's a good person."

"Julie, this is bad judgment. It's the same type of thing that happened with your job. You decided it was going to be fine, but it wasn't, was it?"

The words stung, but I was not about to fight. The sun brightened the leaves on the trees around me, and the pine needles were on display like jewels. It was a beautiful day, and I wanted to focus on that.

"I hear your concern," I told him. "But sometimes you have to trust me."

His jaw pulsed. "It's not easy to do that when I see you make decisions like this."

We walked in silence back to the cabin, and I looked at my watch. I'd planned on going to the office after lunch but to be honest, I didn't feel like being around Tristan if he was going to act like this. It was better to get my work done now and maybe, by the time I came back, he'd be in a better mood.

"Let's talk about it later," I said. "I've got to get to work."

He had already headed up the steps. "Sounds good," he said, and the door clicked shut behind him.

"I have good news and bad news," Nikki said, the moment I walked in. It was nice to see a cheerful face, especially since I'd spent the walk over wondering whether or not Tristan was right, and that I did, in fact, make bad decisions.

"What's the good news?" I asked.

"You were supposed to pick the bad news first," she said, laughing. "So, I haven't found the memory box, but I have put together a presentation for your father about our proposed wedding venue. Would you like to see it?"

My mind was still on Tristan and the way his mood had changed the moment I didn't agree to do what he wanted. It had happened a lot during our marriage, and I hadn't let it bother me until now. It wasn't right to think that the only way we could get along was at the expense of me having an opinion. I was tempted to call and tell him that, but it would just start a fight.

"True love." My voice was thick with irony. "The very thing I want to think about."

Even though I wasn't in the mood to think about weddings, Nikki's presentation sucked me right in. She set it up in the conference room with its rustic wooden walls and floors, which made the pictures of the proposed site by the river all the more appealing. The presentation was beautiful, informative, and had a step-by-step plan to make us competitive in the wedding industry. Not to mention the perfect sprinkling of wedding music to jazz up each slide.

"That was amazing," I told her, once the presentation was over. "Let's get my father in here now so he can see this. It's lunch, so he should be free."

She beamed. "Let's do it. I've been talking with him about weddings for ages now. It might make more of an impression upon him if he can see the facts and figures behind it."

I called him and sure enough, he was headed to his office with an egg salad sandwich in hand. "We'll just take ten minutes of your time," I promised him, and gave Nikki the thumbs-up.

While we waited, Nikki said, "So, I spent a good half hour looking for the memory box this morning." She cued the slide show back to the beginning. "It's frustrating because I remember having it here in the office for the longest time. Eventually, we had to find somewhere to tuck it."

"Who do you think finally put it away?" I asked, running my hand over the bumpy surface of the wooden conference table. "Maybe my mother…"

Nikki snapped her fingers. "Pria!"

"Huh?" I said.

"Pria was here at that time." She grabbed for her phone. "I bet she would know!" Nikki sent a text and grinned at me. "I totally forgot about that. Pria was our intern."

"We've never had interns," I said, confused.

"Never say never," she sang. "One of the big-deal guests needed their kid to have an internship for a college application, so I got the whole thing approved. The girl worked like, one hour three times a week, while her family was on vacation. I remember feeling uncomfortable because she made me do an on-camera interview about the memory box."

"I bet you did great," I said, taking a seat in one of the chairs. "Do you think she put it somewhere?"

Nikki nodded. "One of her projects was organizing the office, so I bet she found some great spot for it that we will never find without a map."

My father walked in, looking rushed but interested. "What's this I hear about a plan to make us a fortune?" He headed towards the table and took a seat, unwrapping his sandwich at the same time.

Nikki didn't waste a moment, just drew the shades and started her presentation. The facts and figures about the potential profit in the wedding industry seemed to pique my father's interest and when she got to the part about the location, he gave a vigorous nod.

When the presentation was over, Nikki brought up the lights and took a seat at the table. "What works and what doesn't?" she asked, fingers poised over her laptop.

My father was still staring at the screen, even though it was blank. "Those facts and figures are accurate?" he asked, turning to her.

"Yes. I started researching this two years ago. It's accurate."

My father looked at me. "I think we've found our solution."

I rushed over and hugged him tight. "You think so?"

He nodded. "Yes. If these numbers are right, I know so."

Nikki's mouth dropped open. "You mean… we can really do this?"

"Dad, there's a ton we'd have to handle before we could break ground but if you're willing, let's get the plans in place," I said. "If we're quick, we could begin construction late October and book our first wedding next spring."

"Go for it," my father said. "If those numbers really are accurate, we should have been doing this for the past twenty years. Nikki, are you going to head this up?"

I looked at her and she smiled.

"I'd love to."

CHAPTER TWENTY-TWO

I spent the rest of the afternoon buried in resort administration, followed by research about wedding venues. The more that I learned about the wedding industry, the more I saw an opportunity. If Nikki and I spent the next few months planning this out, there was a real possibility that Wood Violet's financial problems would be a thing of the past. I could imagine working with her side by side, booking the events, ironing out the details, and setting the stage for weddings that would create memories to last a lifetime.

It was late when I finally made it back to the cabin. I hoped Tristan was in a better mood, because I was more than ready to order in some food and talk out some of our problems. The silence between us had gone on long enough and it was impossible to spend an entire day working on weddings, without wanting to do everything possible to ensure my marriage was where it needed to be.

But just as I walked in, he was wheeling his suitcase towards the door.

"What are you doing?" I asked, coming to a full stop on the porch.

His face split into a huge smile. "Julie, I'm this close to being offered the VP role at Baker and Bromley. I had my third interview last week."

The high-end financial firm was well known in the city, and the opportunity, huge.

I was at a loss for words. "Why didn't you tell me this was happening?"

"I wanted it to be a real possibility." His chest was puffed out, and he seemed focused in that way he got right before he finished a workout. "I've never said no to taking a meeting with other companies if there was potential there, but I didn't expect anything out of this. Then, they asked me back and asked me back again. They called ten minutes ago, and want me to have drinks with the main guys tomorrow. It's a compatibility test, I have no doubt."

"But the Fourth is the next day," I said. "You'll come back, right?"

Tristan hesitated. "Let me just see how this goes."

For the first time all summer, I was tempted to go back to the city. Tristan and I had made such great strides here that I hated to see him go, especially when we could have spent the holiday together.

"Should I come back for a few days?" I asked. "For support?"

"To Chicago? Nah." He grabbed the handle of his suitcase and rolled it onto the porch. "My mind will be there and you've got stuff going on here. It's fine."

It wasn't fine, not for me, but I'd pushed so hard to stay here that it wouldn't make sense to push to go back.

"I had the best weekend with you." Tristan cupped my face in his hands and kissed me.

I hugged him tight. "Me, too."

The image of him grabbing the handle of his suitcase and practically bounding down the steps replayed in my mind as I sat on the sofa, looking out at the water. Our time together had been great, with the exception of our fight that morning, but somehow, that was the image that stuck with me.

*

My father was working late, so I decided to join my mother for dinner. We ordered pizza, which was her favorite, and sat out on the back porch as we waited for it to arrive. The rhythmic chirp of the bugs echoed across the lake through the screen and I tried to match their sense of calm.

"I found a sales deed," she said.

I looked at her. "Huh?"

"The thing I burned."

"A sales deed?" I echoed. Then, I got it. "Dad had signed off on selling some of the land. You found the papers and burned them."

She nodded, putting her hand to her head. "I don't want to sell."

"You won't have to." My voice was firm. "Nikki and I have a whole plan for weddings and we're confident it will bring in the revenue we need."

"That is wonderful. Did you have a nice time with Tristan?" she asked, her words slow and halting.

It was the most I'd heard her say at once since the stroke. The achievement made my throat get tight, and I gave her a spontaneous hug.

"What for?" she asked, laughing.

"Because I love you."

Moths fluttered their wings against the screen and I sat back in my seat on the glider. It had been there forever, and was covered in a floral pattern. When I was a child, I liked to trace the swirling, black stem of each flower, one at a time.

"It was good." I took a drink of water, the precipitation on the side of the glass wet on my hand. It was hot and muggy, but I didn't feel like getting up to turn on the fan. "I've always wanted to spend time with him here like that, but we've never done it."

"Why?" my mother asked.

"Our work schedules didn't match. When they did, Tristan always wanted to take these big, lavish trips. He convinced me it would be our last chance to do things like that before we had kids."

The moment the words were out of my mouth, I regretted them, because my mother's face lit up. I'd never told her about the miscarriages. I would one day, but I didn't want her to get upset.

"Soon?" she asked.

The look of hope on her face changed my mind. "No," I said. "I don't think so."

"Julie," she said, but I held up my hand.

"Before you tell me I'm not getting any younger, I want you to know that I've lost two pregnancies so far," I said, careful to keep my voice steady. "Tristan has not supported me through it and I'm scared to keep trying. I have handled it all by myself, and Mom, it's been…"

She sniffled and immediately, I regretted my words.

"Don't cry." I was mad at myself for sharing such a sensitive topic at a time like this. "I'm sorry, I shouldn't have said anything. I just didn't want you to wonder what was taking so long."

My mother reached out with her good hand and gripped my chin. Turning my face towards hers, she made me look at her. "I love you," she said. "You are never alone."

I tried to avoid her gaze, to fight back the sorrow that had dug deep and rooted itself into my bones, but I couldn't. The memory of the pain that had cut through me in those first moments when I knew something had gone wrong nearly knocked me down. My mother pulled me in close, her good arm strong and sure. I broke, sobbing into her shoulder.

"You are not alone." She rubbed my back in firm strokes. "I am here."

The darkness of the night surrounded the porch on all sides. I held my mother as tight as I could, leaning into her shoulder and breathing in the strength of her love. I wondered what I had been doing, what I had been thinking, trying to carry this burden on my own. My mother had always been there, waiting for me, to find the way back home.

Nikki called me early the next morning when I was in the shower, and left me a message that sounded urgent.

"Julie, can you come to the office as soon as possible," she said. "I have something I'd like to show you right away."

Her tone had been intense on the message, and I hoped that she'd found the memory box. I skipped breakfast and went straight in.

"Did you find the memory box?" I asked, rushing into the office.

Nikki's pretty face looked troubled, and she shut the door behind us. "I was worried you'd think that was it. No, not yet. I've been looking all over for the memory box, and this morning, I stumbled across a box of your grandmother's things." She frowned. "It was in the bottom drawer of this old metal desk in the basement area. There wasn't a key, so I picked the lock. Isn't that awful?"

"It's resourceful." I didn't understand why she looked so panicked. Surely, she didn't think I'd be mad about her looking in the box? "What was in there?"

"Well…" Nikki twisted a strand of hair tightly around her finger, then let it drop. "It turned out to be a stack of old journals, but they weren't personal, more like bird-watching logs and things like that."

Boring, but at least it was a new connection to my grandmother. My grandfather was due back before too long and he might appreciate seeing them, as he and my grandmother used to go bird-watching together.

"There was something in there that concerned me. Some letters addressed to your grandmother." Nikki took a sip of coffee. "I opened one because I wanted to know whether they were trash or what."

"It's not a big deal," I said. "My dad and my grandfather will be happy to have anything that's connected to her."

"I don't know about that."

"Why?" Her tone made my stomach tighten. "Nikki, what's wrong?"

"Julie, I only read the first paragraph and then I stopped. It's pretty clear this was a private issue. I don't know any specifics, but I do know these letters are for your eyes, not mine. They probably don't matter, maybe it's the vitriol of an angry guest or employee, but I'd prefer you be the judge of that."

Reaching into her drawer, she pulled out three envelopes and handed them to me. They did not have a return address but the postmark was from Chicago, and dated eighteen years ago.

My mouth went dry. The letters could have been anything but I could see it in Nikki's face. Whatever they said was not good.

"I'm sorry," she told me. "Maybe I should have thrown them out. But if something like this had to do with my family, I'd want to know."

The bench on the Hut was already warm from the heat of the day, and I settled into the wood with a feeling of apprehension. I'd checked the signature at the bottom of the first letter before leaving the office and it was signed I.K. There was no doubt in my mind that they were from Ivelisse.

Even though Chase had been along with me for this journey, I didn't even consider reaching out to him. We still hadn't had a chance to talk since the bonfire and besides, Nikki's reaction to what she'd seen frightened me. The letter could reveal secrets about my grandmother, the resort, or even Margaret. I wanted to know exactly what they said before sharing them with anyone.

Letting out a breath, I opened the first envelope and started to read. Three sentences in, I could see why Nikki had been horrified.

Geraldine,

I write to you with a plea. The decision you made to protect your family at the expense of mine has haunted me since the day you took my very breath, my very life, and stole it from me. The wicked will always be revealed but they can be saved.

My heart beats outside of my body, somewhere without me, and yet you live on. The threats that you made to me, the lies that you told, will one day face a reckoning.

Forgiveness is sweet, though, and you may still right this wrong. I'm begging you, Geraldine. Return her to me.

I.K.

I stared down at the page, feeling sick inside. I read the letter countless times, trying to decipher its meaning but the final sentence was clear enough to give me chills.

Return her to me.

The lake sparkled in front of me in a distant place, far from the fear racing through my veins. This letter implied that my grandmother had taken Ivelisse's child. That was impossible, though. Margaret was adopted through legitimate means, and the law firm that arranged it was more than reputable.

With trembling hands, I pulled out the next letter, careful to put the first under my leg so that it didn't drop into the water.

The edge of the dock was at least three feet away but I was not about to risk it.

Geraldine,

You ignored my past letter. Did you receive it? Please contact me. I will be waiting to hear from you.

There is nothing that can change the hurt that I caused you. I'm sorry for what I did, that I caused so much pain in your family.

My mistake should not be punished so harshly, as this is unjust. You have me trapped. Have mercy, I beg of you. I would give anything to see her again, so name your price.

I.K.

Did my grandmother have her contact information or was it listed somewhere on the letter or envelope? I flipped over the two letters I'd read, looking for a phone number and then, studied each envelope, praying to find a return address, but there was no information at all. Quickly, I opened the final letter.

Geraldine,

I have received your threat. I will no longer contact you. I would give anything, everything to protect my daughter and that's what I have done, and will do. I know you understand that, because you have done the same on your end. But I tell you this: you will weep at night, and long past the time I am gone, my memory will wail outside your window. In your heart, you will never forget the pain that you have caused and perhaps then, you will salvage the wreckage you have wrought. When you do, I will be waiting.

I.K.

The words were like a knife through my heart. There was nothing that said it flat out, but it was clear. My grandmother had taken Margaret away from her mother, in spite of the fact that Ivelisse had begged and pleaded to be by her side.

I didn't understand how it happened, or why, but the very idea that my grandmother could have done something so unspeakable was hard to process. If these words were true, my grandmother was not the person I had believed her to be. It made me wonder if the same was true for the rest of my family.

Did they know? Was this story common knowledge and my grandfather had played dumb when I asked him about an adoption? I didn't want to believe that but it was possible. Margaret had grown up believing one thing about her family, only to discover that the truth had been hidden, and the same thing could happen to me.

My parents had made a habit of hiding uncomfortable truths from me and my sister. I could see why they'd want to keep us in the dark about this. It was painful, horrible, and I still didn't know the details.

Should I ask my father? Show him the letters and demand the truth? It was possible that he knew nothing about the situation. If that was the case, I did not want to be the one to share the news. Not with my father, not with anyone.

Did Nikki read the letters?

My shoulders tensed. No. She'd said she hadn't read them, and I had no choice but to believe her. Besides, if she had read them, it was doubtful she would have handed them over. It was more likely she would have put them back in the box, locked it, and did what she could to forget what she'd read.

I wished I could, but that wasn't an option. I had no choice but to get to the bottom of the matter, and I had to do it soon.

*

I called my sister the moment I stepped back into my cabin.

"Great timing," she said, as her image loomed to life. "Jon and the kids just went to breakfast. For once, you'll have my full attention."

"I have something I have to read to you," I said. "It's disturbing, but I need to know your thoughts."

Kate poured a bowl of cereal. "I like a little intrigue first thing in the morning."

My sister still didn't know about Margaret, so I wasn't quite sure where to begin.

"There's a lot to this story, so I'll start with the worst part first, because it all ties together." I read the three letters all in a row. When I was finished, my sister sat in stunned silence, the cereal forgotten.

"I know," I said. "You're pregnant, and I would give anything to have a child, and here I am, reading letters that indicate that our grandmother took this woman's baby." It was impossible to wrap my mind around it. "Please tell me I am reading this wrong, or that I'm imagining things."

"You're not imagining things," Kate whispered. "I'm hearing it the same way. I can't believe Grandma would do something like that. You said there was more to the story. What is it?"

I lay back on the bed and stared up at the fan rotating on the ceiling. "Do you want me to send you into early labor or did the letters already do it?"

My sister shifted her body weight to grab a couch cushion. "Please just tell me what's going on."

I looked out at the lake, hoping it would give me strength. "Long story short, a girl showed up here looking for her birth mother. She had adoption papers with Wood Violet's address and a sketch of a pregnant woman that had been drawn by Grandma. I showed the sketch to Claude, and she said the woman had gotten fired. There was a scandal."

Kate peered at me. "You think the woman who wrote the letters is the one in the sketch?"

"Yes," I said. "I think she's Margaret's mother. Margaret is living in the artist-in-residence cabin and I have felt guilty about it every day because Dad doesn't know her history, where she came from, any of it."

"Then tell him the truth," Kate demanded. "Right now. The woman who wrote the letters could be dangerous."

"No, these letters are old. It's not like she sent them last week."

"Read me the first one again," Kate said.

My sister stopped me at the line that read: *The decision you made to protect your family at the expense of mine.*

"There was another thing like that in the final letter." She held up her hand once I'd read: *I know you understand that, because you have done the same on your end.*

Kate's face was stricken. "Julie, I think Grandma was trying to protect Dad."

I blinked. "What do you mean?"

"Think about it," she said. "Dad has always been such a flirt. He could have gotten himself in trouble with one of the employees and, rather than deal with the fall-out, our grandmother helped to cover it up."

The image of my life growing up at home flashed through my mind. Our house smelled like sweet sugar cookies and my parents kissed a greeting at the dinner table during the months the resort was closed for the season. I had no memories of my parents fighting at all.

"That's not possible," I said.

"It is possible. Grandma had to work to keep him away from the women." Kate's neck was flushed with annoyance. "The guests loved him and, more than once, he took it too far. Like, there was that time he kissed this woman whose husband owned a football team full on the lips in the middle of a dance. Everyone laughed—even her husband—because it was Dad, but Mom was furious."

"That can't be true." The room felt stifling with the window shut, and the fan did little to help. "Mom would not have allowed it."

"Julie." My sister's voice was gentle. "Mom accepted it, but that didn't mean she liked it. I'm sure our grandmother liked it even less."

"No." It was too much to consider. "There must have been some situation with a guest, probably someone married. Or what about Grandpa?"

Kate laughed. "Sure, if she could tear him away from his workbench. He wasn't exactly a ladies' man."

My grandfather was strong and stoic, focused on getting things done. He had always had a quick smile for the guests, and they respected him, but my grandmother was the one that everyone adored.

"Then I'm going back to the idea that it was a metaphor," I said. "Grandma had to protect the business, because it was our family's livelihood, so that's how she was protecting her family, like Ivelisse says in the letter. Or maybe Ivelisse changed her mind about the adoption, and decided to take it out on Grandma once she realized it was too late."

"Honey." Kate's tone was gentle. "I know you don't want to think that Dad would have done something like that, especially considering Grandma's role in it all, but people make mistakes."

"We don't have room for mistakes," I told her. "It's one thing to say that this happened almost twenty years ago but if Dad's involved, that won't matter. We live in a cancel culture, and if something like this got out, it could be a disaster for the resort." I let out a breath. "What should I do?"

"Talk to Dad." Kate picked up her spoon. "But at this point, I wouldn't expect the truth."

CHAPTER TWENTY-THREE

Even though I had a lot on my mind, I decided to attend the formal dinner in the dining hall in the hope of seeing Chase. I hadn't seen him since that night at the bonfire and I wanted to make sure that he was okay. It bothered me that he'd seemed so upset but also that I hadn't heard from him since.

I'd stopped by his cabin earlier in the day but the shades were drawn and he didn't answer the door. I wondered if he was going through a depression because of his brother. I wanted to be there for him like he'd been for me but that was impossible if I couldn't find him. If he wasn't at the dinner, one of our friends could tell me what was going on.

I swiped on some lipstick and was just about to walk out the door, when my phone lit up.

Nikki.

Dinner was in ten minutes so I sent her to voicemail. She called right back. Concerned that it was an emergency, I picked up as I headed out.

"Great news!" She sounded delighted. "I found the memory box."

"Really?" The leaves on the trees seemed to dance around me. "That's unbelievable! Where was it?"

"Pria finally got back to me and said she'd put it in the storage room. I took another look and found it in the storage tub beneath the Christmas lights."

I imagined it settled in there, hidden until the holidays. "Nikki, I can't thank you enough. The fact that you kept searching for it means so much."

"It's a little self-serving," she said. "I mean, this was my journey, too. It's a story that so many people who care about the resort were invested in, so I really want to get a few words from him, a reaction and then I'll leave him to it. Can we set up a meeting tomorrow at nine for the big reveal? I'll be here early to help get everything set up for the Fourth, but that's my first spare moment."

I hesitated. "Nikki, this is a very personal thing to him. I think it would be more appropriate if you talk to him after he's had time with it."

"I want to see his face, though," she insisted. "Julie, please. I've been living with this for years. He should be happy to talk about it. This is what he's been looking for; it will be a big moment. There's no reason to not celebrate that."

It really wouldn't hurt anything to let Nikki have her moment, especially when she'd worked so hard to find the memory box. She could have put it on the bottom of her to-do list and forgotten about it. Instead, she kept looking until she got the job done.

"Nine tomorrow," I agreed. "Thank you. Hey, one more thing. I took a look at those letters."

The hurt behind the words flashed through my mind, along with the sketch my grandmother had done. They must have been friends at some point, or my grandmother never would have used her as a subject. I wondered what my grandmother had said to Ivelisse, when she had responded to the letters.

"You did?" Nikki said.

"Yes." I paused. "They were… distressing, but I don't think it's anything to worry about. Still, I'm glad you brought it to my attention. I'm going to show them to my father to see if he wants to get in touch with the woman. If not, we'll just let it go."

"That's a relief." She sighed. "I'm glad it turned out to be nothing."

"Well, I can't wait to tell Chase you found the memory box," I said, stepping off the path from the woods into the main lawn. "He's going to be so excited."

There was a smile in her voice. "See you tomorrow at nine."

I practically raced for the dining hall. To my delight, Chase was there, settling in at a table with Saxon, Leo, and Leo's wife. The waiters had already started to set out the appetizer. It was a baked brie served with crusted sourdough, and a garnish of raspberry. It smelled phenomenal and I grabbed the chair next to Chase.

"Hi," I said. "Is this seat taken?"

Chase looked over at Leo, then back at me.

"It is," I said, suddenly feeling self-conscious. "Sorry. I'll find somewhere else."

I started to get up but he touched my arm. "No, it's fine," he said. "Stay."

The group on the other half of the table was talking about real estate and I listened to the conversation for a few minutes. Then, once it seemed like no one was paying attention, I said, "Where have you been?"

He scraped the bread into the brie and took a large bite. Then he turned to me. "Dealing with some things."

"If you ever need to talk, please reach out. I was worried about you."

Chase took a long drink of water. "Where's your husband?"

"He had to go back to the city."

Tristan was probably having drinks with the team right now. I hoped it was going well, but I had no doubt that it was. He was a natural at making small talk about big ideas, and I had never seen him at a loss for words.

"Well, I actually came here tonight because I really wanted to see you," I said, moving aside as the waiter took the small plate of brie. "I have news."

"Yeah?" The chill that had been in the air since I'd sat by Chase was starting to dissipate. "What's going on?"

My pulse quickened. "Let me preface this by saying that my grandmother passed out a lot of memory boxes."

Chase gave me his full attention. "Yeah?"

"Well, apparently there was some big viral campaign on the Wood Violet social media account about a memory box found in the floorboards of a cabin in the clearing by the river. Do you think you and Garrett would have hidden it there?"

He stared at me. His mouth moved for a moment, as if he was tempted to speak. Then he grabbed the napkin from his lap and swiped it across his eyes.

I beamed at him. "I know you've had a few difficult days. Hopefully, this will help."

"Thank you. You don't know how much this means to me."

"Yes, I do." I squeezed his hand tight. "Trust me, I do."

I met Chase at his cabin at eight forty-five the next morning, my heart practically singing with excitement.

I'd barely slept a wink, with my thoughts fixated on the best time to talk to my father about Margaret, the emptiness of my bed, and the anticipation of the memory box. I couldn't wait to see what was inside but more than that, I couldn't wait for Chase to have the opportunity to connect with the memory of his brother.

He met me on his front porch, the navy in his baseball cap making his eyes look darker than usual. "The idea of seeing this kept me up all night. I kept thinking about my brother, trying to remember the things that we'd gathered up to put in there." His smile lit the morning. "I'm sure everything in there is hopelessly cool, but if it's not, please don't mention it."

"What if it's not yours?" I asked, twisting my hands. "I started to get nervous about it this morning. There were so many memory boxes. Someone else could have hidden it."

He chewed on his lip, something he did when he was nervous. "I'm prepared for that, but at the same time, those cabins were our thing. We were back there all the time and we snuck into them more than once. I can't remember the last spot we hid it, but I do remember spreading out the items on the floor of one of those cabins, and adding a rock from the river. The odds are good."

I nodded. "Well, I don't expect you to open it in front of me. I imagine you'll want to have some time with it, right?"

Chase's eyes met mine. "It means a lot that you understand that."

We looked at each other for a minute.

"We should go," I said, surprised at the intimacy of the moment.

He nodded and headed down the steps, not waiting for me.

The sun was shining brightly. Through the trees, the lake was still, and the water mirrored the depths of the sky. Right as we reached the end of the path, Chase stopped and turned to me. "I wanted to tell you how much I appreciate this. The opportunity to have a new connection, something more than an old voice message I've listened to a thousand times, means everything to me."

The vulnerability on his face made my heart ache. "It's my honor. Nothing has brought me greater joy than the knowledge that you'll have that chance. You deserve it. You are one of the kindest, most caring…"

For a second, I couldn't move. The only thing I could do was look at him. The bright blue of his eyes, the strong shape of his nose, and the kindness in his face that made him so attractive. Something far off in my brain reminded me that I should not be connecting on this level with someone other than my husband but for once, I didn't want to look away.

Chase did it for me. "We should go," he said, clearing his throat.

Feeling numb, I nodded. Something weightless had filled me and I walked along barely seeing anything, only the color of the sky, the path, and trees. We crossed the main lawn and the office came into sight. There was a small group of people standing outside with Nikki, but I hoped she could break away for a minute so he didn't have to wait.

"Julie," Nikki called.

She walked towards us, and in a flash of horror, I realized she was with a camera crew.

"Wait," I said. "What is this?"

With a sinking feeling, I realized it was the local news.

Nikki and a perfectly made-up twenty-something reporter approached us with a bright smile, followed by the camera. The reporter said, "Chase Gibbs, we are thrilled to finally find the owner of the memory box that was discovered here at Wood Violet Resort nearly three years ago. Wood Violet has searched diligently for the person who owned this mystery box ever since it was discovered hidden on the property. You and your late brother buried it together over twenty years ago, is that right?"

Chase stared down at the microphone. His body was rigid. Then he turned to me.

The hurt and betrayal on his face nearly knocked me down.

"Chase?" The reporter's tone turned sympathetic. "This has been quite a journey for Wood Violet Resort and those who have followed the story. Can you share with us the emotions that you're feeling right now? Take your time. I know this is a lot."

For a moment, I thought Chase was going to comment. Then, he reached out and, as politely as possible, pushed the microphone away. Turning, he headed back towards the path. Slowly, at first, before breaking into a run.

"Chase," I called. "Chase, please wait!"

Nikki watched, her face a mix of confusion and concern. There were so many things I wanted to say to her but I didn't dare, for fear I'd burst into tears. Turning, I ran after Chase.

By the time I made it to the woods, he was gone.

*

I looked everywhere for him but he was nowhere to be found. There were so many secret spots in the woods, or by the lake, that I finally had no choice but to give up. I texted Tilly to let her know what had happened and she responded with several broken heart emojis.

I'll keep an eye out for him.

There were several messages from Nikki. I couldn't believe she'd done this and I had no doubt that Chase thought I was in on it. Storming into the office, I found her at her desk, diligently updating our social media accounts.

"Nikki." My voice was quiet. "What just happened?"

"*Right?*" Nikki fiddled with her bracelets. "Why did he freak out?"

"Because this was a private, personal moment for him. Instead of getting that, he walked into an ambush."

Nikki's mouth dropped open. "It was not an ambush! I told you that I wanted to get a reaction from him, maybe a quote. You said that would be fine."

"I didn't know you meant talk to him with a camera crew," I said. "Why would you do that?"

"The social media campaign that went viral was all about trying to find the person who owns the memory box. We found him. It was a great piece of advertising for Wood Violet to have the news crew present."

"This was the last thing I wanted."

I couldn't shake the image of the betrayal in his eyes.

"Julie, you don't understand," Nikki said. "This was a viral campaign. Do you know how difficult it is to achieve that? The amount of publicity this would have gotten the resort would translate into dollars. That's what it's all about."

"That's not what it's all about."

I thought of all of the cases I'd worked on where the insurance companies I'd represented worked on that same principal. There had been so many incidents that had left people hurt or distressed, and instead of helping them, I had helped contribute to their pain. *Never again.*

"Nikki, I've made a lot of mistakes in my career, justifying choices that were wrong because I thought it was my job to serve the company I worked for," I said. "Don't make that mistake. People matter. The heart behind what you're doing matters. If that's not there, it won't make one bit of difference if we have five billion social media followers or if every cabin is booked solid for the next three years. Does that make sense?"

Nikki looked down at her desk. "It does. I'm sorry." She handed me the small, metal memory box. "If you give this to him, tell him I'm sorry."

"Thank you." I held it close. "I will."

It would have helped if I had the first clue where to find Chase, but since I didn't, I took the box to my cabin and stored it in the closet. I couldn't believe this had happened. Forget the fact that Chase was a dear friend, he was also an extremely important guest. My father would have to come up with some way to apologize, on behalf of the resort.

He had texted me last night and asked to meet up at some point today to go over some things, since holidays were always a little wild. I dreaded the idea of seeing my father because I couldn't wrap my mind around those letters.

Picking up the phone, I called him. He answered on the third ring, his voice strained.

"I was just about to call you. Your mother fell during PT. We're about to leave for the hospital. The therapist thinks she broke her hip."

*

The hospital waiting room was practically empty. Its green vinyl seats with the wooden arms were uncomfortable and my father sat next to me, his head in his hands. He had fought tears when the doctor explained the hip fracture required immediate surgery, and the moment my mother was wheeled away, he gave into them, crying into his hands like a child.

I rubbed my hand on his back, fighting my own emotion. It was all too much. It wasn't fair that my mother was facing this, too. Wasn't having a stroke enough?

Tristan chalked up every life challenge as an opportunity to build character or grow as a person, but my mother was already the best person I'd ever met, both in spirit and deed. The idea that she had to suffer another setback wasn't right.

It didn't help that, somewhere in the back of my mind, I wondered if there was more out there, waiting to hurt her. Like the idea that my father could have stepped out on their marriage, and his mother had helped cover it up. It was impossible to wrap my mind around, and in the sterile waiting room, I didn't want to try.

Instead, I put my arm around my father, and held him as he cried.

The news that my mother had made it through surgery without complications made my father jump out of his chair with joy. We followed the doctor back to the recovery room where my mother gave us her half-smile.

"Keeping things exciting." The words came slowly. They were thicker than usual, most likely because of the sedative, and my father kissed her forehead.

"You always do," he said. "How are you feeling?"

Her expression was sad. "I've had better holidays."

I squeezed her hand tight. My father and I did our best to chat and entertain her, until it was obvious that she was getting tired. The nurse suggested that we go get a bite to eat, which was our cue to leave until she got some rest.

"Your mother is strong," he said, once we'd gotten sandwiches and were seated at a small, Formica-topped table next to gray walls. The sterile setting was a far cry from the warmth of the resort. "She'll get through this."

"It doesn't seem fair that she has to," I said. "Hasn't she dealt with enough?"

"That's not for us to decide." My father picked at his sandwich but didn't make a move to eat it. "Sometimes, life isn't fair."

I stared down at my chicken wrap. "Speaking of that. I have something to talk to you about."

"What is it?" my father asked. "Tristan?"

"No." I took a bite of the chicken wrap, the lettuce loud in my ears.

Even though this had nothing to do with Tristan, the insult from the forest ran through my mind. The one where Tristan said I make bad decisions. It was possible that talking to my father about this was a bad decision, since he was already dealing with enough.

Maybe it should wait until another time, when my mother wasn't recovering from surgery. On the other hand, there would never be a good time to talk about this, and I needed answers.

"I'm going to ask you a question." I set down the wrap. "Please answer honestly."

My father nodded, as if honesty was the only option. He gave the impression of being such a wholesome, upstanding family man that my suspicions bothered me even more.

"I found some old letters. Do you remember a worker name Ivelisse?"

He squinted. "She got fired for something or other, some scandal. Did she send the letters?"

"Yes. Turns out, Ivelisse got pregnant while she was working here, and Grandma put the baby up for adoption. I think she changed her mind, got upset, and threatened Grandma."

My father's face darkened. "What? Let me see them."

"They're back at Wood Violet. They were from a long time ago, but they also gave the impression that…" I braced myself. "That you were involved with her. While you were married to Mom."

My father looked bewildered. Then, confusion seemed to dawn on his face, followed by disbelief. "You think I was involved with someone other than your mother?"

He stared at me, the betrayal in his eyes so deep that I cringed.

"Your mother has been my rock for the past thirty-five years," he said. "I would never do something like that to her, ever. And the idea that I am having this conversation with my daughter…" My father moved from hurt to anger. "How dare you?"

Even though he was angry, I felt such a sense of relief. The idea that he was behind this mess would have been too much to take.

"I know you had nothing to do with it," I said quickly. "But it scared me to think Mom could have seen the letters and thought the worst."

My father ran his hand across his face. "No, she trusts me. If she had doubts, she'd ask."

We sat in an awkward silence for several moments.

"Dad, I'm sorry."

"Me, too." He let out a hearty sigh and rubbed his eyes. "I don't know why this woman would say that. I had nothing to do with her. Barely even knew her."

"I don't know," I said. "It was alluded to in the letter, but not said. The thing about it is, though, is that the baby that she gave birth to… I think it was Margaret. The girl living in the artist-in-residence cabin."

My father squinted. "You lost me."

I pushed my lunch aside, appetite gone. "Dad, I made a bad decision. I've been waiting for the right time to tell you the truth and there hasn't been one. The letters are tied into it all."

My father's expression became darker with every passing word as I told him the whole story about Margaret. "I didn't think you could tell me anything that would surprise me more than your first question. Or make me this angry." He squeezed the edge of the table, as if tempted to knock it over. "You had no right to make that decision, to let her stay in that cabin. Your grandmother has a legacy as an artist that deserves to be honored. That's why that cabin exists. Not for this."

"I know and I'm sorry." My cheeks burned with shame. "But Margaret really is a talented singer. You've heard her. It's helping her to write music and work through this. She came here because she wanted to find her mother and we were her only lead. Either way, I'm sorry. I should have told you the truth."

"No kidding." My father's tone was rigid, his shoulders tense. "If my mother helped someone years ago, it's her business, not ours. It was one thing for you to lie to us about the cabin but quite another to do such a thing for a runaway with this type of agenda. The idea that my mother could have been involved with this and that you would practically accuse me..."

"Dad, I—"

"I don't care to hear any more." He got to his feet and paced to the window that looked out over the parking lot.

I looked around the cafeteria in embarrassment. There were only a few people in there, reading books or talking in low tones with a partner. No one was paying attention to us.

My father returned to the table and sat down. "The girl is to leave first thing in the morning. I don't like this situation and I never would have agreed to it. She is not welcome at the resort. If Tilly has a problem with that, she can talk to me."

I started to interrupt but he held up his hand. "Julie, I appreciate that you tried to help someone in need but this situation feels too erratic, like it could blow up in our face at any moment. I don't need that kind of stress, considering the fact that we're already standing in a hospital, and your mother *certainly* doesn't need it."

He looked at his watch. "I'm spending the night here. You need to get back to the resort and help handle the holiday festivities. I want her gone by tomorrow. I'm sorry to say this, Julie, but I'm disappointed in you. I expected more."

The thing that hurt the most was that I had given him the best I had.

CHAPTER TWENTY-FOUR

It would have been impossible to talk with Margaret when I'd returned from the hospital, as the resort was bustling with Fourth of July activities. Without my father there, I was pulled in fifty different directions, helping with everything from sparkler distribution to coordinating the Taps performance at sunset. The fireworks display across the water was spectacular but of course, I didn't have a moment to watch it, as there was too much to be done. Throughout it all, I couldn't shake the memory of the look of betrayal on my father's face, which only made me put my head down and work even harder.

I fell into bed somewhere around two thirty in the morning and was up at dawn to ensure the celebration from the night before had been removed with care and perfection. Then, I returned to the cabin and texted Margaret to see if we could get together later in the day. Once she texted back with the thumbs-up emoji, I pulled the curtains and slept for half the day.

My stomach was in knots by the time I walked through the woods and knocked on the door to her cabin. I thought back to that first morning when she'd refused to go to breakfast without her bag, back when I didn't know the secret she was hiding. Our relationship had developed since that point and, on some level, I felt we'd become friends. I hated to see her go, and to imagine what her reaction was going to be.

"Hi," Margaret sang, throwing open the door. "I'm glad you stopped by. I've been working on a new song."

I followed her inside, noting the cozy set-up she had in the living room. There was a throw blanket on the couch, her writing notebook was next to it, and a cup of mint tea steamed on the coffee table.

Margaret flopped on the couch. "Can you believe I'm not scared to play in front of you? That whole thing by the beach was transformative. I have like, this need to share my music now."

I leaned forward, my hands on my knees, as she sang:

> *The fog fades in and the day begins*
> *But my questions are not new.*
> *I wonder at the trees, the grass,*
> *The wonder that is you…*

I settled back in the chair, listening. Her voice was so smooth. I could have sat there for hours but she stopped after the second verse.

"That's all I've got."

"It's beautiful," I said. "Margaret, have you ever thought of doing music professionally?"

"Yes, but I don't want to do that. Too unpredictable." She traced her finger around the shimmering pearl inlay on her guitar. "I think I want to be a surgeon or something. I'm kind of worried that I couldn't cut it, though, you know?" She cracked up. "I really didn't mean that as a joke."

It was great to see her in such a good mood but it also made the discussion we needed to have so much harder. I'd planned to talk to her first thing, but that would just spoil the night. Instead, I decided to bring it up when the time was right.

Margaret cradled her cup of tea and took a sip. "Ready to lose at Risk?"

We hung out until it was dark, playing board games, and ordering in Chinese. Halfway through dinner, Margaret's text alert chimed and she was quick to pick it up.

"Hold on. Let me answer this." She tucked her feet under herself on the couch, and was on her phone for at least five minutes. When she finally went back to the crab Rangoon, she gave me a mischievous look. "So, Pete isn't with Kelly anymore."

"Is that the boy?" I asked, spearing a dumpling.

"That's the boy." She gave me a sly look. "We've been texting."

I took a bite of chicken. "Where are they now?"

"They'll be in Yellowstone tomorrow. He wants me to come meet up with them."

Seeing my opening, I set down my chopsticks. "Margaret, I need to talk to you about something. This isn't easy and I've been trying to work up the nerve the whole time I've been here."

She gave me a questioning look. "What's up?"

"I told my father the truth about how we met."

Her eyes widened. "What did he say?"

"He said you have to leave."

The silence stretched between us.

"I don't understand. I told you I was sorry about lying about what happened with my mom. You said things were okay." Her eyes filled with tears. "Can't you ask him to let me stay?"

"I did," I said. "It's not about the lie. It's because my family is going through a lot right now with my mom and the resort, and my dad can't handle any more stress. He was furious that I'd found you living in the cabins by the river, and now, he's worried about liability."

"I won't do anything." Margaret looked young and helpless. "I just want to find my mother!"

Guilt cut through me. If she was being sent away regardless, should I just tell her that I knew her mother's name? Let her research it from there?

I couldn't. I still didn't know the whole story, and Margaret had shown me her temper more than once. If she ever learned my grandmother might have kept her from her mother, I could only imagine what she might do.

"I'm so sorry," I said. "He thinks you're a brilliant singer and a nice person, but he's trying to run a business. That's all."

Margaret stared down at the food. "I should have known you'd do something like this. This isn't fair! I had an appointment set up with the county clerk in three days to see if they could tell me anything."

"It's not my choice," I said. "I tried to convince my father to let you stay. He won't do it."

"How convenient for you." She got up and stood at the window, staring out the lake. "You should go."

"What?" I said. "Listen, I know you're upset, but—"

She turned to glare at me. "Just *go.*"

I turned to leave, feeling sick inside. For a moment I stood outside the cabin, paralyzed by guilt, then I trudged down the steps. The stars were dim and even the insects seemed subdued.

I hadn't expected her to be happy about the situation, but I hadn't expected her to shut me out. It served as a reminder that Margaret was young and volatile, and sharing the information about her mother without knowing the whole story could be a disaster.

There was one person who would understand how I was feeling about all of this. Even though it was late, I headed to Chase's cabin. I'd sent him several texts that he hadn't responded to, but now that he'd had time to think it through, maybe he'd be willing to let me apologize about the memory box in person.

The lights were off when I walked up the steps. Still, I knocked, hoping that he was in the bedroom or something, reading. He didn't answer and finally, I texted Tilly.

Have you seen Chase?

The response bubbles were immediate but it took a minute for her to finish the text.

Yes. Julie, I'm so sorry, I meant to reach out to you but we did the camping excursion today and in the midst of lugging around that tent, trying to avoid being eaten by a bear, and stomaching these foil cooked chicken nachos I'm supposed to be excited about, I totally forgot. So, Chase left.

The words made my stomach drop.

It was all too much for him. I'm sure he'll reach out to you soon, he's just dealing with his grief. If you want to come camping, you know where to find us. Please remind me never to do this again, there's only so much nature a person can take.

I couldn't believe it. Chase left because he felt ambushed and betrayed.

No, Tilly must have misunderstood.

Maybe he had a day trip, something that he had to take care of. I knew he was upset, but I refused to believe that he would leave without saying goodbye. We'd been through too much together.

I walked in silence to my cabin. Inside, I stood at the window, thinking of all the things I'd discussed with him, the conversations we'd had and the laughs that we'd shared. It was impossible to think that was over.

Picking up the landline, I contacted the front desk. "Hi, it's Julie," I said, when one of my favorite front desk workers picked up, a man who had been with us forever. "Can you check on the duration of a guest's stay for me?"

"Yes, absolutely. Name?"

"Chase Gibbs." I heard his fingers tapping at the computer.

"He checked out today but was paid up through the summer. Something must have come up. Do you need me to contact him?"

Through the screen, the symphony of the lake on a summer's night was being performed at full volume. Frogs croaking, fish jumping, mosquitoes humming, and moths banging against the screen. For once, it felt as loud as it did back in the city.

"No." I let out a breath. "Do me a favor, though. Credit the remainder of his stay back to his card, and please send him an email letting him know that we've done so."

It was the least we could do. Not that it would restore our relationship with him. I had no doubt that Chase Gibbs would never talk to me, or set foot on this property, again.

The next morning, I texted Margaret flight information to the airport nearest to Yellowstone so that she could meet up with her friends and the link to the e-ticket I had purchased for her. Then, I scheduled one of our shuttle drivers to take her to the airport. When I didn't hear back from her, I texted:

Would you like me to ride to the airport with you?

Her reply was curt.

Nope.

I took a hot shower, trying to ignore the nagging voice trying to tell me that it was wrong to let her leave without the truth. But I pushed it back, firm in the decision I'd made.

Tristan called while I was in the shower, and I called him back on the way to the hospital to see my mother. The shuttle car that took me there was a cozy sedan and my driver seemed content listening to classical music, so I didn't feel rude about being on the phone.

"Hey," I said, happy to hear his voice. "I'm so glad I got you."

It had been a day or two since we'd connected. I still hadn't heard about his meet and greet, so I was interested to see how it had turned out.

"Hey, let me video-chat you," Tristan said. "Hold on."

When the video blurred into focus, I could see Tristan standing in the office at our loft, tossing a foam basketball back and forth in his hands. The moment he saw me, he shot it into the basket on his desk. "They offered me the VP position," he said, beaming. "You're looking at a vice president."

"Tristan, that's so wonderful," I said. "It's a huge step."

"I wanted it, Julie." His eyes searched mine. "It's going to change the rest of the summer and I'm sorry about that."

"What do you mean?" I asked.

It was quite likely that he'd have to attend training sessions, which meant it wouldn't be easy for him to get back here again. It was a disappointment but I knew this job was an incredible opportunity. The firm was so well known and the idea that Tristan was the vice president was more than a little impressive.

"I know you wanted to stay and help your parents."

"Yes," I said. "Would you believe my mother just broke her hip? They need my help more than ever."

"They like your help. They appreciate it. They don't need it, though." Tristan sat down in his desk chair, and his face became large in the screen. "You've had a great summer break, built some good memories, but it really is time we get back to real life."

"Tristan, I can't," I said. "We've had this conversation."

"I need you here!" Tristan hit the desk and the driver jumped at the loud sound. "You belong at home."

"Sorry," I told the driver. To Tristan, I said, "Let me call you back. Not on video."

He picked up on the first ring. "Look, this is going to be a big change for me. I'm going to need you by my side. There are going to be a lot of dinners, meetings and events right away and I can't exactly say *sorry, my wife's away on vacation*. I need you home."

The words filled me with dread. I didn't want to walk away from the peace of the woods, the smell of the air after a rainstorm, and the feeling of the hot sun on my face as I swam in cold water. I couldn't even imagine trying to return to the noise and dirt of the city, the crush of people, and the panicked feeling that everything was too much.

"I'm sorry," I told him. "I'm not ready."

Tristan's voice went low. "I'm not asking."

Outside the window, the trees had become less dense and the smell of campfires faded, as the driver brought me further away from Wood Violet. I tried to imagine what it would be like to return to the city when the resort was the only place I wanted to be. But I could tell by the tone in Tristan's voice that he meant it. I needed to return home or it could put us right back to where we were before his visit, if not somewhere worse.

My parents didn't need me, not really. They had a solid system in place and, even though I had more than enough to do each day, Nikki could handle it without my help. My mother was coming home from the hospital tomorrow and as much as I preferred to hug her, our visits could happen just as easily over the phone. I also had no doubt that Wood Violet would make it out of its financial slump, now that my father had committed to the wedding venture. Even the secret about the adoption and the letters Ivelisse had sent didn't matter, because my father now knew the whole story and Margaret had left. Things would be just fine without me.

Slowly, I nodded. "I'll come home."

"Really?" He gave a mock frown. "No fight?"

"Congratulations on the job," I said.

"It's going to be good for us, Julie. You'll see."

The driver pulled into the hospital parking lot right as I hung up. Summer was over. Time for real life to kick in.

My parents were understanding in a way that I didn't expect when I spoke to them about it at the hospital. My mother was sitting up in bed and the color in her cheeks looked good. Still, it hurt me to think about leaving her.

"He's your husband." My mother patted my cheek as if proud of me for making the right choice. "Of course you should be with him."

"What about the projects, though?" I asked. "I hate leaving everything unfinished."

"Nikki will take over," my father said. "You've laid down the law, so I think she'll follow your example."

I sat in silence, feeling miffed. "You're really not going to try and talk me out of it?"

My parents looked confused. "Honey, your stay was never permanent," my mother's words were still coming slowly, but it was getting so much easier to understand her. "Why, were you thinking it would be something more?"

"No." The reality made my heart ache. "It's just going to be hard to say goodbye."

"It always is," my mother said.

I nodded and pulled my parents in for a hug. We set plans for me to leave within the next two days, and my mother made me promise to call often. We were laughing by the end of the conversation but as I left the hospital, I had to admit to myself that the exchange had left me feeling empty.

It would have been nice if they had asked me to stay. Invited me to run the resort with them on a permanent basis, like my father and I had discussed.

Is that what you want?

The more the thought bounced through my head, the more I realized it *was* what I wanted. The thing that had made this summer so important to me wasn't just the relationships I'd built, but the idea that I had become a part of the place that had shaped me. Walking away would not be easy, and it frustrated me to think that I was leaving for Tristan.

Turning on my heel, I went back to my mother's room. My parents were talking and when I walked back in, they looked at me in surprise.

"You guys, I want to stay here," I said. "Dad told me that I could stay and become a part of the resort. I want to do that."

"Julie." My father looked baffled. "You need to get back to your life, to your marriage, not waste your time here."

"Wood Violet is everything to me. There has to be a solution," I insisted, the beat of my mother's heart monitor keeping pace with my thoughts. "I could commute back and forth to the city. Make it work."

My father shook his head. "Not during the summer. What would be the point of being a part of it at all if you had to hire a manager because you couldn't be on site?"

"There has to be something I could do," I insisted.

"I wish there was," my father said.

We all stood in silence in the sterile room, the reality of the situation settling upon us. My parents were getting older. The resort wouldn't last much longer and there was nothing I could do about any of it, because my window of time to be involved had closed.

The thought made me feel so helpless. It seemed that nothing had worked out the way I would have liked. I should have learned how to speak up when I had the chance, asked for what I wanted, and taken control of instead of trusting that life would take me where I was meant to go.

So now, it was time to grow up. I had a great husband, a nice home, and a busy life in the city. Yes, I'd wanted to stay longer and help my mother. I'd wanted to spend more time trying to understand what had happened with Ivelisse, and determine whether or not to keep trying to find her for Margaret. I'd wanted to spend more time outdoors and less time trapped in an office. Instead, I was going to have to trust that my mother had the help she needed, that the situation with Ivelisse might be better left unresolved, and that being present for my career was simply part of being a grown-up. Ultimately, I needed to be grateful for what I had. Taking a deep breath, I gave my parents another round of hugs.

"What are you going to do?" my father asked, watching me with concern.

"What I should've done a long time ago," I told him. "I'm going to go home."

CHAPTER TWENTY-FIVE

Being back in Chicago was a whirlwind. I jolted awake in the morning to the sound of honking cabs and went to bed at night with pinched feet from the designer sandals I wore to the millionth networking event Tristan dragged me to. His new job kept him extremely busy, and if we weren't out on the town, we weren't together.

The fifth day back home, I claimed a headache and skipped dinner at one of my favorite tapas bars. Tristan was irritated about it, but I needed a break. It was too much to go from the relative ease of Wood Violet to all of this.

While I lay in bed, my thoughts turned to Margaret. It still bothered me to think of all the things I hadn't told her. Earlier in the week, when Tristan was at work and I had nothing to do but hunt for a job I didn't want, I had visited the apartment building on Fullerton where Ivelisse had once lived. My arms were covered in goosebumps as I stood outside, thinking about the pain Ivelisse had felt, yearning to be with her daughter.

Pulling the sheets close, I thought about how badly I'd wanted to talk to Chase in that moment. I hadn't heard from him since he'd left Wood Violet.

We had become such close friends in such a short period of time, and I hated it that our time together had been cut short by a misunderstanding. He had proven to be one of the kindest, most compassionate people I'd ever known, and I admired him. I hoped he'd received my texts, and that they had given him some sense of how much I'd appreciated our time together and how sorry I was about what had happened.

Now, as I stared out at the skyline, I started to type out a text to him, explaining what had happened with Margaret, but it was much too long. I was about to write a shorter one when Tristan returned home from dinner.

I wasn't in the mood to talk to him, so I pretended to be asleep. He must not have fallen for it, because he sat on the edge of the bed and pressed his hand against my forehead. "You don't have a fever."

"I'm not sick," I mumbled, into the pillow. "Not anymore, I mean."

"I brought home a bottle of wine." In the dim light of the room, I saw the outline of a popular, high-end red wine that I had always favored. "Let's go up on the roof and drink it."

The idea was romantic. It was the type of thing that had made me fall in love with Tristan and the city in the beginning of our relationship. Now, I didn't feel like sitting up on the roof having the wind whip hair across my face, when I could be in bed.

"Please." Tristan took my hand. "I'd like to spend some time with you. We can look at the stars."

"What stars?" I said, but got out of bed and bundled up.

Out on the roof, Tristan opened the bottle of wine and we settled onto a blanket. He looked handsome, dressed in a custom-made button-up and a pair of casual slacks. He poured me a glass of wine and passed it over, before tapping his glass against mine.

The wine was complex and I rolled it around on my tongue before looking up at the sky. There were no stars. It was a foggy night and the sky was covered in a blanket of gray.

"No stars." I thought of the brilliant display that hung over Wood Violet each night. It was so hard to believe that only a week ago, I'd been there.

"I see one." Tristan found a pinpoint of light. "It's just moving very fast. Look, there's another one. They're everywhere."

"Those are airplanes," I grumbled.

"Huh." Tristan squinted up. "You might have missed your calling. You would have been a spectacular air traffic controller."

A hint of a smile tugged at the corner of my mouth. He looped a strong arm around me and pulled me in close. "I know it's hard to be away from Wood Violet, Julie. You planned to have the whole summer there."

I rested my head against his shoulder. "I did."

"Thank you for choosing to be here for me."

The idea that Tristan appreciated the sacrifice didn't make it easier. The fact that he was being funny and charming only served to make me feel guilty, because I couldn't offer the same to him. Time would change that, it had to.

He pointed at the sky. "Shooting star."

Letting out a breath, I pointed at a building where the lights were bright on the roof.

"Isn't that Cassiopeia?" I asked.

Leaning over, he kissed me.

My sister had her baby at the end of August, while we were out having dinner with clients. The men were eating steaks, the wives picking at salads, and I stepped out of the restaurant to return my parents' call. My father was over the moon, telling me all about the chunky baby boy she'd brought into the world in less than five hours. The streetlights blurred as I listened, and I stood out on the street for a few moments to pull it together before walking back into the bustling restaurant.

The look I got from Tristan when I returned to the table was nothing short of irritated, because he didn't like for me to leave the table at all during our dinners. I signaled to the waiter for a drink and pretended to jump right back into the conversation the wives were having about the local private schools. I realized that every single one of the women at the table had kids.

I'd always wanted children because of the simple life my sister and I lived at Wood Violet. I'd wanted to give that same type of existence to my children. I'd never considered having children the next step in a career plan but I had no doubt that it bothered Tristan to think that when it came to the family quadrant of success, he couldn't jump into the conversations about private schools, soccer practice and family ski trips.

It hit me that he would want to try again soon, because he would want us to fit in. I wanted a family more than anything but I was not willing to go through that heartache again. Not with Tristan.

Not with Tristan.

The fact that I'd even think those words filled me with fear. I stared down at the bright green pieces of avocado on my blue crab Cobb salad, half-wondering if the women had the ability to read my mind. The thought made me feel sick and I wished I was back outside, away from the crowded table and the smell of hard-boiled eggs.

I looked over at my husband. Tristan was the very picture of success. The carefully chosen pocket square, the cut of the jacket... these were all things that he'd put an immense amount of time and energy into because it mattered to him. Tristan was a guy who liked money, achievements, and the ability to bypass those who'd been handed the advantages that he'd had to fight for. He was a man with a point to prove.

He wasn't perfect but he tried so hard, and he was a good person. It was just... he wasn't the right person for me. I'd known it for a while since I'd been back, but I couldn't admit it to myself, and I had a strong suspicion that when it came down to it, he felt the same.

The words Chase had once said came to mind. *Our marriage would have failed, whether we chose to remain in it or not.*

I wasn't in love with my husband anymore, and I had no idea how to tell him.

When we got back home, I climbed into bed without bothering to brush my teeth, which was something I hadn't done in years. I faked sleep. Once again, Tristan sat on the edge of the bed and stroked my hair.

"It's hard to see you like this," he said. "I thought we were done with all of it."

"All what?" I mumbled.

"Being depressed." He adjusted his cufflinks, as if getting ready to be photographed for a menswear display.

"I'm sorry," I told him. "I know you need support right now, but…"

I fought back tears. Tristan got up and walked over to the closet, the set of his shoulders rigid.

"It's not exciting to go to these dinners, Julie," he said. "I get that. Especially since the women are expected to pick at the food and skip dessert."

The criticism was apparent. I'd eaten every bite of my salad and when the dessert tray came, accepted a mini éclair when the other women had passed.

"However, it's literally two hours of your life. It's not like you have anything else that you have to be back for. It's not like we need to get the kids to bed."

So, it was on his mind, too.

Putting the kids to bed was the conversation that had closed out dinner, the wives complaining that their sitters were hopeless, that the kids would still be up when they returned home.

"Let's try again." Kneeling down, he took my hands. "It's time for a family. We're both ready and I think it will happen this time."

"My sister had her baby tonight," I said. "That's why I stepped out."

Tristan gave me a blank look and I started laughing. "You didn't even know she was pregnant, did you?"

"Of course I did," he said quickly. "You've been so excited for her."

For some reason, this only made me laugh harder.

"What are you laughing about?" He walked over to the closet and started to get undressed. "I knew she was pregnant, I just forgot. I have a lot of things on my mind, these days. Seriously, Julie. Why are you laughing?"

"Because I don't want to cry."

I'd said it quietly but it didn't matter. Tristan had already headed into the bathroom to brush his teeth.

There was a stale taste in my mouth when I woke up the next morning. Fog cloaked the city, the ghost of the lake hovering somewhere behind it. Tristan was not in bed; given the time, he was probably just finishing up a run.

Sure enough, the key turned in the lock in our front door. I heard him hang his keys on the hook in the living room, blend a fruit and veggie smoothie, and then he headed into the bedroom, probably to take a shower.

"You're up." He sat on the edge of the bed, his hair damp with sweat. Heat radiated off his body. "I really wish you'd join me one morning."

He leaned in for a kiss and I drew back. "Sorry," I said, surprised at myself. "I… I haven't brushed my teeth."

"Since when has that mattered?" he asked.

"Did you make coffee?" I asked, moving to get out of bed.

"Wait." He put his hand on my arm, his face lined with suspicion. "What's going on? Don't you want me to kiss you?"

I stared down at the platinum band on his hand, and considered the promises we'd made to each other. For better or worse, in sickness and health…

"Seriously, Julie." His voice had a warning tone. "What is it?"

"This goes deeper than whether or not I want to kiss you," I told him.

The muscle in his jaw pulsed. "I don't follow."

The sense of betrayal I'd felt after the miscarriages, when he had pulled away, ran deep. Instead of getting angry at the time, I had made excuses for him: he needed to handle his own grief before he could support me in mine; he didn't understand because it wasn't his body, or worst of all, that I needed too much.

"When we lost our first baby—" I started to say.

"Oh, come on." He leapt to his feet. "Julie, we've dealt with this."

"We haven't, though," I insisted. "We need to talk about it."

"Talk about what?" he practically shouted.

I hesitated, not sure where to start. "I know that I should be happy for my sister, but…"

Tristan let out a hearty sigh, and rested his hand against the concrete wall. The urban design of our loft was one of the features that was supposed to be so cutting edge but to me, it had always felt cold.

"Of course you should be happy for your sister." His tone held exaggerated patience. "Why wouldn't you be?"

I leaned back against the pillows, pulling the comforter close. "It's hard hearing that she's on baby number three, while we haven't even made it to baby number one."

Tristan yanked off his shirt and dumped it into the laundry basket. "Well, it sounds like you're ready to try, then."

The words made my body go numb. "No. When I think about that day, when—"

"You know what?" Tristan moved to the bathroom door. "The fact that you want to relive things that happened well over a year ago, to wallow about them for so long, means you have deeper issues. I'm sorry you've latched onto this, but you need to book a therapy appointment. You need someone to talk to. Someone other than me. It's too much."

In a voice so calm that it scared me, I said, "You want me to pay someone to talk about my feelings because you don't want to deal with them?"

Tristan flipped on the lights of the bathroom. "I'm going to take a shower."

"What do you mean, 'it's too much'?" I demanded, getting to my feet.

The sharp lines of his face, typically so handsome, were set with anger. "Look, I married you because I believed we were a match, that you were committed to excellence, to living the best life possible. Now, I don't even recognize you. You have barely looked for a job since you've been back, you won't let go of your grief, you'd most likely move in with your parents if they asked you to. It's too much."

The words felt like a punch to the stomach. There were so many things I could have said, but it didn't seem worth the effort. Without a word, I moved to the closet and pulled out my suitcase.

"What are you doing?" Tristan demanded.

"Going back to Wood Violet."

His face went dark. "No. You can't spend half of your time there and half—"

"I don't want to spend half my time there." I gripped the handle of the suitcase and turned to him. "I want to spend all my time there. I'm done."

"Done?" he echoed.

"I want a divorce."

I hadn't meant to say the words out loud but they hung in the air, like a shot fired between us.

"Julie," he whispered.

Letting go of the handle of the suitcase, I sank onto the bed and put my head in my hands. Moments later, Tristan's arms wrapped around me and pulled me in close. The spice from his deodorant, the smell of his hair, it was all so familiar.

I swiped at my eyes, not wanting to give him another reason to find me lacking. Then I realized he was crying, too.

His chest heaving up and down, he buried his lips in my hair. "I'm so sorry," he whispered. "I love you."

We sat in silence, holding one another. It had been so long since we'd taken the time to connect on this level that some far off part of my brain hoped that maybe, it was still possible to work it out. To talk, to heal, to find our way back to one another.

"I don't know why I said that," I whispered. "I'm sorry."

Tristan didn't answer. His silence became heavy, and a slow, numbing sorrow began to move down my shoulders, through my body, and to my toes. I pulled away and looked up at him.

"Is it what you want?" I asked.

His voice cracked. "I think it's what we both want."

The pain that cut through me was so sharp that I leaned into him once again. We held one another so tightly that I could barely breathe. Finally, we slowly moved back apart, and let go.

CHAPTER TWENTY-SIX

The pine trees crowded the shoreline with their multitude of green, yellowed, and burnt rust nettles. The tree trunks were a mix of bright white and clay brown, stretching tall to a turquoise sky dotted with wispy white clouds. The lake sparkled a deep gold, reflecting the sun, and I stopped the car and took it all in.

There had been so many years when I had wished to be here, to make this my home. I had tried to follow a path that wasn't mine, fighting as it tightened and became sharp with weeds that blocked the way. I had thought it was brave to push through, in spite of the pain, because I'd said I could reach the destination. Now, I understood that true courage came from admitting that it might be time to change course.

I walked into my parents' house and hugged myself as relief rushed through me. Finally, I was home. The familiar smells hit me, and I relished the scent of the fresh flowers on the table in the living room, the laundry detergent my parents had used my entire life, and the ever-present pot of decaf that filled the kitchen with its rich scent.

My mother wheeled herself into the living room. Her face broke into a half-smile and I burst into tears. She led me to the couch, indicating I should take a seat. There, she tucked the rough yarn of the orange and yellow afghan around me.

"Forgive yourself." She rested a warm hand on my shoulder. "You struggled. All summer long. Not all things can be resolved."

Tears streamed down my face, salty on my upper lip. The image of Tristan on our wedding day danced through my mind, the moment he lifted my veil and kissed me with such tenderness. That day, we had such a different vision of how things would turn out.

Even though I regretted that our life hadn't taken that path, this was the right one for me. I belonged here, in the place that made my soul sing.

"One promise should not tie you to a lifetime of unhappiness," my mother said, her voice quiet. "Forgive yourself, forgive him, and move on."

I pulled the afghan close and reached for her hand. We sat in silence watching the water. In spite of the disappointment that weighed so heavily on my heart, there was nowhere I would rather be.

The small cabin my parents had given me to live in was on the edge of the forest, close to their house. It was decorated just like the cabin I had stayed at over the summer but they had given me license to add to it however I wanted to make it feel like home. So far, I'd left it the way that it was because, to me, it was already perfect.

The freedom of being at Wood Violet on a permanent basis was such a relief. It softened the hurt and reminded me that life wasn't over just because I'd taken a wrong turn. I spent as much time as possible at the office, working on the tasks assigned by my father, as well as working with Nikki to finalize the plans to break ground on the wedding venue.

My father had made the formal decision to move forward with the wedding industry once my grandfather had returned from his trip overseas. The two had sat down to discuss the decline in earnings at the resort, and my father had asked for his opinion. He hadn't wanted my grandfather to know how close the business had come to falling apart, so it was a difficult step for him to take, and I was proud of him.

My grandfather was as pragmatic about the issue as ever. He encouraged my father to move forward with the new business approach and to only sell the land as a last step. Since then, Nikki had booked a startling number of reservations based on the venue plans alone. It was a pretty clear indicator that this new venture would be a success, and that Wood Violet's financial situation was about to turn around.

Still, there were moments when the hum of work died down and I noticed the pictures of Nikki and her family on her desk that I felt a deep sense of shame.

There was the embarrassment of the divorce, the hurt it caused both my family and Tristan's, and the idea that I had failed. Those feelings weren't easy but whenever I wondered if I'd made a big mistake, I thought back to that restaurant with the women talking about their kids, when I had panicked at the idea that Tristan would want to try again. That moment had made it so clear to me that it was time to let go.

Even though I knew I'd made the right choice, it was hard to accept our love story as it had played out compared to what I'd once dreamed it could be. There were nights I fell asleep with my wedding album cradled to my chest, my cheeks stained with tears, wishing I could go back in time and get it right. Surely, the wisdom and experience I'd gained along the way could change things? In the morning, though, as I stared out the window at the view of the trees stretching to the sky, I understood there was no going back because it wasn't where I was meant to be.

Those moments, I spent time reimagining my future. It wasn't hard to do. I knew I wanted to spend my days at Wood Violet with my parents and my grandfather, working at the resort. I wanted to slow down, invest time in the people and moments that made me happy, and let go of the rest. I did hope that love was out there for me, but I wasn't in any rush. I'd found my way home, and everything that I needed was right here.

CHAPTER TWENTY-SEVEN

I had been back at the resort for a few weeks when I opened the bottom of a file cabinet, searching for a stapler, and found the memory box. I'd tucked it away in the office before returning to Chicago, in the event that Chase might try to contact the resort to receive it. It sat there still unopened, still waiting to be discovered.

"Chase never asked for this?" I asked, holding it up.

The metal was heavy in my hands.

"No." Nikki nibbled at a cookie. "I hoped we'd hear from him, but we didn't. What should we do with it?"

I held it, weighing our options. It was the thing that had hurt him so deeply, because he'd thought I was willing to capitalize on his pain. I couldn't even imagine what he'd felt when he saw that reporter. He must have thought I'd held him with such little regard.

Every part of me ached to pick up the phone and offer another apology. Instead, I packed up the capsule and included a short note.

Dear Chase,

The leaves have changed on the trees here at Wood Violet, bringing a new season. It's a new season in my life, as well. I have officially left the city and will be at Wood Violet on a permanent basis, as my husband and I have chosen to separate. It's a big change, but the opportunity to be at Wood Violet is what I have always wanted.

I think often of the disappointment that you must have felt, with the assumption that I deliberately caused you pain. I've already said it in my texts to you, but in the event that you didn't receive them, I want you to know that I had no idea that such an important moment was going to be turned into a public spectacle. For that misunderstanding, I sincerely apologize.

Chase, I will always value the time I got to spend with you this summer. It was unexpected, and made this summer yet another I will never forget. Thank you for everything, and I hope you discover that Garrett's memory lives on in this capsule.

Best wishes to you,
Julie

There was a lot to get done, but I hopped into the car and drove the package straight to the post office. Chase deserved that closure. I didn't want him to have to wait on it any longer.

There were so many projects to fill the time at Wood Violet that the days flew by. The task that took the most time was digitalizing the paper records, the thing my mother had been working on prior to the stroke. I was back in the records office, sorting through the next batch of files on my list, when Nikki poked her head in, a funny look on her face.

"There's someone here to see you," she said.

Chase walked in. His hair was shorter, and the scruff on his face had grown in enough that it had touches of gray. His eyes were the deepest, darkest blue I'd ever seen, brighter than the depths of the lake.

Nikki shut the door and for a moment, we just looked at one another.

"I'm sorry," he said. "I shouldn't have left like that."

"Don't apologize," I said. "We're the ones who owe you an apology."

His face held a hint of a smile. "Nikki gave me the twenty-minute version. I'm good."

I grinned. "I'm glad to see you."

He walked in and took a seat on the ground next to me, before opening his leather messenger bag. He pulled out the memory box and set it on the floor between us.

"So, you won't believe what was inside," he said.

I patted the metal box with affection. "Tell me everything."

"So, this came in the mail along with a letter from you. It took about two weeks for me to feel brave enough to open either one of them. When I finally did, I felt like my brother was there, cheering me on, watching over my shoulder." He traced the edge of the metal, nearly brushing against my fingers. "I tried to remember the details before I opened it. It had seemed like we'd stuck a bunch of stickers from packages of bubblegum all over the outside but they weren't there. Figured they'd probably corroded away. Then I opened it."

With practiced fingers, he popped open the lock on the box to reveal a bulky manilla envelope. Inside, bubble wrap surrounded a single plastic bag with a piece of paper carefully tucked inside.

"You guys only buried a piece of paper?" I said, confused.

He grinned. "It's not our memory box."

"Chase!" I actually gasped. "You're kidding. After all that? You must have been crushed."

"I was, for a minute." He chuckled. "Then I laughed for days. It was ridiculous. So much drama and it ended up not even belonging to me. Garrett never would have let me live it down. It was like, the ultimate practical joke."

One of the most impressive things about Chase was how he found the good in everything. "So, you got to have your time with him anyway."

Chase nodded, then he turned serious. He slid the paper to me across the old carpet.

"You might want to read that."

His tone pulled my attention straight to the page. The first words read: *To my unborn child.*

"What is…?" I said, confused.

Chase took my hand and led it to the bottom of the page. There, in neat penmanship, was the signature of Ivelisse Kroll.

"Ivelisse?" I blinked. "Wait. I don't understand. How could this be in here?"

"It turns out that Ivelisse made a memory box of her own. You said it was found down by the river, right?"

"Yes, in one of the abandoned houses."

Chase touched the metal lid. "It makes sense, I guess. Your grandmother must have drawn her when she was five or six months pregnant, so she would have been at your grandmother's studio in the fall. I bet it was beautiful down there, until it wasn't. That's when she hid the memory box."

"What do you mean, until it wasn't?"

Chase handed the letter to me. "Take a look."

To my unborn child:

One of the worst parts of not knowing you is that I will not have the opportunity to explain to you what it means to love.

Your father is the definition of love. Kind, generous, and so quick with a smile. I have never met a man that I could both desire and admire at the same time. Suddenly, there he was. His hands had built the very place I slept, his mind had created this perfect paradise, and yet, his heart was pledged to another. Still, I could not stay away.

Every moment I was in his presence it felt like I could barely speak, barely think, just love. It was as if the very forces of natures insisted on our collision. There was nothing that could have kept him from me, until reality came to call.

We were found out. I was given the choice to be deported for my lack of citizenship or say goodbye to him… and you.

I couldn't return home. My mother was gone. I had nothing. I had lived that life and wanted more for you. The only choice I had was to place you with a family that could care for you with every breath.

Your father never knew. I was not allowed to tell him that you were to be a part of this world.

My darling child, one day you will understand that the heart is only as fragile as the choices we make. I tell you this now—we will make surprising decisions for love. Ones that can tear our heart out and leave us begging for answers. The most painful choice I've ever made, my dearest, was to say goodbye to you.

Margaret, I write this as a blessing and as an absolution as I leave this place, this prison. I love you, my sweet darling, and I always will.

Ivelisse Kroll

I held the page tightly in my hand.

"Ivelisse wanted to be with her," I whispered. "Chase, this is… it's heartbreaking. She loved this guy and more than anything, she wanted to be with Margaret."

"Yes." Chase studied me. "You okay?"

"The letters." My heart started to pound. "They were true."

"What letters?" he asked.

"Ivelisse wrote my grandmother three times, begging for information on how to find Margaret. I think she'd changed her mind about giving her up for adoption and since my grandmother had set it all up, thought that she'd be able to reverse things."

Chase glanced down at the page in his hand, then back up at me. I could see he was struggling with something.

"What is it?" I said. "Say it."

Carefully, he set the letter on the floor. "I don't want to, but out of respect for you and your family, I think I have to. It's important to tell you what I'm hearing as I read this."

"Of course," I said. "Tell me."

Chase had come all this way to share what he'd found, and I'd barely let him get a word in edgewise. He'd probably been thinking about the letter for days.

"I hope I'm wrong here," he said. "But I've read this at least fifty times." He paused to let out a breath. Then, he said, "Julie, I think the man that she's talking about is your grandfather."

CHAPTER TWENTY-EIGHT

"My grandfather?" I echoed.

The records closet suddenly felt too hot. Quickly, I reached for the letter. I skimmed the words, trying to understand.

"Why do you think that?" I said. "What...?"

"This," Chase said, pointing at a line. "*His hands had built the very place I slept, his mind had created this perfect paradise, and yet, his heart was pledged to another.*"

"That's... She's being poetic. She's..." The perspective Chase had given the words filtered through. My stomach dropped. "No."

I willed the words to return to the poetry I'd heard the first time. Try as I might, the puzzle piece had clicked into place and it refused to let go. I got to my feet and stood stock still, unable to determine what to do next.

"Julie."

The concern in Chase's voice answered that question for me: Run.

I threw open the door, and rushed into the office. The air conditioning was icy against my heated cheeks. Nikki sat at her desk, blissfully working away with her earbuds in.

I thought of the worry that had clouded her face as she'd handed me the letters that she'd found. That worry would become shock once she learned the truth about my family.

The room started to spin and I pressed my hand against the wall.

My poor father. I couldn't begin to imagine how it would affect him to learn of his father's infidelity, to discover that he had a sister younger than his daughter, to think that his mother had separated a woman from her child.

Or my grandfather, to have to face the fall-out of a mistake nearly twenty years after the fact, to learn that he had a daughter, a child he had never even seen. To have everyone know that he'd betrayed my grandmother and the life they'd built.

My grandmother. To have her memory…

My grandmother.

The wall felt like rubber beneath my hand.

Yes, I was furious at my grandfather for hurting my grandmother, for breaking his wedding vows, but what she had done was so unfair that I could barely process it. The horror of it all made me feel sick.

"Julie?" Chase sounded tense. "It's a guess. I—"

"No, you're right." My voice was flat, and I glanced at Nikki. I couldn't risk that she'd overhear the conversation. "Let's go back in."

The records closet smelled stale and stuffy. I shut the door and sank to the floor, my back against the wall.

"I have to tell my father," I said quietly. "He might not want to tell Margaret. But she deserves to know. No more hiding, no more protecting the truth. This isn't the type of secret that should stay hidden."

"I'll support you no matter what." Chase's gaze was strong and steady. "That said, I do think you should talk to your family before you talk to Margaret. Decide together what to settle on."

"I'm settling on the truth."

"Which is a good choice," Chase said, nodding. "But I do think it's important to talk to your father first. Maybe even your grandfather."

"No." The word came out too loud, and Chase drew back. "Sorry. I just… I can't talk to my grandfather about this. I can't."

Chase fiddled with the lock on the memory box.

"What if they all know?" I asked. "What if every single person in my family knows about this except for me and my sister, and they planned to sweep it under the rug?"

I didn't want to think that way, but my grandfather could have talked to my father about this years ago. They might have agreed that it was better to leave it unsaid.

"It's possible," Chase admitted. "But now, you could lead them in the right direction."

I buried my head in my hands. The scandal behind this could cause such harm to the resort. Still, it was only a business. There had been so many times in the past few years where I'd put the needs of corporations before the needs of people. No more.

Margaret had said that all adults were liars. Well, in this case, it was time to speak up for the truth.

Chase glanced at me. "You okay?"

"Not yet," I said. "But I will be."

My mother was awake and reading in the living room when I arrived at the house. I kissed her on the cheek, hoping I didn't look as upset as I felt. I must have, because she reached up and touched my forehead, as if checking me for a fever.

"Is everything alright?" she asked.

"I need to talk to you and Dad," I said, pacing the living room. "It's going to be a shock, so be ready."

Part of me wished Chase was still with me. He'd headed back to the hotel he'd booked for the night in town, and planned to return home in the morning.

"I can meet for dinner," he'd said, before leaving. "If you decide you need that, please don't hesitate to call."

Now, I waited until my father came out of his office and gave me a peck on the cheek. He looked freshly showered and rested in a way that he hadn't during the height of the season.

My palms started to sweat and I couldn't decide what would be worse: If he had no clue what had happened or if he'd chosen to keep it quiet.

"Is everything alright?" He settled next to my mother on the couch. "You sounded strange on the phone."

"It's a lot to take in," I said carefully. "I'm sorry to be the one to talk to you about it but it's a continuation of the issue I spoke with you about that one day at the hospital."

"Margaret?" my father said.

I took a deep breath and told him what I'd discovered, scared that he'd be furious that I'd found something my family had worked hard to hide. But once I'd shared the story, it was clear my father had not known. His skin and lips were pale, and once I stopped talking, I could hear that his breath was shallow.

"Dad, put your feet up," I said quickly. Racing to the kitchen, I grabbed an orange soda from the fridge and brought it to him. "Drink this."

The click and hiss of the can cracking open was the only sound in the room. My father looked down at it then let out a breath. "I'm going to need something a little stronger."

I returned to the kitchen for a bottle of whiskey and poured us both a drink. My father downed his. It took a minute, but the color finally returned to his cheeks. Then he had me tell him everything again, interrupting to ask questions along the way.

Once we'd gone through it all again, he shook his head. "It's the idea that my mother could have kept my father from his child. Kept the child from both of her parents. It's horrible."

"People make mistakes," my mother said, in her halting voice.

"This wasn't a mistake, though." His eyes rimmed in red. "This was…"

"She was devastated that Grandpa had betrayed her," I said. "The idea that he was having a child with another woman?" I shuddered. "I can't even imagine what that would feel like."

Even though Tristan and I hadn't stayed together, it would have broken my heart if he'd had an affair and, worse, had a child with her. Especially after all we went through to have one of our own. I had always been pretty sure my grandparents had struggled with their pregnancies; I distinctly remembered finding two baby blankets in the closet, blankets that were never used. When I asked my grandmother about them, she said she'd knitted them for the children she'd hoped would come but never had.

"There are so many factors." My father poured himself another drink. "My father doesn't know he has a child. Margaret is hoping to meet her parents, I understand that, but at what cost? This might be too much for him to take."

I considered my grandfather, so strong and stoic. Yes, it was hard to imagine how he would react to this revelation. Not only that his wife had learned of his affair, but that she'd sought retribution against him and his unborn child. Or maybe, he would see it that she had tried to protect him and their family. Either way, the revelation would change the way he kept his wife in his memory, but the truth had been buried long enough.

"Yes, it's going to be a shock," I told him. "But he's missed out on the opportunity to know his daughter for long enough. I think he deserves the opportunity to have that knowledge and make his own decision."

My mother took my father's hand and they looked at each other. "You have a sister."

My father drained his glass. Finally, he said, "I need to confirm all this before I talk to my father. How do we find this woman?"

"The staff files," my mother said, and I nodded.

"The information on file is no longer current and her address was for an apartment where she's no longer a tenant. No forwarding address."

"Let's ask the team," my mother suggested.

"What?" My father drew back. "We can't tell them."

"No, but Ivelisse would have had friends. Most of them roomed together, to save money. Someone has to know."

"Claude," I whispered. My mind shifted to the sharp look Claude had given me when I'd asked about Ivelisse. It had never occurred to me in the moment, but it was possible she knew the details. Not everything, but enough.

My father squeezed his hands so tightly the knuckles turned white. Then he handed me his phone. "Call her."

Claude answered on the third ring, grumbling and complaining. "You best not be calling to chat. I have too much to do."

"Claude, it's Julie," I said.

"Oh, hi honey." Her tone turned to sugar. "I thought you were your father. Do you need something, precious?"

My father cleared his throat. "I'm here, too, Claude."

She laughed her throaty laugh. "How can I help you, sir?"

Letting out a breath, I said, "Do you remember that day I was asking you about Ivelisse, that woman in the photograph? I wanted to know if you have a way to get in touch with her."

Claude paused. The seconds passed and I held my mother's hand tight. "Yes, Miss Julie." Her voice was quiet. "She left me with a PO box address. Said she would never change it, and to pass it along if anyone came asking. You must be anyone."

My throat felt tight. "Yes," I managed to say.

My father grabbed a pen. "We're ready."

CHAPTER TWENTY-NINE

Ivelisse burst through the office doors like the picture come to life. Short, black hair with streaks of gray, high cheekbones, alabaster skin and cheeks flushed with red. She looked to be in her late fifties. Her gaze held mine with suspicion but at the sight of my father, she gave a smile that I recognized.

It was the same as her daughter's.

My father had sent a letter to the address Claude had given us. It took ten days, but he finally received a call from her. She still lived in Chicago and wanted to meet with us right away. My father set up a time after hours in the main office, in the conference room, and we met her in the front hallway.

"Thank you for coming," my father said.

She stopped short. "You look just like him now." Her tone had such a sense of pain and history that it nearly took my breath away.

I walked down the hall in silence, wishing Chase could have been there. He had gone back to northern Wisconsin to handle the ice-cream business, but we had talked on the phone nearly every night. He had been a rock through all of this, and it surprised me that I was already thinking about what I'd say to him when he called.

Ivelisse adjusted her black leather jacket. It smelled like lily of the valley. The scent was soft and delicate, a sharp contrast to the no-nonsense look on her face. The three of us walked to the conference room in silence, where my mother was already seated.

"You are tricking me," Ivelisse said. "This woman is too old to be my daughter."

My mother laughed. "I remember you. Hello, Ivelisse."

Ivelisse smiled. "Hello, Lilian. It's good to see you."

If Ivelisse wondered at the change in my mother's physical appearance, she didn't comment. Taking a seat at the conference table, she squeezed her fingers. Her nails were painted a deep, shimmering coral but her skin was weathered and worn.

"Would you like a cup of coffee?" my father asked.

She shook her head.

"Then, let's get to it," he said. "We called you here today because the circumstances behind…" My father spoke as if he'd prepared a speech, then he stopped, dropping the formal tone altogether. "Ivelisse, we pieced together what happened with your daughter. On behalf of our family, I cannot tell you how sorry I am. She came here this summer, looking for you, and that's when the truth came to light. I was hoping you could fill in the blanks, tell us what happened and then, assuming this all matches up, we'd like to introduce you to her."

"She's not here now," I said quickly. "She's at school but I can get her here as soon as tomorrow."

"It is true, then." Ivelisse put her hands to her face. "I will meet her. For that, I thank you." Emotion colored her features and she took a moment, patting her face with a tissue.

My father clicked on the air conditioning, and its steady whir cooled the conference room.

"I do not blame you for what happened," she told my father. "We both have suffered, now. I'm sorry for that. My actions were motivated by love and I fooled myself into thinking it was okay. It was not."

"Two wrongs don't make a right," I told her. "You never should have paid such a price. We hope…" I glanced at my father.

My parents and I had spoken in depth about the effect this could have on the resort if the story got out. He was more concerned that it would harm the reputation of my grandmother than the business itself. In spite of what she'd done, she was still his mother.

"I can be angry at her, Julie," he'd told me. "Furious. But I will never stop loving her."

"We hope that you will one day forgive our family," he said. "I'm sure my mother did what she thought was best at the time. Unfortunately, it was wrong and now we want to do whatever we can to make things right."

She stared down at her hands. "Thank you."

The four of us sat in silence. Then, Ivelisse said, "There are so many times I have relived that summer in my mind. My work visa was almost expired but my friend had worked here the summer before and had loved it. She had gotten a good job at a big hotel in Chicago after and thought I could do the same if I came here. I did not expect the workers to be young. They seemed so silly. Then I met McGregor." She glanced at my father. "He was so wise, so kind. We connected on many levels. When I think back, I remember our talks most of all."

My father stared down at his hands, his ears flushed. He looked so much like a little boy that I had to look away. It was hard to see him so vulnerable.

"Your grandmother was close with members of the staff." Ivelisse shrugged. "Someone tipped her off about what was happening, and I was fired." The words came out monotone. "I sent McGregor a letter about the pregnancy without knowing that your mother collected the mail. She called to say that she had video of me stealing from one of the cabins and I would be arrested for theft, if I didn't do exactly what she said."

"There are no cameras in the cabins," I said. "There never were."

Ivelisse winced. "I did not know. I had stolen; a few dollars here, make-up, and once, a cheap ruby necklace. My visa had expired and if I'd been arrested, I would have been deported. I could not give my child a good life. I had no money, no home, and no family. What could I do?"

I couldn't begin to imagine the agony that must have caused Ivelisse, and I felt grateful that Margaret was not here to witness this conversation. I couldn't imagine what she must think of our family.

"That's when she convinced you to give the baby up for adoption," I said.

Ivelisse nodded. "Geraldine requested that I return here and stay in a cabin by the river, next to her art studio, until I had my baby. McGregor never went back there, since she did not want him near her art studio, so he would not have known."

I shivered. "How did that work? The cabins were shut down. There was no heat. There would have been snow, ice…"

"The heat was on." Ivelisse turned to me and I was once again startled at her beauty. Deep lines around her eyes and her mouth added such a depth of character, and I could see Margaret in her. "Hot water. Geraldine brought three warm meals a day. I was older so there was a risk that there would be trouble with the baby. Geraldine had a doctor visit every few weeks, even weekly at the end. I appreciated that and believe it or not, she and I became friends. We talked often and spoke about McGregor and all of the things that we loved. We made plans for Margaret, and it all felt quite mature and reasonable until late at night, when my hands rested on my stomach as I fell asleep."

I handed her a tissue, before taking one for myself.

"I prayed she would have a change of heart," Ivelisse said, staring down at the table. "Let me keep my child and trust that I would not return but she refused to take that risk. If McGregor knew, he would not allow her to send the child away."

"Why didn't you tell him?" I demanded. "Break free and tell him?"

Ivelisse wrinkled her brow. "She would have found a way to report me and I would have been sent back to my home country. If that had happened when I was pregnant…" She straightened her shoulders. "It was not an option. It hurt me every day but I could see that she was hurting, too." She looked at my father. "Each day, I do try to find a place in my heart to forgive her."

"Ivelisse, I know your daughter," I said. "She will be proud that someone like you—that you—are her mother."

My father cleared his throat. "Did you love him?"

"Oh, yes." Ivelisse rested her cheek against her hand. "I never stopped, much to the detriment of the men that have crossed my path since. I was once married, I became a citizen, but… no one was like him. I cried to learn he was gone."

My mother squinted. "Gone?"

Ivelisse's dark eyes were cautious. "You said he was gone."

I peered at her. Then it hit me. When my father spoke to her on the phone, he'd said my grandfather was gone, but he'd meant on another vacation. This time, to Canada, to see the changing leaves.

"Ivelisse, he's not dead," I said. "He went on a bus tour. He'll be back tonight."

Her face turned pale. Then, bright pink.

"Do you think…" She turned to my father. "I do not mean to disrespect the memory of your mother—"

"Would you like to see him?" he asked. "It might do him good. Let him hear the truth from the source."

Ivelisse reached for his arm and squeezed it with such force that the skin turned white. "I can't thank you enough. Finally, I can tell him we have a daughter. But most of all… Please. I want to meet her."

Margaret sent me to voicemail three times before she finally picked up the phone.

"Do I have to block your number?" she demanded.

It felt so good to hear her voice.

"Don't hang up," I said. "I know you're mad and I get it. I'd be mad, too. But I have some things that I need to talk to you about."

She paused. "What things?"

"I'll come visit you, if that's all right," I said, squeezing the phone tight. "Can you tell me how to find you?"

"If you tell me what it's about."

"I'd like to talk in person," I said. "Please. I just need you to trust me."

She was silent. "I'm not sure I do," she said. "But you can come."

I drove to visit Margaret at Northwestern the next day. My father called when I was on the drive, to tell me that my grandfather had reunited with Ivelisse that morning.

"Grandma told him what happened a few weeks before she died," my father said. "She had been stricken with guilt for years and said she only did it because she was afraid he'd choose to be with them instead of me and her. She wasn't well by that point, and as a result, couldn't remember the name of the law firm that had handled the adoption. She begged him to try and find Margaret to make things right. He was so shocked by the whole thing that he walked away from the resort altogether." My father's voice went quiet. "I'd always wondered why he'd left the place that he loved so much."

He paused, then said, "You texted him about the adoption a few weeks ago."

"Yes." I gripped the steering wheel. "So, he did know something."

"You really threw him. He didn't know if you were talking about something different or the situation Grandma had revealed to him, but he said he was just about to talk to you about it when this all hit. He's so happy, Julie, and wants to see her more than anything."

"I'll do my best," I said, already worried at how she would react.

My father was silent. Then, he said, "That's all that any of us can do."

Margaret's classes were done at noon, and she took me to her dorm room. It smelled like freesia from a potpourri set and everything was decorated in purples, pinks, and turquoise accents, to match her bedspread. It was a cheerful, fun room that matched Margaret's bold personality.

I was nervous and I could tell that she was, too, because she flitted all over the room, showing me stuff.

"Look at this," she said, pulling out a drawer.

It was crammed full of enough snacks to make Tilly proud.

"Do you want Twizzlers?" she asked.

"Tempting, but no."

"Your loss." She flopped on the bed, candy in hand, and indicated I should take the hot-pink beanbag chair in the corner.

"This is all so cozy."

I settled into the crunchy beanbag and studied her. It was hard to believe that this girl was my aunt. I'd spent so much time thinking about how much she looked like Ivelisse and, now that I knew the whole story, I realized she and my father had the same mouth and even the same ears.

The entire thing was hard to take in.

"So, I figured out my major." Margaret bit into the red piece of licorice. "Human biology. You know what that means…"

Margaret had said that she wanted to become a doctor, but was worried that she wouldn't make the cut. It was great to hear she was going to take the risk.

"I'm so proud of you," I said. "Dr. Margaret."

She rolled her eyes. "I knew you'd say something stupid."

"You'll have an amazing bedside manner."

Margaret laughed, and ripped into another piece of licorice. Her skin was shiny, her smile bright, and she was the picture of a happy college student. Was it fair to tell her all of this? She'd been the one seeking her mother but she'd also jumped into that right after learning she was adopted. She could have changed her mind.

"So, did you ever say anything to your parents?" I tried to sit up straight on the bean bag, but it was impossible. "About the fact that you'd learned you were adopted?"

"No." Margaret twisted her wavy hair into a knot on top of her head. "It didn't feel like the right time. Did you find a new job yet?"

"Yes. I'm working at Wood Violet."

"Oh." She looked confused. "Your husband-guy is okay with that? I thought you lived in downtown Chicago."

"Not anymore." My cheeks flushed, as they did every time I had to talk about this. "We're getting a divorce."

"Oh." She considered the last bite of licorice and then, looked at me. "Do you want my honest reaction, or for me to say what's expected?"

It was rare for Margaret to offer such a courtesy. "Hit me."

"I'm glad." She shrugged, her gray T-shirt practically swallowing her thin frame. "I mean, you never seemed happy when you talked about him or when I saw you with him. He kind of seemed like a jerk, no offense."

The memory of Tristan standing outside Margaret's cabin, arms crossed and face creased with frustration, didn't do much to refute her theory. Still, she had only seen a quick slice of life, not the whole picture. Tristan wasn't a jerk. He was a smart, impressive guy who handled life, love and grief in a different way than me, and we couldn't find a way to meet in the middle.

"He was a great guy but not a great partner," I told Margaret. "I miss him, but we didn't belong together. It's for the best."

"Yeah." She started to stretch out on the bed but then she sat up and squinted at me. "Wait. Why are you here if you don't live in Chicago? Wood Violet's a hike."

Outside the window, the leaves on the trees had changed to vibrant shades of red, orange and yellow, while the sky looked bright and cheerful. I wished I could be out there, enjoying the day, instead of delivering such heavy news.

"Well, I have to talk to you about something." I pulled my bottle of water out of my purse and took a sip. It was hard to steady the bottle in my shaking hands. "Do you remember that day that we went out on the boat and you told me you knew I had looked in your bag and found the adoption papers?"

"What about them?" she asked.

"Well, I um…" I let out a breath. "I did some research and they led me to your mother."

Margaret brought her hands to her mouth. "You're kidding." Her eyes went through a series of emotions. Disbelief, excitement, fear, confusion… "Where is she?" She got to her feet and moved towards the door, as if expecting her to be waiting outside.

"Wood Violet," I said. "She wants to see you, but I have some things to tell you first."

Margaret put her hand to her mouth. She was smiling, but looked scared. "This is wild. How did you find her?"

"Well, I was curious about why Wood Violet's address was on the paperwork. I'd assumed my grandmother had helped out a guest who needed it but learned it went a little deeper than that. So, I started to look into it."

She sat back on the bed and pulled a pillow to her chest. "Why didn't you tell me you were doing that? It's the whole reason I was there."

So many excuses flashed through my brain. The fact that I was scared of what I'd find and how it would affect the resort. The fact that I didn't trust Margaret, and how she'd handle the information. In the end, the truth was worse than anything I could have imagined, but the only thing that mattered now was bringing the two women together.

"I made a mistake," I said. "I should have told you, and there were lots of reasons I didn't, but the biggest was that I was scared you would be disappointed. That your mother wouldn't want to meet you or that I wouldn't be able to find her at all. Please keep in mind, this was at the time I was trying to protect you, because I believed the story you'd told me about your adoptive mother kicking you out of the house."

Margaret looked down at her hands. "How long have you known?"

"I've known her name for a while but I didn't know how to find her," I said. "It turns out that she worked at Wood Violet the year you were born. Her name's Ivelisse."

"Ivelisse." The name sounded like a song when Margaret said it. "That's beautiful."

"Yes." I picked at the fabric on the beanbag, wishing I could leave it at that. "I'd found her name but her contact information wasn't current. Long story short, my mother thought to ask one of the staff who had been close to her if she knew anything. It turned out, your mother left her with the address to a PO box that never changed, in hopes that you would come to find her."

Margaret frowned. "Then why did she give me away? If she was so eager for me to get in touch, she could have just kept me."

"Because your mother had an affair with my grandfather and things got messy."

"Your *grand*father?" she said, dropping the pillow.

"It's not as bad as it sounds," I said quickly. "Age-wise, I mean. She was forty and he was mid-fifties. Of course, my grandmother was furious. She did some pretty terrible things."

Margaret watched me with her haunting eyes. "What things?"

I swallowed hard. "My grandmother did not give your mother the choice to keep you. She threatened to turn her in for stealing if she didn't put you up for adoption."

Margaret put her hand to her mouth. "What?"

"I know," I said. "It's awful. Your mother went along with it all because her work visa had expired. She was afraid she would get sent back to Colombia and wouldn't be able to give you a good life. She contacted my grandmother several times, later in life, without any luck. My grandfather never knew about any of it."

Margaret stared at me. She had picked up a plastic licorice wrapper and was slowly scrunching it. The shock on her face slowly changed to rage.

"I know," I said, holding up my hands. "I agree with you. My family is horrified that my grandmother did something like this. The only positive is that your mother would give anything to meet you, and my grandfather feels the same. I don't know if you'll ever forgive my family, but we wanted you to know the truth."

Margaret slid off the bed and walked to the window. With her back turned, she said, "How could something like this even happen?"

"I don't know."

Margaret nodded.

"This is a lot," she said quietly. Then, she shouted, "It's a lot!" Letting out a loud cry, she bent down to her knees.

My stomach twisted into knots to see her hurting like this. I moved to the edge of the bed.

"Margaret, I'm so sorry," I said. "It's not right. It's—"

She shot to her feet. "No, it's not right!" The rage on her face pushed me back. "None of it," she cried, then punched her pillow again and again and again.

"I can't tell you how sorry I am," I said, fighting the lump in my throat. "Why don't you take a few minutes and—"

She crossed her arms. "Leave."

"Wait," I pleaded. "You have to see your mother. Please."

Margaret clenched her fists. "You. Need. To. Leave."

Eyes blurring, I rushed out into the hallway. My heart ached, hearing Margaret scream into her pillow. The sound was raw, and heartbreaking. Then came the tears.

I sank to the floor, my knees drawn to my chest.

What could I say to Ivelisse if Margaret refused to come? It would crush her. Ivelisse had spent years of her life wanting nothing more than to be with her daughter, but this was all new to Margaret. She was perfectly within her rights to walk away. Maybe the best choice was for me to leave and check back in a few days.

I had just risen to my feet when Margaret came to the door. Her face was etched with pain. Still, she had the backpack I had bought for her slung over one shoulder, and a pair of sunglasses perched on her head.

She stopped short at the sight of me. "I thought you'd left."

"No," I said. "Do you have class?"

"No." She lifted her chin and walked towards the elevator. "I was headed to Wood Violet. I want to meet my mother."

Margaret set a plan to meet her mother and her father at my parents' house that afternoon. I pulled up in the car and we sat outside for several minutes before she nodded, and opened the door.

"Ready to go?" I asked.

She let out a breath. "Let's do it."

I looked at her with admiration. This was such a tough situation for anyone to be in, let alone someone her age. I was proud of her for handling it with such grace and bravery, when so much of her life had changed.

Now, as Margaret and I walked into my parents' house, I saw that my grandfather was sitting on the couch with Ivelisse, holding her hand. They got to their feet and my grandfather gently nudged her forward. Margaret, who had walked in with that full, confident swagger, stopped and stared.

"You're my mother," she whispered.

Ivelisse nodded.

The two women stood in silence. The only sound I could hear was my heart beating. Then, their faces crumpled.

Margaret and Ivelisse rushed forward and held one another tight. They spoke in quiet words, brief thoughts that we couldn't hear. Then, Ivelisse began to cry huge, gasping sobs as she held Margaret close.

"It killed me to leave you," Ivelisse said. "There was no choice. I had no choice."

The lump in my throat was painful as well as the hurt in my heart. My mother and I reached for one another at the same time. Leaning into her familiar warmth, I couldn't imagine not having her as a part of my history.

I pulled her close, scared to let her go. My father stood next to us, his face raw with pain. My mother squeezed my shoulder and reached her hand up to hold his. My grandfather finally stepped forward, and held out his hand. Margaret rolled her eyes, walked right up, and hugged him.

"Let's give them their time," my mother whispered, and we all headed into the kitchen.

Soon, the laughter and shouts that came from the living room had us looking at one another in surprised delight. It felt so strange to think that there was room for celebration in the midst of such pain, but life was long. There was still plenty of time for Margaret to get to know her birth parents, and for my grandfather and Ivelisse to get to know who she was, and who she planned to become.

EPILOGUE

One year later

The sweet notes of 'Ave Maria' rang out across the forest, their beauty clinging to the trees like the flower buds of spring. The bride and groom-to-be held hands and gazed at one another with adoration. Margaret stood next to the river, her hands clasped and her eyes closed, as she finished the haunting final notes.

"Now, you may kiss the bride."

The pastor smiled at the couple that stood beneath the wooden arch woven through with fresh wildflowers. They kissed and their parents applauded from the seats we'd set out for the wedding rehearsal.

"Perfect!" Ivelisse's commanding voice rang out, and she stepped forward with her clipboard. "Now, you'll turn and exit down the white runner to the gazebo for pictures and head to the reception. Then you live happily ever after. Voilà!"

The couple beamed at each other, as Margaret looked at me with a big grin. I gave her the thumbs-up sign as Ivelisse gathered the bride and groom together again to discuss additional details of their exit.

"We did it," Nikki said, giving me a high five.

Even though Nikki and I had worked diligently on the wedding project for the past year, it felt like a miracle to see the venue not only ready but resplendent for the first wedding of the season, and the first wedding ever at Wood Violet Resort. The reception hall was rustic yet modern, nestled like a forgotten castle at the edge of the forest, and the landscape artist had added the perfect amount of flowers and foliage by the river to create a wedding wonderland.

We had interviewed for weeks, trying to find the perfect wedding coordinator, when my father had suggested Ivelisse. She had worked for years managing corporate conferences and was delighted at the offer. She'd made the transition to Wood Violet in March, and Margaret had spent several weekends here, with plans to spend the summer working at the resort the moment the school year was complete.

Her adoptive parents had encouraged her to do so, because they wanted her to get to know our family. They had offered Margaret nothing but love and support once she told them about her discovery and her journey to find her birth parents. Her adoptive parents planned to stay for two weeks in late June, and I couldn't wait to meet them. They seemed like great people. My mother was already hard at work planning the menu and what treats to bake for their visit, as her stamina and abilities continued to grow.

Margaret walked over and slid on her sunglasses. "I never knew I'd add wedding singer to my grand list of life accomplishments."

"I'm so glad you have," Nikki told her. "You sing beautifully."

Instead of deflecting, Margaret smiled. "Thank you."

Ivelisse signaled to Nikki that the group was about to head over to the reception hall.

"I can take it from here, if you'd like," Nikki told me. "You have somewhere to be."

Margaret elbowed me in the ribs. "I can't wait to spy on you all summer. I expect a full report."

My cheeks colored. "Go help your mother," I said, ruffling her hair.

The pastor needed a ride back to the main area, so he and I boarded one of the golf carts, and took the ride through the woods. We'd had the path widened and graded as part of our development project, and the way was smooth. The sun shined down, the birds chirped, and the promise of spring was fresh in the air.

"It should be a beautiful wedding," I told the pastor.

"Love is always beautiful," he said. "It's the greatest gift of all."

The dock echoed beneath my feet over the silence of the water. The rustic bench in the Hut was waiting. It had survived wind, hail, sleet and rain, and it still stood strong for our family.

The trees that surrounded the lake were bright with the bloom of new beginnings, the chill of the winter was far behind, and I closed my eyes, basking in the warmth of the sun.

So much had changed but in my heart, so much remained the same. I was grateful to have found the way back to the place and people that I loved, and I looked forward to the future with a sense of peace that I hadn't felt in years.

There had been times since I'd been back where I missed Tristan, but mainly, it was the idea of what he and I could have been. There was so much we'd hoped for in our marriage, including our careers and creating a family. It hadn't worked out and when that image crumbled, the gravity of it all made it impossible for us to recover. In the end, it had been for the best.

It hadn't made for an easy year, especially given the heartache that my grandmother's secret had caused. It had been hard on everybody, my father in particular, to work through so many conflicting emotions. But we all welcomed the continuation of that journey, because in the midst of such change, our family had discovered even more room in our hearts to grow.

A duck skimmed the surface of the lake, drops of water shimmering beneath its wings.

The echo of footsteps on the dock made me sit up straighter.

This year had taught me that I was not alone, yet I could be perfectly happy on my own, for a lifetime, really. But I didn't want to be. I wanted to be with the one who filled my heart, the one who made me feel that the simplest moments in life were the ones that mattered the most.

Chase poked his head around the corner of the wooden shanty. He wore my favorite baseball cap, the one that made his eyes as blue as the deepest sea. He settled in next to me and we stared out at the water.

The distance between us felt too great and I closed the gap, resting my head on his shoulder. He put his arm around me and pulled me in close. We didn't move for what felt like years. Then, he spoke, his voice as familiar as my own heartbeat.

"Sorry it took me so long to get here."

I squeezed his hand. "It took me a long time, too."

His eyes searched mine then he leaned in and kissed me.

The kiss transported me to the past and collided with the future.

Beyond the two of us, the lake was smooth as glass. A fish jumped, its rings shattering the stillness. The rings ebbed and once again, the surface was still. I settled into his arms, waiting for another fish to jump. The surface would continue to shatter but with his arms around me, it would feel like no time at all until it was smooth once again.

A LETTER FROM CYNTHIA

I am so delighted that you read *The Choice I Made*. If you enjoyed it and want to hear about future books, sign up for my newsletter here. Your email will never be shared and you can unsubscribe at any time.

www.bookouture.com/cynthia-ellingsen

The thing that I will always remember about this book is that it was written during the pandemic of 2020, where I spent months at home with my precious family, my computer, and my thoughts. (And several pieces of candy, but who's counting?) The time spent writing this story was a wonderful escape from the weight of the world, and although the content was sometimes heavy, my goal was to share a feeling of joy, love, and most of all, the importance of connecting with the ones that we care about even in the most difficult times.

I've always said that I've done my job if my books can warm your heart or make you laugh out loud. I hope you walked away from *The Choice I Made* feeling like you wanted to read more, because I have plenty more for you to read! Check out my backlist, starting with the Starlight Cove series. I also have a new book coming out very soon.

If you liked *The Choice I Made*, it would also mean so much if you'd leave a review on the site where you bought it. I read every single review—it helps me learn what it is that you like about my books, so I can do more of that the next time. That way, I can keep making your reads better and better.

Thank you again for everything, especially the time you've taken to read this book. All the best to you and yours,

Cynthia

[f] cynthiaellingsen

[twitter] @CynEllingsen

[globe] cynthiaellingsen.com

ACKNOWLEDGMENTS

There is nothing greater than the opportunity to write books for a living, and I could not do it without the incredible support and encouragement of my readers. Thank you for buying my books, writing reviews, and the kind words throughout the years. I am so lucky to have you!

Brent Taylor, Super-Agent, you always make it happen. I have endless respect for your brilliance, work ethic, and your uncanny ability to hear what I want and somehow, make it happen. Thank you for everything, from the bottom of my heart.

Lucy Dauman, the stars must have been shining on me when you decided to become my editor. Your ability to bring out the best in my work is incredible. You have taught me so much already and I can't wait to work with you on the next one. Thank you for being such a ray of light, and for letting me be a part of Bookouture.

To everyone at Bookouture, I am infinitely grateful to you. Thank you for welcoming me into such a smart, innovative company. Your professionalism, aspirations and hard work are so impressive, and I am delighted to be a part of the team. From the contracts to the cover art to the title and marketing, I cannot thank you enough for all that you do.

Jennifer Mattox, Stephanie Parkin and Frankie Wolf, I am so lucky to have a writers group with the best group of women in the world. Thank you for the countless hours, dedication, and wisdom. You have been there through it all, and I am delighted to call you my friends.

Much gratitude to Suzanne Shaffar of Embry, Shaffar, Merritt, Womack, PLLC for being my go-to legal expert and friend. All mistakes are my own.

As always, thank you to my mother. You and Dad invested such time and love in our family, and made me believe it was possible to achieve the impossible. I'll forever be grateful.

Ryan Ellingsen, reaching for the stars is easy when you're the one lifting me up. I love you with all of my heart. Thank you for our beautiful children and sharing this wonderful life with me.

Made in the USA
Monee, IL
25 November 2024

71088814R00184